The Dandelion Clock

Jay Mandal

BeWrite Books, UK
www.bewrite.net

Published internationally by BeWrite Books, UK.
363 Badminton Road, Nibley, Bristol. BS37 5JF.

© Jay Mandal 2002

British Library Cataloguing in Publication Data.
A catalogue record for this book is available from the British Library

ISBN 1-904224-25-3

Digitally produced by BeWrite Books.
Also available in eBook and CD-ROM format from www.bewrite.net

Exclusive cover art by Shelley C. Smith

"Look at that," Rob added, pointing to a dandelion which had already gone to seed. "It's perfect. You can't cut it yet."

David remembered his own childhood games of telling the time by a dandelion clock. "All right," he conceded, feigning reluctance. "You can weed them out next year when we get twice as many growing."

It was an empty threat: Rob wouldn't be here then.

Then they'd fallen quiet for a while, and David dozed a little. When he woke up, he was again extremely aware of Rob. It was almost as if he knew how his body would feel to the touch, the skin warmed by the sun. He had only to reach out his hand to see if he was right ...

He reached out.

Lookout Magazine: "Written in the sympathetic, amusing and inimitable style which has become Jay's trademark. All the characters are well drawn and, in almost every one, a reader will easily identify someone they know. Jay handles dialogue extremely well and is a master of quick-witted repartee."

Neil Bartlett, Artistic Director, Lyric Theatre Hammersmith: "I read with pleasure."

Ned Sherrin, CBE, writer, director and producer: "Congratulations. I enjoyed ...."

Hanif Kureishi, writer of *My Beautiful Launderette*: "Wonderful story."

Alan Sinfield, Professor of English and American Studies, Sussex University: "Shrewd and thoughtful. I enjoyed it."

Matthew Parris, columnist, broadcaster and former MP: "Well-written: a good attention-grabbing narrative style."

Susannah York, actress and writer: "Very engaging. You characterise your people well through their speech, and sympathetically. I'd guess this would adapt well for radio, too."

A collection of sixteen short stories published under the title *'Slubberdegullion'* is available through Rabbit Books, 6 Chaplin Grove, Crownhill, Milton Keynes MK8 0DQ.
(www.rabbitbooks.com)

Busy writer Jay Mandal is from Southern England. After grammar school, he joined a City bank and worked in Europe. He's written two novels and over seventy short stories – three of which have been adapted into plays – and '*Slubberdegullion*', a collection of short works. ***Speakout*** magazine have published at least one Mandal story in each issue, and his short stories have been featured in popular publications such as ***Passport*** and ***Lookout***.

Also by Jay Mandal

A Different Kind of Love BeWrite Books 2002

The Dandelion Clock

ONE

1986: not so very long ago. But things were different. The USSR, Czechoslovakia and the old Yugoslavia were still shown on maps. Inequalities in the age of consent persisted despite the ever-increasing powers of the European Union which went by a different name. And people still had record collections.

It was the year Argentina won the World Cup in Mexico, *Today* was launched, and the Greater London Council abolished. It was a year of explosions: Chernobyl, Challenger and the Stockmarket's less earth-shattering 'Big Bang'.

And trains were still run by British Rail.

He got to the departures board just in time to see the indicator for the train he'd hoped to catch being removed. The next one wasn't up on the board yet, so he waited.

His glance fell on a young man standing a few yards away. Everyone else was either staring, mesmerised, at the notice board or walking purposefully along the concourse, but he was looking towards the shops at the rear of the station. Just the usual: a chemist's, a stationer's, and a café together with signs indicating Tickets, Travel Centre, Underground.

David stared at him for a moment and then turned back to the board. After a few minutes, David decided he might as well have a cup of tea while he was waiting, as it would be at least half an hour before the next train was due.

He'd bought himself some tea and a couple of sandwiches, and found a free table, when a party of Italians entered. They bought coffee and were looking around, wondering where to sit.

As they debated loudly in their own language, the young man who, earlier, had been on the station concourse, stood up and gestured to them that they could sit at the table he'd been occupying.

They nodded their thanks while he moved to a seat opposite David. As the din from the next table, now surrounded by Italians – six seated and another three standing – erupted, the two Englishmen exchanged brief smiles of amused tolerance.

David immersed himself in his book, but after a few minutes he became aware that he was being stared at. Surely the man opposite wasn't trying to pick him up? After all, it was still early and Waterloo, of all the London termini, was scarcely renowned for that sort of thing. Besides, he hadn't looked as if ... Still, how could you tell?

Eventually he looked up and realised with relief that he'd been wrong. The young man's interest was obviously fixed on the sandwich on David's plate, but he had the grace to look away when he saw David had noticed.

A few minutes later, a middle-aged woman pushing a trolley appeared, collected a cup that had been there when David had arrived, appeared to dismiss the idea of wiping the table and asked David if he'd finished with his plate.

He had.

"If you don't want it ..."

But the woman had already swept the plate from the table, tipped its contents into a small bin, stacked the plate on the pile on her trolley, and moved on to the next table.

David looked at his unknown companion with renewed curiosity. "I'm sorry. I hadn't realised you were hungry. You were welcome to it."

The young man, or boy, really – David decided he could be no more than twenty-one, and might easily be several years younger –

smiled self-consciously.

"Probably a lucky escape. After all, it was a British Rail sandwich."

But there was something in his eyes that led David to believe he was sorry the woman hadn't heard him.

David glanced at his watch, and then at the indicator board where he saw the sign "Train Cancelled" in red letters. Already there were more people milling about the concourse, those waiting for delayed or cancelled trains joined by new arrivals. Time for another cup of tea, he thought with the sort of philosophy that comes to all delayed travellers.

At least he didn't have to put up with this day in, day out as the regular commuters did. Still, perhaps they were used to it, hardened by years of unexplained delays. Had it been like this in 1848 when Waterloo Bridge, as it then was, opened? He'd come up to London today, Friday, to visit some bookshops. His father was a keen reader, and David had inherited his love of books.

David stood up, went over to the counter, and bought more insipid-looking tea.

He returned to the same table and found its occupant watching the trolley lady wipe the surface with a cloth that had seen better days.

David waited for her to finish.

At last, he was able to sit down and push a cup of coffee and a pre-packed cheese sandwich across the table.

"I didn't ..." the young man began to protest. "I can't pay you."

"It's all right."

They looked at each other.

"Thanks." And he smiled as if it was the nicest thing to have happened to him for a long time. Perhaps it was.

He had been hungry. David could see that from the way he'd eaten the sandwich, hardly chewing it at all, and from his surprise when he'd realised he'd finished it so quickly. And then his face had become serious as if he would have rationed himself if he'd thought about it earlier.

"When did you last eat?" David asked.

"Yesterday," came the reply, accompanied by a brief smile to show it wasn't that bad.

"Haven't you got any money?"

The boy's face registered a slight struggle before he answered. "Yes, but I'm saving it for an emergency."

Their eyes met, and suddenly both grinned as it crossed their minds that if being hungry didn't constitute an emergency then what did?

"I can buy you another sandwich if you're still hungry," David offered.

"No, it's all right. Thanks, though."

"Don't you have a job?"

The boy shook his head. "I was working in a hotel, but that was only part time so I thought I'd come to London. I'm not sure I want to work here but beggars ..." he smiled at the word "... can't be choosers."

They continued talking. When David next looked at his watch, he found he'd been so absorbed that he'd missed his next train. Still, he was in no hurry and, much as he liked books, he was intrigued by his companion's story.

Apart from ordering cups of tea – it was cheaper than coffee – the boy hadn't spoken to anyone in two days and he liked having someone to talk to for a change. Funny how the more people there were, the less they spoke to each other. Perhaps you had to be more careful to preserve your own space, your own identity.

"It's expensive, living in London," David agreed. When there was no reply, he asked: "You have got somewhere to stay?"

"Not yet."

"So what will you do tonight?" It was too late to do much, he thought.

"Well, the same as last night, I suppose. Stay here as long as I can and hope I can get some sleep." He hoped he sounded more blasé than he felt. "I feel a bit of a fraud. It's only my second night, after all. Some people have been sleeping rough for months, even years." His eyes looked bleak, and then he smiled. "Anyway, thanks for the coffee. Here's to another night on a crowded platform."

While David went back to an empty house. Stupid, wasn't it?

He'd spoken aloud, and they avoided each other's eyes, each suddenly uncomfortable.

You couldn't just ask for a bed for the night, no matter how much you needed one.

You couldn't just offer a bed for the night, no matter how much you sympathised with someone.

They had spoken together for some time, but they were still strangers.

They went back to discussing neutral subjects. David talked about books, and his companion told him some of the funny things that had happened or he'd heard about in the hotel he'd worked in. They relaxed again.

The café had filled up in the meantime. Disgruntled office workers moaned about another day of train disruption, while others resigned themselves to a long wait. A few muttered about wasting money on tarting up the buildings rather than sorting out the trains. Indeed, it was a very curious thing: it was as if, by painting the stations red, the passengers would fail to notice the late arrival of their trains.

When David next looked at the departures board, he decided he ought to be making a move if he planned to get home that night.

"I'd better go," he said, standing up.

"It's been nice having someone to talk to," his companion said disarmingly. He suddenly looked about fifteen and very lost.

"Me, too. Goodbye, then."

"Bye," the young man said reluctantly.

David turned towards the door. He always wondered afterwards what made him do it. Perhaps the same impulse that had prompted him to buy the coffee.

"Look," he said, rather abruptly, turning back. "If you've really got nowhere to go, you could stay at my parents' house. For a few days at any rate."

"Where d'you live?"

David told him.

There was a long pause, during which he had no idea what was going through the other person's mind. Eventually, though, the boy said, "I suppose it must be cheaper than London. It's as good a place as any to look for a job. All right."

Back on the platform, they checked the board again. This time, to David's relief, there was a platform number shown against his train which was due to leave in just under ten minutes' time.

"How much is the fare?"

David told him.

"Oh."

"Here." David took out his wallet but couldn't find anything smaller than a twenty pound note.

"Thanks." The eyes were suddenly wary. "Are you homosexual?"

Despite all the people there – ticket collectors, commuters, vendors – it was as if they were suddenly alone.

David hesitated for a moment. "Yes." It was a fair question given the circumstances. He objected to the implication, but he'd probably have asked the same question if he'd been in the boy's shoes. And would have refused the offer, too. "I'm sorry – it was a stupid idea. You're right to be careful."

The boy held out the twenty for David to take back. He looked oddly disappointed.

"No, keep it. Find somewhere safe to stay tonight." David smiled, and ignored his own feeling of disappointment.

"Thanks." The boy was grateful and something else. Surprised? His faith in humanity restored?

"Well, I'd better go. Time and British Rail wait for no man."

They looked at each other, then David added softly: "Take care." He turned and walked away towards the platform.

The young man stared after him, still with the money in his hand. He was undecided for over a minute, then he turned abruptly and made his way across the recently cleaned station concourse.

David sat on the train, trying to read. He wondered why he'd made such an offer. Concern? Sympathy? A feeling of empathy? He wished his offer had been accepted. He had been offering only somewhere to stay, nothing else, but who in this day and age is prepared to believe such an innocent motive? It was a pity. He could have done with some company.

He glanced up as someone sat down opposite him.

"I changed my mind. Is it still all right?" Anxious eyes searched David's face for his reaction.

David smiled, glad to see the boy. "Yes. My name's David Rees, by the way."

"Rob Greenaway. Here's your change."

"It's all right. Keep it."

Rob hesitated, then put the money away.

Suddenly there was nothing to say.

The seats next to them were soon taken as commuters spilled out from the mouth of the staircase which led from the tube train platform – where forty-year-old Waterloo & City rolling stock still laboured from Waterloo to Bank and back – on to the platform itself. Then there was an announcement requesting passengers to close all doors as the train was ready to depart. The grille at the top of the stairs was closed, leaving latecomers to watch impotently as their train pulled away without them. At the end of the platform, a few hardy train-spotters jotted down numbers in notebooks. Behind them, they left the NatWest Tower and, on the other side, the Post Office Tower.

Rob looked out of the window while David kept his eyes fixed on the page he was supposedly reading. Why on earth had he suggested this? He didn't know anything about the boy. He could have lied about his name. He could be a thief. He could be mentally unstable. He could be violent. It wasn't even David's house, it was his parents'. They would never have believed he could be so irresponsible. How would he explain having invited a stranger into their home?

He glanced up, just in time to notice Rob look away. He realised Rob was probably thinking along similar lines. After all, he knew nothing of David either, except that he was homosexual. You weren't likely to lie about that. Christ! You'd have to be desperate to accept under those circumstances. David suddenly felt sorry for him. Surely he was too young to be living rough?

"How old are you?"

"Nineteen. Why?"

"I just wondered." He looked down again at his book. He'd been at university when he was nineteen, not accepting a cup of coffee from a complete stranger. He wondered whether Rob's parents knew where he was. Surely they'd help if they knew he didn't have any money? Why hadn't he asked them? David supposed there'd been a row. Just because he got on well with his parents didn't mean everyone did. Jeremy and his parents didn't, for a start. Judging from what Jeremy said, his parents were pig-headed; and, as for Jeremy, well, he didn't exactly bother about meeting people half-way. David's own mother had made a few choice remarks about him. His mother had never really understood why David and Jeremy remained firm friends; and David thought his father probably suspected there was more than just friendship between them. It was one of life's little ironies: the only close homosexual friend David had, and he didn't want anything other than friendship even though Jeremy had often suggested more. Mostly he'd been joking. David thought that, on the whole, Jeremy was probably as realistic as he was about things – they were too different in most ways and too similar in others ever to be compatible in the long term.

He watched as a fellow traveller across the aisle struggled with a window that was letting in the chilly autumn air. Eventually the exasperated man banged on the metal lip, pulled down the window and then quickly pushed it up again with all his strength, this time managing to shut it.

Perhaps he'd better not ask about Rob's parents.

Perhaps they'd asked him to leave.

Why, oh why, had he suggested Rob stay at his house?

He told himself he was being stupid. Until Rob had got on the train, David had been wishing he'd accepted his offer. As soon as he had, David had begun to wish he hadn't! David had said he could stay for a few days – how did he think Rob was going to find somewhere else so soon? What was he going to do if Rob couldn't find a job or anywhere else to stay – drive him back to Waterloo so he could sleep rough again? Cardboard City was no place for anyone, let alone someone still in their teens. It would be winter before long – how on earth did people keep warm and get enough to eat when they were homeless and jobless? But why should David go out of his way to help Rob? He knew nothing about him. They probably had nothing in common and David would find his life totally disrupted. And that was ignoring the likely awkwardness of the situation. He'd scarcely be able to get straight out of the bath and then go into his bedroom to get dressed in case he met – and embarrassed – Rob on the landing. He wouldn't be able to call the house his own any more. Still, at least he had a home, he thought, putting aside his own worries for a moment.

Straight, light brown hair, direct blue eyes and a pleasant face –

Rob didn't look like a thief, especially when you remembered that he'd innocently admitted having some money and that he'd tried to return David's to him. Neither did he look unstable – a little nervous, perhaps, but that was understandable. He didn't look as if he'd be dangerous either; of the two of them, David thought himself the stronger. Although a few years older, he knew from his games of squash that he was fit, and Rob still had the slightness of youth. He could always hide the carving knife, David thought, smiling to himself. Or, if he got really paranoid, put it under his pillow.

"Where d'you come from?"

The train was just pulling out of a station and the seats next to each of them had been vacated, making conversation easier.

Rob told him, a little uneasily.

"I've been through there, but I don't really know it."

"It's quite a nice place to live. Less built up than down here. What's your parents' house like?"

"Oh, detached. Quite a large garden when you compare it with those of the houses they build nowadays. A fairly quiet road. I've lived there since I was eight. I like it."

"What about work? Are there plenty of jobs around?"

"I think so. I mean, there often seem to be notices at the Job Centre or in shop windows. There's supposed to be a shortage of school-leavers. But then they said a few years ago that we were going to have more leisure now that computers could do so much but that didn't seem to happen. Apart from the people who couldn't find a job and had too much." He smiled. "What sort of job did you want?"

Rob shrugged. "Oh, anything. The hotel I worked in was nothing special – long hours and poor pay. The staff were friendly, though. What do you do?"

"I work in an office." David mentioned the company's name, but Rob hadn't heard of it.

"Have you been there long?"

"About six years. Before that I worked somewhere else for a year, but I didn't really enjoy it so I moved."

"And now?"

"Yes, I'm happy where I am. I wouldn't stay if I wasn't."

They smiled at each other, then Rob turned his attention to the passing countryside, where the dying leaves were shades of bright yellow and dry brown with the occasional fiery red, and David went back to his book.

After about ten minutes, he looked up, too. "Next stop," he said as they sped past a station whose name Rob didn't have time to read.

"D'you live near the station?"

"About ten minutes' drive."

The train began to slow, and David unconsciously stretched. It must be a trigger mechanism, he thought, smiling to himself. Like when a film has finished and the lights come on.

Rob yawned.

"Tired?"

Rob nodded.

"Well, you should be able to catch up on your sleep tonight."

People nearby were putting on coats and collecting briefcases from luggage racks or from spaces between the seats. Commuters apparently sound asleep suddenly opened their eyes and stretched. Others moved through the carriage so that they could alight as near to the ticket barrier as possible.

David fished out his ticket and closed his book.

"What are you reading?"

" 'To Kill a Mockingbird.' "

"That was a film, wasn't it?"

"Mmm. Gregory Peck, I think."

"Who wrote it?"

"Harper Lee. A woman," he added, as the name didn't seem to

19

mean anything to Rob.

"What's it about?"

"Childhood, I suppose. She reminds you of things you'd nearly forgotten. It's strange how much your perspective changes as you grow older." He got to his feet.

As he followed David off the train and then out of the station, Rob was seized with doubts. He hesitated by the car, then he got in.

Was he completely lacking in common sense? To accept a complete stranger's offer of a bed for a few days? Especially when that stranger had admitted he was gay.

He must be out of his mind. It must be safer spending the night in London where he'd at least be with other people. Safety in numbers.

Why had David kept looking at him on the train, and then avoiding his eyes? Why had he asked him his age? Had he intended handing him over to the police if he was too young, or had he hoped Rob was over the age of consent? Would he be deterred that Rob wasn't twenty-one yet?

Telling himself that David's open admission was evidence of good faith didn't help reassure him; neither did the fact that, despite being alone in a car with him, David hadn't attempted anything.

Oh God! he thought, suddenly realising that David might have jumped to conclusions and interpreted his acceptance to mean that he was willing to sleep with him for the sake of a roof over his head. No wonder he hadn't bothered to try anything in the car, when he probably thought he was onto a sure thing.

By the time the car drew to a halt and David announced this was it, Rob was in a state of panic.

He stared at the house – it looked solid and well-cared for, mellow brick, a shiny, blue front door with four panes of glass at the top, large, white-framed windows, all seemingly innocuous –

and made no attempt to get out. Hoping to gain some time, he said: "I didn't think it would be so big." Christ, he thought, he couldn't have said anything that had more sexual overtones if he'd tried!

"It's my parents', really. They're abroad."

"So it's just you living there." He swallowed and gave no indication of any desire to move from where he was.

"Got everything?" David asked.

Rob nodded, unable to speak. They got out of the car and walked to the front door.

As David looked for his key, Rob blurted out, "Look, I don't know …" and stopped abruptly.

David, not having paid much attention to him while he'd been driving, suddenly realised Rob was worried about something.

"Why don't you phone someone and let them know where you are?" he suggested. "There's a phone box on the corner, and you'll be able to see the name of the road from there." Although it was only just beginning to get dark, the street lights were already on.

Rob considered the idea. Who could he call? There was no one. He shook his head. "No, it's all right," he said miserably.

"I'm not Jack the Ripper," David assured him.

Was he just a Good Samaritan? Rob wondered. "I suppose not." As he shut the door behind him, Rob wondered what he was letting himself in for.

"I'll make some coffee," David said, talking his coat off and hanging it on a hook in a hall that must have been at least twice the size of that in Rob's parents' house. "Is that all you've got?" He was looking at the small holdall Rob had just put down.

"No, I've got some things in a left-luggage locker. I can go back for them tomorrow." It would be an excuse, if he needed one, to leave.

They went into the lounge, where David put down his book,

and Rob looked about him.

It was a pleasant room. Although most of the furniture was obviously expensive, nothing seemed ostentatious and everything looked comfortable. It was a room that was lived in.

It felt like a nice house, he thought, following David through to the kitchen, which was warm and reminded him how hungry and how tired he was.

He sat down at the kitchen table, and then stood up again to take off his coat. Although the room was full of gleaming pots and pans and electrical appliances, he smiled as he noticed some unwashed dishes by the sink.

"I didn't get round to doing those before I left," David admitted, noticing what had attracted Rob's attention.

"No dishwasher?" He looked about, apparently trying to sort out the various gadgets.

"Yes, over there, but it doesn't seem worth it when there's just me. When my parents are at home, we use it. Dad works in America a lot, and my mother usually goes with him now. He started working overseas when I was about fifteen, but my mother stayed here until I left school. No," he corrected himself: "No, she didn't go with him until after Holly, our Labrador, died."

They both smiled at the thought that David's mother had viewed the dog with at least equal concern.

For a moment, Rob believed once more that David's motives weren't as suspect as he'd imagined.

When the coffee was ready, David brought it over to the table, where, for a while, they sat companionably sipping their hot drinks.

"Would you like a biscuit?" David asked.

"Yes, please." He took a chocolate digestive from the tin David held out. Biscuits had become luxury items.

"How old are you?" Rob asked.

"Twenty-eight."

Somehow that worried Rob. He'd thought him younger.

"Why are you still living at home?" he said with the directness of youth.

David grinned. "Various reasons. I get on well with my parents, they need someone to look after the house when they're away, I've never ..." He stopped, amazed to find himself about to say that he'd never met anyone he'd wanted to live with. Only minutes ago, he'd been thinking of Rob simply as someone he'd been fool enough to invite to his home; now it was as if they were back in the anonymous intimacy of the café at Waterloo. "I've never wanted to move," he finished lamely.

"There's really only one bedroom you can have," he said, changing the subject. "We've got four, but one's just used for storing things in and as a rather cramped study."

"Oh, anything's better than sleeping on a bench. Or not sleeping at all. You don't appreciate a roof over your head until there isn't one." Despite its being hot, he drank the coffee quickly.

"D'you want some more?" David offered.

"No, thanks."

"I'll finish this and then I'll show you the room."

Upstairs, David pointed out the bathroom to Rob, and then opened the door of the spare bedroom.

"Well, here we are."

Rob stepped inside.

It was much larger than his bedroom at home. It was mostly blue – light blue walls, dark blue curtains and carpet, and the patterned duvet cover contained blues and mauves. The furniture was mostly white – a white bedside table, white wardrobe, a white chest near the window with a blue and green rug thrown over it – though there was an obviously old brown chair in one corner.

David was saying something about putting the radiator on, when Rob looked at the bed and froze.

He turned to David, his eyes hard. "It's a double bed," he said very quietly. "Look, when I changed my mind about coming here I didn't mean that I intended ..." He stopped, not wanting to put his fears into words.

"Neither did I," retorted David, beginning to lose his temper at the unjustness of the accusation when he was in fact trying to do someone a good turn. "But the only single bed in the house is in my room and I'm damned if I'm giving it up. If it's not to your liking, you can sleep on the sofa." His anger died as quickly as it had come when he took in Rob's expression. He hadn't realised the kid was petrified. He was only young, after all. Perhaps this was the last straw.

"I'm sorry," he went on. "But, honestly, this is the only room you can have."

He could see the struggle reflected in Rob's face as he tried to make up his mind whether to believe him. Perhaps at the station someone had tried to pick him up and now he was wary. It was an unusual situation, to say the least, and he could hardly be blamed for expecting the worst.

Rob looked round the room again. It was a nice room. Not too fussy or cluttered, not so recently decorated as to feel more like a show piece than somewhere you could feel comfortable. Why did he have to make such a fuss? If David was sincere, Rob was surprised he hadn't been thrown out of the house in view of his remark. And if he wasn't? It didn't bear thinking about. What alternative was there, anyway?

"Is there a key?" he asked at last.

"What?"

"To the door. Is there a key?" He stared at the empty keyhole as if one would materialise. At least he could try to minimise the risks, he thought. Perhaps he could barricade himself inside.

"I'm not sure. There might be one downstairs. I can have a look."

"It's a nice room," Rob conceded slowly. He put his bag down at last. He'd made his decision. He'd made his bed, he thought wryly. "Thank you."

"I'll make us something to eat. You're welcome to have a look round the house or watch television." Now that it came to it, David didn't quite know what to do with his guest.

"Could I have a bath?" ventured Rob.

"Yes, of course. I'll find you a towel."

"And could I use the washing-machine? Someone spilled beer over me last night."

"That's all right. Leave everything you want washed outside the bathroom and I'll put them in for you. You can borrow a dressing-gown," he added.

Rob balked at the idea of a dressing-gown: he would have felt vulnerable. "Could you lend me some clothes instead? Just a pair of trousers and a pullover, I mean."

They were about the same height. "Yes, OK," David agreed. From his room he got an old, but clean, pullover and a pair of trousers he'd not worn much. He gave them, together with a towel taken from the airing cupboard, to Rob.

"The water's been on since six, so it should be hot. Supper won't be ready for at least half an hour so you should have plenty of time. If you leave your clothes outside, they can be washed tonight and dry by tomorrow."

"Thanks." Rob smiled awkwardly and closed the bathroom door behind him. The bathroom was pleasant, with its relaxing warmth and restful green walls and tiles. A plant whose name he didn't know cascaded from a high ledge. He thought he'd better wash his hair, too, so he opened a cabinet and searched for some shampoo. There was a mirror on the cabinet door. He looked at his reflection as if he hoped he could see his future. He turned away. He was being fanciful.

After fetching some clean sheets and leaving them in the spare room, David went downstairs and searched for something to eat.

n intending to have fish, but there wasn't enough for two.

d a couple of pork chops in the freezer so he took those out and defrosted them in the microwave.

The potatoes he peeled and put in a saucepan to boil, while the chops he put under a low grill.

Then he took out some frozen peas, put enough for the two of them in another saucepan, but didn't light the gas as they wouldn't take long to cook.

Upstairs he found Rob's discarded clothes, a pair of socks being the most intimate item Rob had chosen to leave outside the bathroom door, which he took downstairs and put in the washing machine.

He'd set the table in the dining room, opened a bottle of wine and was doing the washing-up from that morning when Rob reappeared. David didn't hear him enter.

"I used some shampoo – I hope you don't mind."

"No, of course not." David dried his hands and turned round.

He was unprepared for the sudden rush of desire he felt. Rob stood there, his hair still damp, his feet bare, smiling a little self-consciously. Perhaps the fact that he was wearing David's clothes made David feel some sort of intimacy.

David hurriedly turned towards the cooker before Rob noticed. "Why don't you go and sit down? I've just got to do the peas and then we can eat."

"OK." Rob went out and David busied himself with supper, trying to put all wayward thoughts out of his mind.

Rob had, although luckily David was unaware of the fact, registered the effect his presence had had on David; but he'd also realised David's profound confusion and the way he'd dealt with the problem. In a way, he supposed, it was a compliment. But it was also a complication.

By the time he'd dished up, David was in control of his emotions again.

He carried the plates into the lounge and then poured out a glass of wine for each of them. He decided that he'd better not offer to replenish Rob's glass in case it looked as though he was trying to get him drunk.

Rob looked at the table – the full plates, the shining cutlery, the wine – and the room, and for a second he was close to tears. Reaction setting in, he told himself, trying to pull himself together, to the sudden change from being homeless. Utterly ridiculous; he'd slept rough only one night. It must be the prospect of continuing to sleep rough.

"Are you all right?" David asked as Rob just sat there, not eating. Was he a vegetarian? Surely he'd have said if he was?

"Yes, I'm fine." Rob picked up his knife and fork and began to eat.

"Oh, I found the key, by the way. I put it in the lock."

"Thanks."

"I think some of the keys are interchangeable, though. I'm sure I remember my cousin locking himself in when he was young, and Mum and Dad finding another key to the door. But I'm not sure which room that was. Oh, that reminds me – I usually turn the burglar alarm on at night. It's connected to the front and back door, and to some of the downstairs windows."

Rob ate hungrily.

David, trying to make him feel more at ease, talked about work.

"Would you like something else to drink?" he asked eventually, as Rob had taken only a sip of wine. "There's some orange juice in the fridge."

"Yes. Thanks."

David went out to the kitchen, got another glass, poured some orange juice into it, and then returned.

"I'm not really used to wine," Rob explained apologetically, accepting the glass David offered. "Thanks." He drank the orange juice quickly.

After they'd finished eating, Rob looked up awkwardly. "I'm sorry if I offended you earlier. It's just ... I don't know you."

"That's OK." David grinned. "Honestly, the only thing you need worry about is whether or not I defrosted the pork chops properly."

Rob looked at him, assessing what he'd said, and then suddenly he smiled and his face lit up.

For a moment David was engulfed, not by the desire he'd felt earlier, but by a bitter-sweet longing for something intangible. "Anyway," he continued more soberly, "you'd have to be mad nowadays to sleep with someone you didn't know."

"Almost as mad as inviting a total stranger to your house," Rob joked a little warily.

David grinned. "Mmm. I can't say I didn't have second thoughts."

"Just say if you'd prefer me to go." Although what he'd have done in a strange place at this hour, he had no idea.

"No. You're welcome to stay."

"Thanks."

David stood up. "I'm going to make a cup of coffee. Would you like some?"

Rob nodded.

While they drank their coffee, David noticed that Rob could hardly keep his eyes open. His head would start to nod and then jerk back as he tried to stay awake, whether from politeness or just putting off going to bed, David didn't know.

"Why don't you go to bed?" suggested David gently, although it wasn't late.

"What about the things in the washing machine?"

"Oh, I'll see to those. Don't worry."

"Thanks." Rob put down his empty cup and stood up. His eyes searched David's face. David wondered what he saw.

"Have you got everything you need? I left some sheets in your room."

"Yes." He looked young and shy again. "Well, goodnight, then."

David smiled. "Goodnight."

TWO

It was gone ten o'clock before David heard any movement upstairs. He'd been in the kitchen, watching the rain trickling down the window pane. Rob must have been tired – he'd slept round the clock.

He collected Rob's things, went up, and knocked at the bedroom door.

"I've brought your clothes," he said.

"Just coming."

David heard what he took to be a chair being moved from behind the door, then the sound of the key turning. The door opened a few inches.

"Thanks," Rob said as he took the pile of clothes David held out. He closed the door quickly.

His shirt and trousers had been ironed, and they and his pullover had been neatly folded. He felt churlish and ungrateful.

When he went downstairs, David asked him if he'd slept well.

"It took me a while to drop off, but then I slept like a log." He didn't mention that he'd lain awake waiting for the sound of footsteps on the stairs and then the turning of the door handle, but that he'd eventually been overcome by tiredness. Why did reason desert you at night? The door had been locked after all. He'd have heard the chair being knocked over if someone had tried to get in. And there was something about David that made Rob want to trust him, to believe that he was merely being kind.

"Do you want toast or cereal?"

"Toast, please."

David smiled to himself at Rob's obvious disappointment at not being offered both. "We'll have an early lunch," he promised and, from the way Rob visibly brightened at the prospect, he knew Rob had indeed been hungry. "Tea or coffee?"

"Coffee, please. I was drinking tea at the station. It's cheaper." He looked down at the table. "It felt like I'd been there for ages. Stupid, really."

When David joined him, he asked, "Aren't you having any breakfast?" David had just a cup of coffee in front of him.

"I've already eaten. I've been up since eight."

"You should have woken me. I expect there are things you want to do today." He spread marmalade on his toast.

"Nothing special. You looked last night as if you could do with a lie-in, so I let you sleep." He sipped his coffee.

"Thanks for ironing my clothes. You needn't have gone to all that trouble."

"It didn't take long," David said easily.

"Still, it was good of you." Rob ate a piece of toast. "The bed was comfortable," he added, then he felt his face grow hot as he wondered if he'd made it sound like an invitation. "But then I suppose anything would seem comfortable after spending the night on a bench." Damn. Now he sounded rude. He realised David was trying not to smile. "I'm sorry," he apologised, laughing at himself.

"Forget it," David answered.

"D'you mind being homosexual?" Rob found himself asking unexpectedly.

David gave him a level look. He nearly replied that that was none of Rob's business but something prompted him to be more open. "No," he said. "No, I don't. I can't imagine being any other way. And I don't particularly want to."

"What about prejudice, though?"

"Perhaps I'm lucky. I haven't really come across any. Maybe –

Well, I suppose I don't broadcast the fact. Not usually. It's not meant to be a secret, it's just that I don't see why people have to know. It's a private thing. It shouldn't make a difference."

"But you're afraid it will?" Rob asked perceptively.

"I suppose so, if I'm being honest."

Rob finished the last piece of toast. "I haven't behaved very well towards you."

"I can hardly hold it against you if I tell you to be careful and then you are!" David grinned.

"I suppose not," Rob conceded.

Again David was aware of a feeling of empathy. He'd never spoken to anyone other than family – and Jeremy – about his homosexuality: he'd never wanted to. He found Rob a receptive audience.

"I'll get the rest of my stuff after lunch," Rob said. His doubts seemed to have evaporated overnight.

"Have you got enough money for the fare?"

Rob nodded, but was touched by David's concern. "Can I do anything? The washing-up or something?"

"You could Hoover your room. It hasn't been done for a while. You'll find the Hoover under the stairs. There's probably some polish there as well."

"OK."

Rob went out, and David washed up and then started preparing lunch. After a while, he heard the sound of the vacuum cleaner. When he'd finished, he went into the lounge. Rob was standing by the window, watching the steady, weekend rain.

"Typical!" David said in mock disgust.

"What? Oh, the weather. Yes. I like the garden, though." Despite its sogginess, it was green and peaceful.

"Yes. It's not overlooked, either – not that I've got any complaints about the neighbours. They've been here nearly as long as we have. It faces south-west, so you get a lot of sun, too – when it's out," he added pointedly. "What's your parents' house like?" Damn, he thought, remembering his resolution not to mention Rob's family in case it upset him.

"Oh," Rob turned from the window, not seeming annoyed. "It's a lot smaller than this. It's got three bedrooms but they're all small and the garden's tiny." He changed the subject. "Can I do anything else?"

David shook his head. "I was going to clean the car but there's not much point at the moment. Lunch'll be about half past twelve. You can do what you like till then."

Rob looked uncertain, so David added, "Today's paper's somewhere around. Or you could go for a walk. Although perhaps not." The rain had suddenly become heavier. "You can watch television if there's anything on, or help yourself to a book – there's loads upstairs."

"I noticed." Rob felt a little guilty at having glanced into some of the upstairs rooms already even though David had told him he could look round the house. He'd opened the door to what was obviously David's room – he saw the single bed – and then closed it quickly, fearing his curiosity might be taken as prying, but not before noticing the full bookcases. Another bedroom, decorated in pinks and greens, was Mr and Mrs Rees' room, while the fourth room housed a desk with a computer on it and assorted furniture, abandoned in a somewhat haphazard way. And more books.

Rob watched David, who'd settled down to continue reading 'To Kill a Mockingbird', for a moment, then rummaged under the coffee table and pulled out Saturday's newspaper.

After lunch, David washed up and Rob dried. It was still raining, and David wondered whether Rob had changed his mind about going up to London.

"What time are the trains?" Rob asked suddenly as if he knew what David had been thinking.

"They're every half-hour – well, they are during the week. I think they're roughly the same on Saturdays. The timetable's in the lounge." David found the timetable in a drawer, and showed it to Rob. "You could get the one at twenty-to," he said.

"You're sure it's OK for me to stay for a while?"

David nodded. "I'll give you a lift to the station if you like. You'll get drenched otherwise."

"Thanks."

David dropped Rob off outside the mainline station. "Here," he jotted his number on a scrap of paper. "Give me a ring when you get back and I'll pick you up."

Rob watched as David reversed the car and then drove off. Then he bought a single to Waterloo.

At ten p.m. David bolted the front door and set the alarm. He knew he felt let down at not being trusted. He'd checked Rob's room and found he'd left nothing behind. Perhaps it was all for the best that Rob had decided not to come back.

He sat down on the sofa and picked up his book. It would have been difficult, he had to admit. Not the physical desire he'd felt last night – that was controllable, although he'd been shocked at its intensity. It wasn't really desire for Rob, he scarcely knew him. No, it was the way that Rob's being in the house had served to underline David's rather solitary existence. It was easier to live without such a reminder.

He read a few pages.

It was a pity, he thought. He'd liked Rob.

He hoped he'd be all right. If you didn't have anywhere to stay and you didn't have any money, what did you do? The answer was disturbing.

How bad did things have to be, he wondered, before you considered theft or prostitution a reasonable way of earning a living? How many men would Rob talk to before one of them wanted something in return for buying him a cup of coffee?

He put the book down on the coffee table.

Were his own motives so pure?

He'd acted out of compassion, true, but was it just coincidence that Rob happened to be young, good-looking and male? He thought not. Still, you'd hardly invite someone to stay if you couldn't stand them, he thought, smiling. And living under the same roof as a relative stranger could turn out to have hidden pitfalls.

No, it was probably better that Rob hadn't returned.

That didn't stop him being worried.

Rob had got cold feet, both metaphorically and literally. He was also wet.

He'd gone back to London, still with half an idea of returning to David's parents' house. He had enough money to buy another ticket although it might have been cheaper to have bought a return, he realised. But he hadn't wanted to commit himself.

He'd wandered around Waterloo, trying not to look as if he'd nowhere to go, but hoping not to lose his place on a bench. He passed some time looking in WH Smith's at the array of books and magazines on offer and wondered if he should spend some of his meagre resources on something to read. Boredom was as much an enemy as hunger. If he'd thought about it earlier, he could have asked David if he could borrow a book. But then he'd have had to return it somehow. And, anyway, if he'd planned to go straight back, he wouldn't have needed a book. He wanted to trust David, but his head told him he was being stupid. How could you possibly trust someone who'd admitted they were gay and then had invited you back to an empty house? Especially when they'd obviously got aroused just by looking at you? He'd been lucky that nothing had happened last night.

At eight o'clock he'd left the station and had gone for a walk to pass the time. The rain, which had eased off, started to pour and he'd got soaked. He'd bought some soup and a cheese roll to try and cheer himself up. If he spent much more time there, he'd have to ask someone if there really were soup kitchens.

Back at Waterloo, as he took out his handkerchief to wipe his face, a piece of paper fell out of his pocket. He picked it up. It was the note David had given him. He threw it in a nearby bin. The numbers had smudged, anyway.

He spent a miserable night without any sleep. He saw the trains carrying newspapers pull out of the station. He kept thinking his watch must have stopped, but, no, the four-faced clock suspended near the Waterloo Road exit showed the same time. By six o'clock on the Sunday morning, all he could think of was the warmth and peace he'd felt on waking the previous day. David had bought him a coffee, paid his train fare, cooked him supper and lunch, ironed his clothes and, finally, driven him to the station. He'd done it all in a perfectly natural way, not as if he expected anything in return. And Rob hadn't even bothered to phone him to say he'd changed his mind.

He was a bastard. And during that time David hadn't so much as tried to lay a finger on him. There'd been plenty of opportunity – the car, the bedroom, the kitchen – there would have been no witnesses. And what had David talked about? Sex? No. His parents. His job. A Labrador they'd once had called Holly. They didn't seem likely topics of conversation for someone who wished him harm. David had even suggested he call someone to let them know where he was. How could he question David's integrity? He was an ungrateful, suspicious bastard and he had no one to blame for his sleepless night but himself. He wanted to cry.

Lunchtime came, well, midday, to be more exact; he didn't eat anything. How could he go back? he thought. David had offered hospitality and he'd taken it. Then he'd walked out. He could scarcely go back as if nothing had happened. What was supposed to have taken place – twenty-four-hour amnesia?

By six p.m. Rob knew he couldn't face another night sleeping rough. He wondered what would happen if he struck up a conversation with someone else. Perhaps they would buy him a cup of coffee.

David looked at his watch. Nearly nine o'clock. He'd forgotten to take the sheets off the bed Rob had slept in. Oh well, he'd do it next weekend. He was just getting up to go into the kitchen and move some of the food he'd bought yesterday out of the fridge and into the freezer when the doorbell rang.

"You're soaked!" He looked at Rob. "How did you get here?"

"I walked from the station." His tone was somewhere between defiance and defeat. It had taken him ages to get there, partly because he'd come on foot and partly because he'd got lost several times and had to ask people for directions. Once, he'd turned left instead of right and had had to retrace his steps.

"Come in." David closed the door and hung up the damp coat which Rob had taken off. Neither said anything about the intervening twenty-four hours.

"I lost your phone number. And I couldn't remember how to spell your surname." He didn't mention how the number had been lost and that he'd not wanted to waste his money on a phone call. Or that yesterday he'd been afraid his resolution not to return would crumble if David had been sympathetic. Or that today he hadn't phoned in case David had had enough of being messed around.

David smiled gently at the bedraggled figure in front of him. Why hadn't he looked in a phone book? It wouldn't have been too hard to track down the number. "Go and have a bath," he said quietly, "I'll get you some beans on toast when you come down."

s." Rob swallowed and picked up the hold-all he'd
‿‿ with him two days previously, together with the one he'd
collected from left luggage, and turned to go upstairs.

"Have you got some dry clothes to put on?"

"Yes ... well, unless the rain's soaked through." He bent down
to unzip one of the bags and felt inside. "No, they're dry." He
stood up.

"The towel's in the airing-cupboard next to the bathroom."

They stared at each other, then Rob turned quickly and went
upstairs before David noticed that it wasn't just rain that had made
his face wet. He felt about as confident as a five-year-old on his
first day at school.

David went resignedly into the kitchen. Was this what was meant
by déjà vu? Well, at least he hadn't changed the sheets.

He turned on the switch for the hot water in case Rob used it all
up and then put some bread in the toaster and got out a tin of
beans.

Poor kid, he thought, realising what a difference a nine-year
age-gap meant. Where had Rob been last night? What had made
him come back?

When he came down, Rob was very quiet.

"Tomorrow."

Rob looked up from his plate of baked beans.

"Tomorrow, I'll get another key cut for the front door. I'll turn
off the alarm before I go to work. You'd better use the kitchen
door if you want to go out. Make sure you lock it behind you,
though." David wasn't entirely happy leaving Rob on his own in
the house, but he had no option. He couldn't keep him locked up
just to be sure he didn't steal anything. Anyway, he'd had ample
opportunity to have done so already.

"I'm sorry," Rob mumbled, staring unblinkingly at the table.

David realised he was upset. "It's all right." He stood up. "I'll leave you in peace. I've got to sort some things out for work." He went out.

Eventually Rob joined him in the lounge. "Coffee?" David asked.

"Yes, please, if you're having some."

They drank it, watching a programme David had videoed on Thursday. When it finished, David collected the cups and said goodnight to Rob. "I've locked up," he added.

Rob sat for a few minutes, staring at the blank television screen, then he, too, went upstairs.

As he'd done on the Friday, he locked the door and put a chair against it.

He couldn't sleep. He was overtired. After a while he got up and, very quietly, moved the chair and unlocked the door. He crept along the corridor and opened a door. He listened for a moment in case he'd woken David. Then he picked up what he'd come for and left, closing the door softly behind him.

When he got back to his room, he again locked the door and replaced the chair. He looked to see what book he'd taken from the unused bedroom and found it was David Copperfield. They'd read it at school. It seemed a long while ago, now. On the whole, he'd enjoyed school. He'd been willing to learn, although he'd struggled with French and economics. French he could never pronounce quite right; and economic theories just confused him.

Well, at least the television set was still there, David said to himself, reassured, as he returned home. He always assumed that that would be the first thing any self-respecting burglar – or stranger invited to the house – would steal. It was like coming back after a holiday: first, you looked to see if the house was still standing, and then, inside, you checked whether the television and video had disappeared.

During the next couple of weeks, Rob looked for a job. David lent him some money to cover the bus fares into town, and Rob promised he'd pay him back when he was able. He checked the situations vacant section in the papers, but his lack of skills and qualifications precluded the better paid jobs. Not that he was fussy, but when he did ring up, the position had always been filled.

He was still quiet. He always asked first if it was OK if he made himself a cup of tea or watched television. He knew David liked reading and he was afraid the sound from the set would distract him despite David's assurance that he didn't really notice it. Sometimes when David came in he would find Rob guiltily switching the television off.

"It's just some Australian soap," Rob said once, shrugging.

He spent a fair bit of time in his room in the evening. It was David's home – David had only offered Rob somewhere to stay temporarily and he probably wanted to relax when he got in from work. Rob would come down for supper and help with the washing-up, then he'd stay to watch television for a while – David usually turned it on for the news or for something like M.A.S.H..

He'd also look through the local paper to see what sort of accommodation was available. Well, to be honest, how much it cost. It would be a lot cheaper to find something where he came from; even more cheap to live at home. Still, maybe Mr Micawber was right: perhaps something would turn up.

When David got home one evening, Rob announced he'd found a

job. It was only in a record shop, but he could start on Monday and he'd be paid at the end of the week ... which was the important thing. He'd be able to move out once he was earning some money.

"Wait and see if the job's OK," David advised.

"Are you sure you don't mind?"

David said he didn't.

The following week, Rob started work at the record shop, and in the evenings he went to see accommodation advertised in the local press. The places he liked were beyond his means; the others depressed him.

On the Saturday's pay-day, he put some money on the coffee table. David looked up.

"It's what I owe you," Rob explained. He gave David a list that included exact bus and train fares – and the change he hadn't returned to David – as well as some money for his board. There was even an amount to cover the cost of having had an extra key cut. "Let me know if I haven't allowed enough for the food," he added.

David was on the point of saying that he didn't want the money; after all, Rob couldn't have anything left out of his first week's pay; but then he saw that being able to repay him meant a lot to Rob. "Thanks. It covers the food." He glanced at the list again. "You've forgotten the cup of coffee I bought you, though."

It was a moment before Rob worked out from David's expression that he was joking. "I thought you were serious!" he said, relieved.

"No. You can have the coffee on me."

"Thanks. Not just for the coffee."

They were silent for a while, both a little embarrassed, and then David asked curiously: "What would you have done if you hadn't come here?"

"Oh, gone home, I suppose," Rob replied, his eyes showing that he was thinking about the past.

It couldn't have been too serious a rift, then, thought David, but he didn't pursue the matter.

"Not that I wanted to go back. Not yet."

"Are you looking at any places tomorrow?"

"Yes. There's a couple of houses in the same area which have rooms to let. I thought I'd go round in the morning."

"Where are they?"

Rob told him.

David's expression changed. "Oh," he said expressively.

"What's wrong?"

David paused. "Well, it's not a very salubrious part of town. In fact, it's got rather a bad reputation – fights on Saturday nights, that sort of thing. Still," he finished more positively, "the houses you're going to see may be OK."

"I hope so. They've got one major advantage to start with." When David looked puzzled, he added: "At least I can afford them."

After they'd eaten, they watched a film on television, but David fell asleep on the big, comfortable sofa half-way through. He woke up only to find he'd missed the ending. "What happened?"

Rob told him.

David grinned. "I keep doing this – going to sleep in the middle of a play or something and waking up only when the credits are rolling. I suppose I ought to video everything. I must be getting old," he joked. "At university I used to study until three o'clock in the morning sometimes. That is, if there wasn't a party to go to."

"You haven't been out much lately." Rob had spent three Saturdays there and David hadn't gone out in the evenings.

"No. I suppose I haven't these last few weeks." He didn't add that a 'relationship' – he wasn't over-enamoured of the word and it didn't quite sum up the low-key nature of the particular friendship – had finished about two months earlier. Jeremy was going out with someone new, so David hadn't seen him much over the past couple of months. And Mike and Carol had recently moved house, which had taken up most of their free time and had meant that, because of the distance, it wasn't so easy to arrange evenings out.

"Still, it's not too long till Christmas." To judge from the shops, it had already arrived. "Usually there are quite a few things going on then. Office parties," – he grimaced good-naturedly – "drinks down the pub, even two or three birthday parties." He wondered what Rob would do at Christmas. "It can get a bit too quiet sometimes when my parents aren't here. Not that I object to my own company, but it's a nice change having someone here." He stretched, swung his feet onto the floor, and stood up. "Tea or coffee?"

"Tea, please." Tea had become more palatable since its price had ceased being the determining factor.

There was a companionable silence as they sipped. Rob was glad he was no longer – at least for the moment – in David's debt; and David was still in a pleasant, relaxed state after his doze.

In bed, Rob read for a while.

David, however, went straight to sleep.

"Well? What were they like?" David looked up from the Sunday magazine and wondered if he was the only person to be aware of the world shortage of staples.

Rob pulled a face. "A bit grim." The first one had been a large, gloomy room in a large, gloomy house with high, nicotine-stained ceilings. The place was old and dilapidated, furnished with tables and chairs that had seen several monarchs come and go but which would never be classed as antiques. Dusty curtains hung at the window and there were spots of condensation in the bathroom.

The second room he'd seen was in a modern house and was cheerful but tiny. Even his meagre belongings would have filled it. His room at home had been bigger.

"You were right – it's not a very nice area. The bus service is good, though, and it's not far from the station. I said I'd let them know."

"Are you thinking of taking one?"

He shrugged. "I haven't decided yet." He changed the subject. "D'you need a hand with the dinner?"

"What's the time? Oh, yes, you could peel a couple of potatoes and put them on."

After lunch, David's aunt phoned to find out if he'd be coming to them at Christmas. His parents weren't sure if his father would be able to take enough time off work to make it worthwhile flying home, and so it had been agreed that, if they returned, they'd spend Christmas with David's uncle and aunt. David said he'd come, even if his parents couldn't get away. He wondered whether Rob had any plans. Probably Christmas was a long way down his list of priorities.

When he put the receiver down, Rob asked if he could make a call.

"Yes, of course." David wondered if he was phoning home at long last. Of course, he might already have done so while David had been at work. Then David noticed that he was reading the number from a piece of paper. Having greeted the person at the other end, Rob said he'd take the room if it was still available.

When he came off the phone, David said, "I thought you didn't like either of the places you saw?"

"Well, hopefully it won't be for too long."

"Which one have you chosen – the large, gloomy one or the small, bright one?"

"The large, gloomy one." Already he was regretting the

decision.

"Well, it won't be forever. When can you move in?"

"Anytime. I thought Tuesday. It'll be my day off." If he worked Saturdays, he got one day off during the week.

Outside, it was still damp from the previous evening's rain. David put the garden table and chairs in the garage and then collected up bean sticks and netting which had been used during the summer. These he put in the shed. Having pruned the rose bushes and the buddleia, he put the cuttings in a green sack that he'd take down to the dump when full. As the afternoon was sunny and mild, he decided to creosote one of the fence panels. Most were all right – he and his father had done those not obscured by shrubs and climbing plants a couple of years ago – but this one had had ivy growing over it so they hadn't bothered. The ivy had died off for some reason. His mother said she'd never liked it and perhaps the honeysuckle would spread now it didn't have any competition from that side.

He changed into an old shirt, rolled up his sleeves and began. As he worked, he realised he'd have the house to himself again. He'd miss Rob, he thought, even though he hadn't been there long and he'd been a bit on the quiet side. Shy, rather. Still, he was only nineteen. David had been relieved that the desire he'd experienced that first evening hadn't been repeated. He hadn't felt awkward, either, despite Rob's being aware of his sexual preferences.

The area where Rob intended living wouldn't have been his first choice. But then money wasn't a problem for David. Also, renting was always a Catch 22 situation: you couldn't afford to buy, so you rented a place; you couldn't save, so you still couldn't afford to buy. Meanwhile, house prices went up more than salaries. In fact, his father worried about David not getting a foot on the property ladder and had assured him he wouldn't lose out just because he remained at home to take care of the house. David had replied, jokingly it seemed at the time, that maybe it wouldn't always be like this – maybe one day house prices would even fall. It would make more sense for Rob to stay on while he saved at least enough to be able to rent somewhere decent.

He stopped putting wood preserver on the fence as he considered the idea.

It had made a pleasant change, having company, and he found Rob easy to get on with. The only problem had been that Rob seemed reluctant to treat the place as home and that, in turn, had made David feel slightly uncomfortable. As if he always had to act as host. What would Rob think David's intentions were if he suggested staying on? He mentally shrugged. If Rob thought they were anything other than honourable, then maybe it would be better if he did move out.

The fence panel completed, he washed the brush and put it and the tin of preserver away in the shed and locked the door.

In the lounge, he found Rob watching television. David sat down on the sofa and gave a sigh of relief. That should take care of the garden for a while, at any rate. He was hot. He needed a bath, too. For a while they both watched a female panda steadily eating bamboo shoots in a forest somewhere in China.

"Rob?"

Rob looked up.

"This place you've taken – is it really awful?"

Rob hesitated. "I suppose it's not that bad," he said.

"You don't sound very keen." In fact, it had sounded as if he'd used as his comparison the Black Hole of Calcutta or the inside of a Turkish jail.

"It's all I can afford," he said simply.

After a brief pause, David said, "Look. You don't have to move out. You can stay a bit longer. It'll give you the chance to save up so you can afford something better."

Rob said nothing.

"Well, it was just an idea," David said, standing up. "I'm going to have a bath." He was very nearly out of the room when he heard Rob say: "Thanks," very quietly. He turned round.

"I've already said I'll move in, though." But he was sorely tempted to take David up on his offer.

David leaned back against the door. "It's stupid to go there if you don't want to."

"But ..." Rob looked searchingly at David and then decided to say what he was thinking. "But won't it be awkward, me being here, if you want to ask friends back?" You didn't need a degree to work out what he meant by 'friends'.

"No, I don't see that as a problem." If they couldn't accept that he could have a platonic (or did he mean 'non-platonic'?) friendship, then any relationship would be doomed from the outset, anyway.

"How long were you thinking of? A month? Three months?"

David hadn't given much thought to the matter. He shrugged. "Well, I suppose you might as well stay until my parents come home. Unless we get on each other's nerves before then!"

"When are they due back?"

"I don't know for sure. Not until next summer, maybe even later." To Rob, this sounded a lifetime away. Next summer ... what would he be doing then?

David unrolled his shirt-sleeves. "We'd have to agree some sort of rent. I don't want to make a profit out of you, just as long as food and other expenses are covered. Then you'd be able to save some of your pay. I don't suppose there'd be much chance of that if you took the room."

"No, you're right."

"Have a think about it."

"OK. David?"

David turned back once more.

"I suppose I should tell you why I left home." He stopped, disinclined to continue. At last he said: "It was just a misunderstanding. Mostly on my part. Things had got a bit claustrophobic and I felt that I had to get away. What I mean is there's nothing for you to worry about. I'm not wanted by the police, or anything like that."

David grinned. "Well, I'm glad the family silver's safe," he said, before he turned again to leave the room and go and have a bath.

David was right when he guessed that Rob wasn't very happy about the room he'd said he'd taken and, although there was still a small, nagging doubt that told Rob to beware, Rob's main feeling was one of gratitude. All right, so David wasn't keen on girls, but so far his actions were all above board.

Financially, it made sense to stay.

Materially – the house as opposed to the room – it made sense, too.

Logistically, it was no worse than the place he'd looked at today.

Logically. He wasn't sure. Nowadays two people of the opposite sex could share a house or a flat without their friends all assuming there was more to it. Why should he feel more wary of David than he would of a girl? David had been honest with him after all and there was certainly no way David could have misinterpreted Rob's intentions.

A couple of months couldn't do any harm. Could it?

THREE

Rob had been wondering how he could repay David's kindness. He felt a bit guilty letting him do most of the cooking, but, as he'd told David, he hadn't had much experience of doing any himself.

He asked Sally for her advice. She'd been working in the record shop only a couple of months longer than he had, and they'd become friends, often going to lunch together.

"What does your friend like?"

"Most things, I suppose."

"And what can you cook?"

A pause.

"Well, that narrows it down."

"I didn't do cookery at school," Rob said defensively.

"Spaghetti," she said promptly, deciding now was not the time to discover whether that was meant as a sexist remark.

"How d'you cook it?"

She laughed. "I'll write it all down for you. When are you going to do it?"

"Tonight?" he said hopefully.

"Have you got all the ingredients?" She smiled as she realised the stupidity of the question. "OK. Well, I'll write down the recipe in my lunch hour and then you can make sure you've got everything. Do I know her?" she added mischievously.

"No, it's not – I mean, I thought I'd do the cooking for a change. It's not really fair letting someone else do it all the time." He'd told Sally that he shared a house.

"I'm only teasing!"

She gave him the recipe as she'd said, and warned him that it might take longer. "All cookery books seem to underestimate the time needed to prepare and cook things."

Rob couldn't remember whether they already had any of the ingredients so, when it was his turn for lunch, he went out to get everything Sally had listed.

That evening, with the help of Sally's instructions and one of Mrs Rees' cookery books he'd found in the kitchen, he attempted to cook spaghetti bolognese.

It didn't taste too bad, he thought, as he sampled a little, but it still tasted like mince. It looked a bit grey, too, despite his efforts with the tomato purée. The spaghetti was sticking together and he didn't know what to do apart from trying to separate it with a fork.

Sally was right, he thought, as he noticed that he'd taken nearly twice as long as the recipe book claimed. Still, it was lucky that it hadn't been ready earlier as David wasn't home yet.

After half an hour of waiting, he dished up his own meal. It was edible, but even he had to concede that it looked unappetising even though he'd done what Sally had suggested. And the fact that David still hadn't returned by the time he'd finished took the edge off what little pride he had in having cooked a meal which didn't go straight from freezer to oven.

By half-past nine, he knew David would have eaten elsewhere and, disconsolately, he emptied the contents of the plate he'd been keeping warm into the bin.

It was just after ten when he heard David's car.

"Hello!" David called from the hall. He went into the kitchen, got an apple, which he washed, and went into the lounge.

"Hello."

"I had a game of squash with Graham," he explained. "We couldn't get a court at lunchtime, so we thought we'd play after work. Then we went for a curry. Have you had a good day?"

Rob nodded mutely.

"Do you want something to drink?" The curry had made him thirsty.

David had noticed the two plates left to drain but didn't appreciate their significance until he went to throw away his apple core and found the bin full of spaghetti. Damn, he thought, also noticing the various spices that hadn't been there that morning and realising that Rob had gone to a lot of trouble. No wonder he'd been so quiet. David wished he'd phoned, but he hadn't expected him to be doing any cooking.

Rob had already gone to bed. He'd apologise tomorrow. Hell. It was Rob's day off. David probably wouldn't see him until the evening.

Rob smiled when he read the note propped up against the kettle. At least his efforts hadn't gone completely unnoticed.

"Sorry, did the phone wake you?" Rob asked as David came into the kitchen.

"No, I was already awake. It wasn't for me, was it?" He started getting cutlery and crockery out of the cupboards. He couldn't think of anyone who was likely to phone so early on a Saturday.

"No, it was Ian to say he's not well and won't be going in to work, so he can't give me a lift."

"I'll take you," David offered, looking at the kitchen clock which said twenty-five past eight.

"No, I've just got time to get the bus. Besides, you haven't had breakfast."

David, who was still in his pyjamas, acknowledged that it didn't make much sense. "I can pick you up tonight, if you like. I was going into town anyway. I'll just go a bit later."

"Are you sure?"

David nodded. "No trouble. See you this evening," he added to Rob, who was half-way to the door.

"Thanks. Bye."

He'd collected Rob, and they were home by the time David remembered something. "Weren't you going out tonight?"

Rob shrugged. "Ian was taking Sally and me to the Borough Hall. There's a disco on."

"How are you going to get there if Ian's not going?"

"Sally said her Dad could take her. I think I'll have to give it a miss. There's no problem getting there, but there aren't any buses back after eleven."

Saturday evenings could seem very long when you were only nineteen and you had to spend them at home while your friends were out enjoying themselves. "I don't mind giving you a lift," David suggested.

"It finishes late. It wouldn't be fair. Anyway, you've already ferried me around enough today." From the expression of amusement on David's face, he realised that what he'd just said could be taken the wrong way.

"I don't suppose one late night would kill me," David joked. "How about compromising at midnight? Is that too early?"

"No, that's fine. But – Look, you don't have to. I mean I don't expect you to."

"I don't mind. Really."

"Well, thanks." Rob looked thoughtfully at the floor. "Why don't you come with us?"

"I'm probably a bit old for discos now."

"We'd look after you. Put you in a dark corner somewhere, bring you a shandy, ask them to play Hi Ho, Silver Lining once in a while," Rob offered, tongue firmly in cheek.

"Thank you. But I was at discos when you were still learning joined-up writing. I don't think it's quite my scene, now," David said lightly.

Rob looked up. "I'm sorry," he said simply. "I didn't know it hurt."

"Only sometimes." For a moment he had the fanciful notion that Rob could see into his soul. He sighed. "I didn't mean it like that. I'm not planning on joining Jeremy on the gay club circuit, either."

"Sometimes I forget. It must be difficult at times. Not being able to do things other people wouldn't think twice about doing. I suppose it's better than it used to be. I mean, twenty-five years ago we wouldn't have been able to have this conversation."

David fought to suppress a smile. "You certainly wouldn't have. And I'd have been more interested in train sets and building bricks."

"I was trying to be serious," Rob complained, grinning.

"I know. Thanks. It's just that sometimes ..." He shrugged. "Sometimes I wish I was settled. With someone. I must be getting old!" he laughed.

But all the same, they both knew that he was perfectly serious.

Presumably the plumpish, fairish girl talking to Rob was Sally, decided David when he arrived at the Borough Hall just before midnight.

He pulled over and opened the passenger door.

"Did you have a good time?" he asked as Rob got in and quickly closed the door on the freezing night air.

"Yes, great." He fastened his seat belt.

"Does Sally need a lift?"

"No, her Dad's coming for her."

David didn't like the idea of leaving the girl on her own so late at night. "We'll wait till he comes," he said, about to switch off the engine.

"That's him now," Rob said as a car pulled over in front of them, and Sally moved towards it. He thought again how lucky he'd been to meet David that day at Waterloo.

"OK. Home, then."

"I thought it was my turn to clean the floor," David said mildly, coming into the kitchen at ten o'clock the next day and finding Rob on his hands and knees by the cooker.

Rob looked round. "Well, you collected me last night, so I thought it was the least I could do."

"Want some coffee?"

"Mmm. Thanks." Rob sat on the floor and leant against a low-level cupboard door as if worn out by his labours.

David grinned down at him. "We do have a mop, you know," he said dryly. "I don't insist on you scrubbing the floor inch by inch."

"I was merely trying to clean between the cooker and the edge of the work-surface," Rob said with all the dignity he could muster.

When the coffee was ready, David handed a cup down to Rob and took his over to the relative comfort of a kitchen chair.

"So what did you do last night?" asked Rob.

"Nothing much. Stayed in. Read. Cooked supper. Watched television. Collected lager-lout from disco before he could cause any trouble."

"I had two halves of lager all night," Rob remonstrated. "And Sally kept taking sips from my glass, so I didn't actually drink a whole pint."

"Too mean to buy the girl a drink, huh?"

"It's equality these days." Rob drank some of his coffee, and suddenly looked serious. "All sorts of equality," he added meaningfully. "You ought to go out more," he said, keeping his eyes fixed on the floor, afraid David might think he was being intrusive.

"You're probably right." David stared absently at one of the Sunday newspapers on the table. "Perhaps I'll give Mike a ring. See if he wants to go to a concert or something."

Rob looked at him with undisguised curiosity.

"Just a friend," David said before he could ask. "I think his wife would object if it was anything else. Come to think of it," he said, grinning, "I expect Mike would as well. I suppose there's no hope of this floor being dry before I cook the Sunday dinner?" He got to his feet, picking up the newspapers to take into the other room.

"I've always preferred my main meal in the evening anyway," Rob countered.

"It's your turn to cook tonight."

"It'll be dry in time for lunch," Rob replied hastily. "Tell you what," he added, obviously not having believed David completely. "You could give your friend Mike a ring while it dries."

Christmas came and went. David had been worried about leaving Rob on his own. He knew that it was a bad time of year – the Samaritans probably didn't get much sleep – and that, despite Rob's protestations about being OK, his usual sunny disposition could sometimes swing into a bout of introspectiveness.

"I promise I won't do anything stupid," said Rob, who'd obviously recognised the lines along which David was thinking. "I'll be spending Christmas round at Sally's, and then I'm back at work the next day. Who on earth decided that the January sales should start straight after Christmas?" he finished in an aggrieved tone.

They put up a tree. David hadn't been going to bother, but then he thought maybe it would make the place more cheerful. When Rob mischievously asked him if he had any fairy lights, David gave him a long-suffering look, got the lights out of the loft, and left him to it.

In the end, David left a phone number where he could be contacted, and went off to his uncle and aunt's. His parents managed to fly back, so there was quite a gathering.

Jeremy phoned while David was still on holiday.

"Who was that?" Jeremy asked suspiciously. Rob had answered the phone.

"Just a friend," David said. Rob had asked practically the same thing.

"Huh. Knowing you, I suppose he's just that. Will he still be there when I come round?"

"I expect so. Remind me: when did I invite you?"

"You didn't. See you about two." Jeremy put the phone down.

As it happened, Rob went out with Sally just before Jeremy called. Jeremy installed himself on the sofa, commandeered the television, and promptly fell asleep in front of the film he said he must watch.

David grinned and continued to read a book someone had given him for Christmas. When he eventually awoke, Jeremy suggested going out for a pizza and his usually sharp observation failed to notice that the house was now occupied by two people, so David was spared an inquisition.

Someone else turned up before David had to go back to work: Mark. Out of the blue, as David had seen him only once since they'd left university. They'd gone out together for a few months, then parted amicably, as both had wanted to concentrate on their studies.

"He seemed nice," Rob said after Mark had left.

"Yes," David agreed.

"You can be so infuriating!"

"I don't know what you mean," David said, feigning innocence.

"Mark. You didn't mention him."

"Nothing to say, really."

"I bet." Rob sighed. "Well, what about Jeremy?"

"Ah, now Jeremy's different, I admit that."

"Oh?" Hopefully.

"You'll see what I mean if you ever meet him."

" 'If'? Why 'if'?" Rob asked.

"He's going out with someone else."

"You don't sound very concerned about it."

"I'm not," David agreed mildly.

Rob shook his head. "A lost cause."

"Have you and Jeremy been comparing notes?"

FOUR

March arrived, coming in like a lion. David had got used to the gentle chaos in the house which Rob's presence meant. They got on well together. He was just finishing his breakfast one Saturday when Rob came downstairs.

"Hello. I'd forgotten you'd got today off. You're up early, aren't you?" David asked.

Rob, still in his dressing-gown, yawned. "Yes. It's a pity to waste a free weekend when it's not often you get one."

"Are you doing anything special?"

"Not really." Rob helped himself to coffee, then poured some cereal into a bowl and added milk. He sat down opposite David. "Are you going out?"

"I thought I'd buy a few books."

Rob grinned. "It's nice to see someone trying to help impoverished authors. Judging from the number of books you've got, you're hoping to do it all by yourself!"

David ignored his remark. The amount of time he spent either in bookshops or reading was a standing joke. "I was thinking of going to Brighton, but of course, if you're going to carp, perhaps I won't bother asking you if you'd like to come, too."

"Where's Carp?" Rob said, attempting to wind David up.

"You don't have to traipse round the bookshops with me – you could have a look round on your own and we could meet up later."

"I'm not even dressed," Rob said. "Won't I hold you up?"

"I can wait half an hour, if you want to come."

When they got to Brighton, they parked near the town centre, had a quick look at the Royal Pavilion with its domes and minarets and then went on to The Lanes. Rob was content to follow David into the numerous bookshops, although, while David searched for particular books or editions, Rob merely browsed. He supposed it would be a nice gesture to buy a book for David's birthday in a few months' time, but he had second thoughts when he saw the price of the hardbacks. Still, he consoled himself, it was the thought that counted. Besides, he didn't know what book to get, David had so many. The road to hell was paved with good intentions.

David caught him day-dreaming.

"Sorry, I was miles away. How many have you bought now?"

"Five. That's it for today." He noticed Rob's face fall as he assumed they'd be driving straight home. "Look, I'll put these in the car, and then we can have a look round properly. Not just bookshops."

After he'd left the books in the boot of the car and collected his camera, they spent half an hour wandering around and then had a sandwich and a cup of coffee for lunch. The café was crowded: Saturday shoppers, groups of teenagers, people sheltering from the elements. They ate hungrily.

"Can we go down to the beach?" Rob asked, putting his coat on as they came out.

"Why not? It's a pity to come to a coastal town and not to see the sea. Mind you, it's not exactly the weather for it."

In fact it was cold and the sky was grey. The sea, when they reached it, was a choppy, uninspiring grey-green which made it difficult to imagine it ever being warm or inviting enough for people to swim in.

They walked along, leaving the Palace Pier behind them and heading towards the West Pier, for a while. The pebble beach was below them, and to their right were the hotels for which Brighton is famous, including the Grand, which was still not open to the public after the bombing a couple of years earlier. There were a few people out. Hardy souls, arm-in-arm, heads covered with scarves or caps; others walking dogs; some patently enjoying the wind whipping their hair about their faces as they strode along.

"So why is it called the Palace Pier, and not the East Pier?" Rob asked reasonably.

"Maybe it was built first."

"Hmm." Rob didn't sound convinced by this piece of logic.

David's knee had begun to hurt, and he hoped it was merely the result of colliding with a wall the previous day during a friendly game of squash with Graham and not the recurrence of an old sporting injury he'd sustained six years earlier. In a fortnight's time he was due to play in a tournament, and he wanted to be fit for it.

A biting wind made him shiver, and he put his hands in his pockets where he discovered his camera.

Absorbed in looking at the sea, Rob didn't notice that David had stopped, taken the camera out of its case, and was aiming it towards him, the dull sea in the background.

"Smile, then!" David called, and Rob turned round.

"No!" Rob turned abruptly before David could take a photograph, and walked away.

When David caught up with him, Rob was standing with his hands on the rail dividing pavement from beach, his face pale and impassive.

"I don't like having my photo taken," he said quietly.

"I'm sorry. I should have asked." David waited.

Eventually Rob said, "It's calming, isn't it, listening to the sea? Almost hypnotic."

David nodded.

They walked on further, David abandoning any idea of using

his camera. Rob was quiet, and seemed to have something on his mind. David wondered whether he should try to find out what was bothering him, but before he could ask Rob said: "Are you all right?"

"Yes. Why?"

"You're limping a bit."

"I ran into a wall."

"Oh." Rob's natural sympathy lost to his sense of humour. "How did you do that?"

David told him.

"D'you want to go back then?"

"The exercise will help. At least I hope it will."

When it started to drizzle, they turned towards the town, and spent the rest of the afternoon looking round the shops. Rob bought a postcard of the Royal Pavilion, saying he'd send it to Sally as a joke. Then he bought another card and said it would do for his parents.

David was glad that Rob had cheered up, and he good-naturedly followed in Rob's wake. It was only fair. After all, Rob had toured the bookshops with him that morning.

The shops were beginning to close when they left. David, who, after only a sandwich for lunch, was beginning to feel hungry again, suggested they stop on the way for something to eat. Rob worked out how much money he'd got on him, and agreed, but was a little taken aback when they stopped outside a small restaurant rather than a pub or self-service café.

Looking at the place – it didn't display a menu – Rob said, "I'm not sure I've got enough cash on me."

"Don't worry, I'll add your share to the rent."

Rob grinned. "OK, Scrooge. I'd hoped you'd pay by credit card."

"I still have to pay it back, you know."

"Really?" Rob asked innocently. "Perhaps I won't bother to

apply then."

"Come on," David said, holding the door open, "I'm hungry even if you're not. And since it sounds like I'll be paying, I call the shots."

"I love it when you're masterful!" Rob said, tongue-in-cheek.

"Watch it, or I'll leave you to do the washing-up!" David hissed as a waiter came forward, showed them to a table, and left them with the menu.

"How's your knee?" Rob had noticed David wince when he knocked it against the table as he was sitting down.

"Hurts a bit," David admitted.

"Um," said Rob, as he read the prices on the menu. He said it again when he read the range of dishes. He looked up in dismay, noticing the understated nature of the place, with its soft, pink tablecloths covered by stiff white squares of linen on which rested sparkling, clean glasses.

David, who privately thought the restaurant wasn't particularly expensive and didn't want to have to find another one, told Rob not to worry. "It can be your turn to clean the bathroom for the next six months," he suggested.

"Gee, thanks. D'you think they'd let me have just soup and a roll? That's about all I can afford."

"Shut up and choose something!"

That, as it turned out, was easier said than done. It might have helped had the menu been in English.

They sorted out which were the starters and which main courses – they were separated by a row of asterisks – and embarked on translating the individual dishes.

Eventually they managed to order, Rob deciding on pâté to start with. "It's a bit rich, isn't it?" he said, having given up half-way through, and started to eye David's starter enviously.

David grinned.

"Oh, all right, you told me so," Rob conceded, leaning forward to help himself to a small piece of melon from David's plate. "You can have some of my pâté."

"If I'd wanted pâté, I'd have ordered pâté," David said reasonably.

"Are you always right?"

"Usually."

"It can be very infuriating," Rob said, smiling.

"I do so agree."

"In fact, I think I ought to be paid to put up with it."

"I thought you were," David said caustically, referring to Rob's insufficient funds for the meal.

Rob had the grace to look abashed for a couple of seconds. "I'll pay you back. I could even get you a discount on records and tapes. I'm afraid we don't have many 78s in stock, though."

"Cheek. Didn't your parents bring you up to respect your elders and betters?" For a minute, David thought he was on dangerous ground. "Sorry."

"Why?"

"For mentioning your parents."

"No, that's all right. Things are getting better. I know I ought to go and see them, but the longer I leave it, the harder it becomes."

"You know they're always welcome to come here," David said quietly. "There's enough room."

"I know. Thanks."

"I could take myself off for a couple of days. If it would make things easier." He shrugged awkwardly.

Rob was touched. "I couldn't ask you to do that. Besides ..." Besides what? He sighed. "I'm not sure I'm ready." He glanced round the restaurant, which had become quite busy since they'd arrived. "What about your parents?" he said, changing the subject. "Will you go out to see them, or do you think they'll be back soon?"

David said he'd probably spend a couple of weeks with them in the summer as it looked unlikely that they'd be home before October. "Maybe I could go when Dad has some time off, then we could travel around a bit. See one of the National Parks or something."

"So what's this tournament?"

David told him.

"Can I come and watch? I don't know the rules, though."

"That doesn't matter. It's not hard to follow."

"Will you be OK to play?"

"If it's just a knock, yes."

"You sound as if you're not sure."

"Well, about six years ago I hurt my knee and had to give up squash for a couple of months. I'm hoping that when I banged my knee yesterday I didn't set off the old injury."

"Is it a one-off competition?"

"No, they've held it the last few years. I came fourth last year. One of the people who was in the first three won't be competing, so I was hoping to do better this time."

"Has Graham entered?"

"No. I said he stood a good chance – he often beats me – but he doesn't like competitions. He says he's never played well in them, and they bring out the worst in people."

"So I can expect you to turn into an aggressive, bad-tempered McEnroe over the next few weeks?"

"I hasten to add that Graham's never played me in a competition."

"He's probably been very wise, then."

David laughed. "You'll enjoy the walk back."

"Anything to get out of cleaning the kitchen!"

"I don't suppose I could tell the difference, anyway."

"I won't bother, then."

David muttered something rude. He was glad they got on so

well together. It could have been a tricky situation, both of them under the same roof. Rob accepted David's homosexuality without any uneasiness. He'd grown up in a climate of tolerance and couldn't remember the time when such a thing was illegal. It was debatable whether AIDS had swung the pendulum back: for every person blaming homosexual men for the spread of the virus, there was another praising them for the way they'd changed their sexual habits or pointing out that a lot of homosexuals had no more partners than their heterosexual equivalents. And how could you blame those who had been promiscuous when no one had known the dangers? Especially those who were now suffering from the virus itself or from the certainty or the dread that they had infected someone else?

The restaurant was called 'L'Abeille'.

"I was stung by a bee once," David remarked.

"Well, you would be. They die immediately after, so they only get the one chance. I've been stung a couple of times by wasps." Rob frowned thoughtfully. "I thought bees didn't usually sting unless you annoyed them."

David was suspiciously quiet.

"What were you doing?"

"Trying to stroke it." He tried hard to look as if it was not a laughing matter, while Rob choked on his half of lager. "I was only four," he said, reprovingly. He started laughing, too. "It wasn't funny at the time. It hurt quite a lot. And Mum hauled me off to the casualty department just in case I was allergic to the sting."

"I thought it was just me that did stupid things!"

They sipped their coffee in contented silence.

David glanced up at Rob, and Rob smiled back, the smile transforming his face from serious to happy. David suddenly thought of the coffee shop at Waterloo.

Rob moved, and his leg caught David's left knee. David reacted immediately.

"Sorry. Still painful?"

"Not too bad." He sounded stoical.

"Shouldn't you get it X-rayed?"

"I hope it'll mend itself. D'you mind having X-rays taken?"

Rob was puzzled for a moment. "Oh, I see what you mean. No, just photos." He finished his coffee, aware that David was still staring at him, the atmosphere subtly changed.

David pushed his chair back a couple of inches, careful not to knock his knee against the table leg.

Why now? he thought. Why after all this time? He stared unhappily in front of him, and it was left to Rob to reply to the waiter's question as to whether there was anything else. David quickly settled the bill, anxious to leave.

David didn't say anything on the way home. He hoped he'd be OK for the tournament. He stared grimly ahead, and kept thinking, why now?

Rob sat hunched miserably in the car. He was receptive to people's moods, and knew that David was upset about something. He was pretty sure he knew what that something was.

That was why David had looked so oddly at him. As if he'd been let down.

If only he hadn't acted so stupidly about having his photo taken. Or if he'd thought more quickly and had suggested he take one of David instead. Now he couldn't blame David for drawing the conclusion that the reason wasn't that he was camera-shy. That it was simply that he didn't want his picture in the photo album of a homosexual.

As soon as they got home, Rob said miserably: "Sorry if I

spoiled your day."

David looked at him in amazement. "What?"

"The photo. I can't help it. I hate it when people take them. That was all it was."

David relaxed. "Don't worry. Plenty of people don't like having their picture taken. Anyway, the light wasn't much good. I've plenty of other photos of Brighton. We can always go again."

Rob stared at him. "Something's wrong."

"No."

Rob didn't believe him, but knew David well enough to realise that if he'd decided not to say anything then Rob's best course of action was to let the matter drop. Rob said: "Goodnight," and went upstairs.

David bolted the front door.

He didn't think he was a very good liar. But he could scarcely have told Rob that he was falling in love with him.

He went into the lounge and sat down. He felt shell-shocked. It had happened so suddenly. He'd looked up, seen Rob smile at him, and it had dawned on him that here was the person he wanted to spend the rest of his life with. When Rob's leg had accidentally touched his own, he'd nearly jumped out of his skin. Funny how Rob had – quite wrongly – assumed it had been his bad leg.

Then when Rob had apologised for spoiling David's day ... for a moment, David had thought he'd guessed.

Why now? he thought again.

Why after all this time? He'd given up hoping he'd fall in love with someone.

Why Rob?

Why not? he countered, thinking of all the things he liked about him. His sense of humour, his fairness, his honesty, his candour, his gentleness and sensitivity. (What was all that about the photo? he wondered absently.) The appealing mixture of shyness and maturity. The way he smiled. His voice. Perhaps even the fact that Rob liked him.

Damn, damn, damn!

The tournament had become insignificant. He thought he'd be fit for it and, even if he wasn't, there was always next year. He'd never been one to cry over spilt milk.

He ought to ask Rob to leave, but he didn't like the idea of Rob having to rent a room in some fleapit of a house. Besides, what reason could he give? Unforeseen circumstances ... beyond my control. That was a joke. With hindsight, it was so obvious.

Anyway, he didn't want him to leave. He'd just have to behave as usual: there wasn't any alternative.

Perhaps it would burn itself out. It was probably only lust. He'd get over it as he'd got over the measles when he was young.

Who was he trying to kid?

FIVE

April came, and with it a spell of good weather.

"I suppose I'd better cut the grass," David said.

"I don't mind doing it," offered Rob, who had a rare free Saturday. "I could do with some exercise. Besides, it's a nice day."

When David finished breakfast, he hunted through the kitchen drawer for the key to the shed where the mower was kept. He frowned. "That's funny."

"Can't you find it?"

"No, it's not that. I've found another bedroom key in here. I must have missed it when I last looked. I thought there was only the one I gave you."

"I put mine back."

David closed the drawer slowly. "Well, here you are." He handed the shed key to Rob. "I'd better show you how the mower works."

Whilst he was doing the washing-up, David watched Rob cutting the front lawn. The grass had grown a lot in the last couple of weeks. He noticed that Rob didn't always push the mower in a straight line. Perhaps there were stones in the way, he thought, and then he realised that Rob was avoiding the clumps of dandelions and daisies. He smiled to himself, amused and exasperated at the same time at such tender heartedness. Then, having finished the front – there wasn't much to do, and David had done some of it – Rob took the lawnmower round the side of the house, and was lost to view. David heard the engine start up again as he tipped the water out of the bowl.

By the time he'd returned from the nearby shop with some fresh vegetables for the weekend, Rob had finished, and was sitting outside in the garden. As the sun was quite hot and he'd got warm cutting the grass, he'd changed into shorts and a tee-shirt, and had promptly fallen asleep.

David got a book from the house and sat down quietly nearby. He felt a strange mixture of protectiveness and desire each time he looked at Rob. He wished ... oh, he didn't know what he wished. It was all so impossible. And yet this bitter-sweet ache wasn't unpleasant. He supposed the need to love must be stronger than the need to be loved. For the first time in his life he was in love. He was happy just to be in Rob's company. He didn't expect anything in return. It was amazing the difference it had made. It was as if his life until then had been in black and white, and now it was in colour. There was meaning to it. Would it last? he asked himself, unsure whether he wanted it to. Oh God, he wanted him so much. He longed to hold him, to touch him, to lose himself. And yet he didn't want Rob to know how he felt.

He tried to read his book. He smiled as he remembered trying to do the same at Waterloo, his eyes even then being drawn to Rob's face. He thought he'd got over the physical attraction he'd felt then, but he hadn't counted on falling in love. It was utterly hopeless, of course, David knew that. What was the point? Rob was far too young; they didn't share the same interests; and he was heterosexual. But none of that affected in the least the way David felt about him.

After a while, he went into the kitchen. As he waited for the tea to brew, he wondered wryly whether you could buy bromide from the chemist's. He thought his self-control could do with a bit of help. He took the tea outside, and the sound of the mug being put down on the paving stones woke Rob.

"Thanks," he said, finding David had made him some tea, too. He smiled.

When Rob had taken a few sips and had woken up properly, David commented, "I see the dandelions have lived to see another day."

"I wasn't sure if you wanted them cut, too, so I left them."

Because this was so patently a lie, they both started laughing. David had to admit that the clusters of daisies and dandelions did look bright and cheerful. He wondered why some flowers were doomed to being classed as weeds. "Maybe I'll leave it till they've stopped flowering," he said.

"Look at that," Rob added, pointing to a dandelion which had already gone to seed. "It's perfect. You can't cut it yet."

David remembered his own childhood games of telling the time by a dandelion clock. "All right," he conceded, feigning reluctance. "You can weed them out next year when we get twice as many growing."

It was an empty threat: Rob wouldn't be here then.

"It just seemed a bit of a shame."

At the bottom of the garden a blackbird clucked. David drank his tea.

They sat outside most of the day, David acutely conscious of Rob's presence. All his senses seemed heightened. He watched the frantic to-ing and fro-ing of the pair of starlings who were nesting in a house nearby.

In the afternoon, next door's cat came into the garden. It ignored David, whom it knew, and made its way to Rob's chair. There, it wound its way through the chair legs several times until Rob leant over to stroke it; then, with the fickleness of all cats, it decided it was bored, and, with graceful speed, it jumped onto the fence and then back into its own garden.

"It comes round here sometimes," David said. "We had to chase it out of the kitchen once – it had smelt the fish we'd had for lunch and come in to investigate."

Then they'd fallen quiet for a while, and David dozed a little. When he woke up, he was again extremely aware of Rob. It was almost as if he knew how his body would feel to the touch, the skin warmed by the sun. He had only to reach out his hand to see if he was right ...

He reached out.

"Thanks," Rob said, holding out his glass so David could re-fill it from the carton of orange juice in his hand.

David was glad Rob couldn't read his thoughts.

"I always wanted a dog or a cat when I was younger," Rob said reflectively. He didn't usually say much about his childhood. David was again conscious of the way in which Rob seemed to sense his mood. "But Mum wouldn't have a cat. She'd had one when she was young and it was always catching things, you know, mice, sparrows, even rabbits, and leaving them on the doorstep. And we couldn't afford a dog. Dogs need a lot of looking after, too. I said I'd look after it if we got one, but I expect Mum was right when she said she'd end up feeding it and taking it for walks."

David told him some of the funny things that Holly, their dog, had done. He liked making Rob laugh. They watched some house sparrows collecting cut grass from the lawn; others tugged at dandelion stalks; while some seemed intent upon generally dismantling the garden. One female, obviously wanting a more desirable residence than her companions, was removing lavender leaves. After a while, David remarked in surprise: "You've caught the sun." Hell. That was just the sort of thing he should beware of saying. But Rob's skin had become browner and the hairs on his arm golden despite it being only April.

"I go brown easily," Rob admitted. "I was fair until I was about ten and if it's a good summer I sometimes go fair again."

"That can't have happened too often in the last few years!"

David said, not wasting the opportunity to complain about the British weather. "Have you ever been abroad on holiday?"

Rob shook his head. "Well," he corrected, "just a day trip to France and it was raining then. It'll be nice to go somewhere different. Maybe mountains. I've never seen a mountain. Snow, ice."

"You could go skiing. You can hire all the equipment. It doesn't have to be too expensive."

"Ian went a few years ago. Came back with a broken leg."

"I understand that's optional."

Rob laughed. "Knowing me, it'd be compulsory! What about you? Have you decided definitely where you're going this year?"

"I think I'll visit my parents. Spend a couple of weeks there and a couple of weeks at home. What about you?"

"I don't suppose I'll go anywhere. Not even on a beach holiday. Can't afford to. I don't know."

"You could go youth-hostelling. That's not expensive. Or you could go to France again. It's easy to get to and it's a lot cheaper spending a week there than in Britain. And some of the travel companies do short breaks ..." Rob began to smile. "No, I'm not talking about skiing accidents, idiot," David said affectionately. "Amsterdam, Bruges, Copenhagen, Venice. You could go in the autumn when it's not so crowded."

"I'd love to go to Venice. That's certainly different. And if money was no object, I'd go to New England for the fall."

"There's an arboretum near here. Not as spectacular, but quite pleasant." They watched one of the starlings which was proceeding rather drunkenly across the garden very close to where they sat, apparently heedless of its own safety. "Where've you been to on holiday then?" David asked.

Rob didn't answer immediately.

"I'm sorry ..." David began, thinking he'd been tactless.

"No, it's all right. Just the usual places. You know, Wales,

Cornwall, the Lake District – with my parents."

"I like Devon."

"Isn't it like Cornwall?"

"A bit. Not so rugged, though. Cornwall's got more dramatic scenery."

"Bloody awful when it rains," Rob said feelingly.

David grinned. "So's everywhere. It's even more miserable if you're abroad – all that money you could have saved and you can't just pack up and go home if you feel like it."

"If the weather was like this, I wouldn't mind holidays at home. It's just so unpredictable. Tomorrow it could be snowing or something."

David wished they could spend the evening just talking, but when it grew cooler towards five o'clock, Rob stood up and said he was going to have a bath before he went out.

"Tenpin bowling. We'll probably eat afterwards, so I may be late home."

David was restless. He dialled Jeremy's number and got no reply.

Then he phoned Mike, who talked for a while but said he and Carol had already arranged to go out that evening. Finally he rang Graham, hoping for a game of squash to get rid of some of his pent-up energy, although he was afraid such a last-minute suggestion was not likely to be feasible – Graham would be busy or the court booked.

"Actually, I'm playing badminton with Jill tonight," Graham said. "Look, why don't you join us? We could play doubles. I'm sure one of Jill's friends could come, too."

David agreed readily.

At the sports centre, David found that Stephanie had been roped in. They'd met before and got on well together. They decided that to have a more evenly matched game it would be better for Jill, Graham's fiancée, to partner David.

David played reasonably well. In fact, because he felt so energetic, he ran for many more shots than he would normally have done and managed to return quite a few of them. As Jill was a steady player, they won the first game and then changed partners whereupon David and Stephanie were soundly beaten.

They had to abandon the third game as they'd run out of time and other people were waiting to use the court. Afterwards they went to the local pub for a drink and something to eat. It was busy as usual after a warm day and they were lucky to get a table to themselves.

Jill and Steph did most of the talking, Graham contenting himself with superior looks over their heads at David until Jill noticed, nudged him in the ribs even though she knew he was only joking and accidentally caused him to spill his beer.

"Women!" he muttered, mopping at his shirt with a handkerchief.

"Sorry," said Jill contritely.

"Well, what is it then?" he asked as she was still looking at him.

"Have you told David?"

"What?"

"You know."

"I'm sure they speak another language," Graham said to David. "I can't for the life of me fathom why I agreed to marry her. Let alone set a date."

"What?" said David.

"Oh, not you as well!" Graham said in long-suffering tones. "All right. Here it is, the official announcement. Jill and I have fixed a date for our marriage: the second Saturday in January."

"And you're both invited," added Jill.

"The more people we invite, the more presents we'll get," Graham said optimistically.

"So it's drinks all round?" David asked.

"I seem to be experiencing a temporary deafness in my left ear," Graham said, shaking his head as if that would clear the problem.

"Don't worry," said Jill, "I know where he keeps his wallet." There then ensued a skirmish from which she emerged triumphant.

David caught Stephanie's eye and grinned. "You can tell who'll be the boss in their house!"

"Well," Graham reasoned, "why should our house be any different?"

"So you think women dominate men, do you?" Steph asked, her eyes shining with the light of feminist battle.

"Only if you say so," he countered submissively and everyone burst out laughing.

"And are you another male chauvinist?" she asked David, smiling to show she wasn't totally serious.

"Oh, I believe in equality for all," he replied mildly. He knew they didn't fully appreciate the meaning of his remark, but it was Graham and Jill's night and not the right time for explanations.

"Useful for painting skirting-boards," added Graham.

"Men! I don't know why we put up with them!"

"Well, I think we should," Jill said. "I mean, Graham's not all bad. For instance, he's paid for our meals."

"No wonder I never have any money now," he remarked gloomily, investigating his wallet. "I didn't realise I had to support my wife-to-be's philanthropic tendencies."

David and Stephanie hastened to produce something towards the cost.

"I think he's only marrying me to get his married man's tax allowance," Jill whispered.

"I'd settle for that," Stephanie whispered back.

They stayed till closing time, then David offered to drive Stephanie home.

"Sorry about the game," she said in the car. "I haven't played in years."

"That's OK. I was grateful for the exercise."

When they reached her house, she invited him in for coffee, but David said he was tired and said goodnight, and watched until she'd gone inside.

He'd driven other girls home, and he always wondered what they thought when he never suggested seeing them again. Relief? Disappointment? Unconcern? Had any of them guessed why he didn't ask them out?

He drove home, glad to have worked off most of his restlessness. In the hall, Rob's jacket hung on a hook. He was home already. He went to bed, passing Rob's door which he now knew to be unlocked, and fell asleep immediately.

SIX

David managed three weeks' consecutive leave that summer. The first two weeks he spent with his parents in America.

It was only on the plane coming home that he realised how much he was looking forward to seeing Rob again. Not that falling in love had had any obvious symptoms. Well, he hoped not, he didn't want to embarrass Rob by letting him discover how much he cared. He certainly didn't want him ever to know about the episode of the shirt. He'd been loading the washing machine one Saturday morning when Rob was out at work, and he'd been about to put in a favourite shirt of Rob's when he found himself holding it to his face and breathing in the faint, pleasant traces of its wearer. Damn, he'd whispered to himself and had placed the shirt inside the machine. Once was understandable. A second time would be inexcusable.

When he reached home, he felt fit and relaxed albeit a little tired from the flight. As he opened the front door and heard the sound of one of Rob's records from the lounge, he smiled delightedly, glad he was in.

Rob must have heard him, as he came out to the hall. "Did you have a good time?"

David nodded. "Very good."

"You look well."

"I could do with a cup of tea."

"I'll make it."

David followed him into the kitchen, hoping that Rob had interpreted his expression as being one of pleasure at having had an enjoyable holiday when it was really at seeing him.

"How was the flight?"

"Oh, going out, half an hour's delay, and then coming back today there was an hour's delay. It's funny how tea never tastes the same abroad," David said, as Rob handed him a cup. "Must be the water."

Rob asked after David's parents and how they liked it out there. David told him. He remembered he'd got some photos which he'd already had developed and he went out to the hall and dug them out from one of his cases.

Rob looked through them. "Where were they all taken?"

David happily explained. Some were of Yosemite National Park: the waterfalls, the sequoias, Mirror Lake. One photo showed David standing under – literally – a giant sequoia that had had a tunnel cut through the base of its trunk. Although David seemed little bigger than a dot in the distance, you couldn't see the top of the enormous tree that had stood, despite the desecration of Man, for centuries.

"The weather was obviously good."

"So was the food. Even on the plane. One of life's mysteries."

"What?"

"How you can never re-pack everything in a airline meal box even though you've eaten most of it. And why they insist on serving you coffee in a tiny plastic cup with a handle too small to use. And why, just when you want to relieve yourself, the aisle is always blocked by someone selling duty free."

"It's probably like British Rail: they're happy to sell you a cup of coffee, but once the train starts moving there's no way you can drink it without spilling it."

It was good to be back.

David spent the first part of the week decorating the downstairs cloakroom, but he'd finished by Wednesday and the weather had improved so he decided not to bother painting the hall. It could wait a few more months.

He went to Wisley Gardens on the Wednesday afternoon, and to Stratfield Saye, the Duke of Wellington's house not far from Basingstoke, on the Thursday. A statue of Copenhagen, the Duke's horse, stood in the grounds, where there was also an ice-house. The weather forecast for Friday was even better: warm and sunny all day.

On the Thursday evening, David said to Rob that he was driving down to the coast the next day. He knew Rob had the day off. Would he like to come?

For once, the weather forecast proved accurate. They set off at eight, spent a couple of hours looking around Salisbury, renowned for its spire, and then stopped to have an early lunch at a pub, where, for once, the wasps kept a discreet distance. David said there was a hill nearby from where you got a good view of the surrounding countryside, and they decided to go there before driving on to the coast.

"It was worth the climb," said Rob, breathlessly, as they reached the top, having passed early acorns, blackberries and hazelnuts, a reminder that autumn wasn't far off.

David agreed.

The air was clear and you could see for miles in all directions. The view was magnificent. Green countryside, dotted with darker hedgerows and trees, stretched out before them. Something – a pond? a window? – glinted in the sun. There was a stillness, a timelessness, about the place as if it had been there for centuries and would be there for centuries to come. There was a sense of peace, too, as if being there cleansed the mind and soul of petty everyday concerns.

David looked at Rob, hoping to see the same reaction. He wasn't disappointed.

"It's like you can breathe up here," Rob said, looking around.

David nodded. He'd been here before. He'd wanted to return with Rob to show him the beauty of it.

"It puts things in perspective. Not just distances." Rob stared before him for a few moments, unseeing. David wondered what he was thinking.

They stood in silence for a long while, then they walked over to the panorama and tried to match the hills and towns marked on it against what they could see. When they'd given up trying to make out one of the words engraved in the metal, they moved away.

Rob lay down, his hands under his head, partly in the shade of a small tree. David sat down with his arms clasped around his knees.

It was quiet up here. They'd passed only a few people, probably on their way down to have something to eat as it was now one o'clock. Even the traffic was strangely comforting and somnolent, too distant to be a nuisance. A bee buzzed around some white clover flowers.

They sat in silence. After a while, David looked round, and realised Rob had fallen asleep. He smiled to himself. The passion was still there and the desire he'd felt only a few months earlier but they had subtly changed. Now, instead of merely being in love with Rob, he also loved him. It was an easier feeling to live with.

Here, overlooking the distant valleys and hills, it was as if they were the only two people in the world. For a moment, he wished that time would stand still and that everything could remain as it was. Just the sky, the fields, the wild flowers growing nearby amongst the grass, lit by a warm summer sun that brought out their colours. And Rob. He almost wished, too, that Rob would never wake up so they would never have to leave.

At last, Rob did stir. He sat up and blinked at the brightness of the sun. "You should have woken me. You don't want to spend the last day of your holiday watching me sleep." He picked up a twig and began peeling off its outer layer.

"No, I suppose not," David said softly.

And something in his voice or his expression – a gentleness – gave him away.

Rob suddenly realised that David had grown fond of him, but, oddly, the discovery didn't worry him.

"I was just thinking wouldn't it be nice if it was always as peaceful as this," David continued, unaware his secret had been found out.

"And if we didn't have to go back to work. And if the weather was always good."

"Mmm. We'd probably get bored, though, without anything to occupy our time."

"And no money."

"End up going somewhere wet for a holiday. And of course it wouldn't be so green if we didn't get so much rain. Still, it's good to come back from somewhere hot and find the weather here's OK. In the past, I've usually managed to time my holidays so that I miss the only heat-wave of the summer."

"You must have been in the sun a lot over the last couple of weeks." David was very brown.

"Oh, just walking about, really. And some swimming – just to keep cool."

Rob grinned. He knew of David's usual aversion to water.

After a while, Rob said: "Actually, I've been thinking. About holidays. I thought I might save all my holiday up and then go home in the New Year for a few weeks."

"Really? I'm glad you've made it up with your parents."

Rob shrugged. "It was never really a row. Just a misunderstanding. I suppose it's been pride that's kept me from going back sooner. Mum keeps asking me when I'll come and see them. Well, she used to. I'd never say when, so now she doesn't ask."

They fell silent again.

"I suppose we might as well head for the beach," said David eventually, his reluctance to join the crowds evident.

"I'm happy to stay here a bit longer." He saw David's eyes light up.

They sat in silence, David looking at the view and listening to the sound of a lark high above them. Tall rosebay willow herb waved in a gentle breeze. Above, the bright sun filtered through green beech leaves.

Rob tried to analyse his own thoughts. He wasn't shocked, he wasn't even surprised. He didn't feel anxious or embarrassed or guilty that he didn't feel the same way about David. In fact, it was nice having someone who cared about him. He knew David expected nothing in return. David deserved better, he thought a little sadly.

"It was a bit like this when I was in Austria," David said. "I went there a couple of years ago. I remember being on a chair-lift, going down, and all I could hear was the sound of the fields being mowed. It had been a bad summer and they were late cutting the grass. It was so peaceful. You could imagine there was no one else for miles." He stared at the ground, then grinned at Rob. "To be honest, I suppose the lift clanked a little when it went over one of the supports. But that just made it seem even quieter when you couldn't hear it."

"Sounds nice."

David nodded. He began to say, "You miss ..." and then broke off.

"Being with someone."

David looked at him then glanced quickly away. "Well," he said, surprised Rob had known what he'd been about to say, and attempting to make light of it, "it's better to have some company when you're on holiday – then you've got someone to complain to when you can't get a decent cup of tea anywhere."

After a while, Rob said, "I phoned my parents a couple of times while you were away. So you'd better sit down before you open the next phone bill."

"How are they?"

"Fine."

"You know you can always take the phone upstairs if you want more privacy. You don't have to phone when I'm out."

"I'm afraid I've been using you as an excuse. You know, 'Better ring off now, David's just come in'. That sort of thing. Not very laudable."

"Only a white lie."

"I don't like hurting people's feelings."

"That's a good reason, then, for not telling the whole truth."

"The road to hell is paved with good intentions."

David had no opportunity to ask whether anything was bothering him, as, at that moment, the sound of several people making their way up the hill reached them. By common consent, they stood up and began heading back to the car.

The beach was busy: parents on holiday with young children; office workers who'd finished early and were making the best of the weather; children who'd rushed home from school and then had come straight down to the sands.

They leant over the promenade rail, happy to be spectators. A toddler smiled up at them, proud of the sandcastle he kept patting with his spade. To the right, a girl in a dazzling pink bikini lay soaking up the sun, her eyes hidden behind huge sunglasses. On their left, a group of teenagers, presumably from the same school as they obviously knew each other well, were playing a game of catch with a beach ball, conscious of their own bodies and those of their friends.

They watched the game, the girls missing the ball far more often than the boys did and laughing far more often, too. They boys showed off their muscles and fitness, and joked with each other while looking at their female companions. The eyes of the girls tended to drift towards one of the boys in particular, the natural leader of the group, a handsome, athletic sixteen-year-old in blue shorts.

When the game ended, most of the players stripped down to swimming trunks or bikinis, and ran down to the sea where the boys pushed reluctant, screaming girls into the water or picked them up and unceremoniously dropped them in. The boy in the blue shorts had lifted a dark-haired, elfin-faced girl into his arms and stood poised about to let her fall into the water, but then he let her down slowly so that only her feet got wet. Then the two of them turned and walked along the shoreline, holding hands, oblivious to their friends.

Young love.

David watched their neat, adolescent bodies, with the curious analytical detachment reserved only for people you don't know.

"I'll wait while you go for a swim," he said to Rob.

"I don't think I'll bother, it looks quite cold." The swimmers hadn't stayed in very long; the girls took their revenge on those who'd made them take an unwanted dip by hiding towels or threatening to throw them in the water. "Didn't you bring your camera with you?"

"No, I forgot."

Rob smiled inwardly. David wasn't a very good liar. That was kind of him, though, not to bring it just because of Rob's irrational dislike of being photographed.

"Maybe we could buy a postcard."

They'd found a fair a little way along the beach. David didn't like fairs much. He thought the food tended towards the unhygienic; the games were probably rigged; and he had doubts about the safety of the rides. Nowadays they struck him as too noisy, with pop music blaring out. What had happened to traditional fairground music? he wondered. Or was he just getting older?

But when Rob said excitedly: "Can we go in?" he smiled and said: "Of course," aware once again of the difference in their ages.

However, Rob's enthusiasm was infectious and they went on several rides until Rob owned to feeling queasy and said he thought he should stay on solid ground for a while. He agreed it didn't appear consistent with his purchase, five minutes later, of some candy floss.

"When I was young ..." Rob said.

"Methuselah."

"Stop interrupting. When I was young, about four, my parents bought me some candy floss but I wouldn't eat it. I didn't like the look of it."

"So you're making up for it now."

They walked round the rest of the fair, sometimes just looking, sometimes trying the more gentle pursuits of rifle-shooting and hoop-la.

Rob said he was still hungry and bought a bag of chips.

"Didn't you eat yesterday?" David asked.

"I always eat when I'm happy," Rob said, partly ignoring the question.

David smiled.

While they watched the Ferris wheel turning majestically, Rob shared the chips with David, who rejoiced in the innocent pleasure of his fingers touching Rob's.

On the way home, they stopped at a service station for something to eat. The sea air seemed to have made them both ravenous. For months afterwards, David could recall precisely what Rob had eaten. As for himself, he couldn't remember.

Both were quiet in the car.

It was late when they got back. Rob made coffee for both of them.

As David sipped his, he glanced across at Rob and thought how easy it would be to tell him. Sometimes the temptation was very strong. But he resisted it. He didn't want to spoil everything.

"Thanks," Rob said. "I've enjoyed today."

"Thank you for coming." Some people might have thought twice had they been aware of his sexual preferences.

"It beats doing the washing up." There was a pile of dishes in the sink awaiting Rob's attention. They grinned at each other, and Rob yawned.

"Tired?"

Rob nodded. He finished his coffee. "Work tomorrow," he said, getting to his feet. He stood, uncertain, wondering if he should say anything to David. If he'd jumped to the wrong conclusion, he'd feel like a complete idiot. And if he was right and told David it didn't matter to him, it might embarrass him or give him hope when there was none. It was complicated enough already. "Well, goodnight, then."

" 'Night, Rob."

David sat quietly. He wondered how long it could all last. He smiled to himself, remembering Rob's childlike enthusiasm on seeing the funfair. Perhaps he could suggest going out again. In a few months' time. After all, he didn't want to make Rob suspicious.

They never did go out again, not properly. Yes, there were joint shopping expeditions to the supermarket and sometimes to the local DIY store. And some evenings they strolled to the pub for a quiet drink. A trip to the arboretum had to be called off when the day dawned foggy and damp.

David continued to try to hide his feelings; and Rob pretended not to know how he really felt. Occasionally it went through Rob's mind that it was time to move on. For a while he'd needed David's kindness and his hospitality, but now he thought he could stand on his own two feet. Not only could, but should. He owed it to David, too. The longer he stayed, the more painful it would be for him when he eventually left.

He'd asked David about his friends. David seemed not to mind telling him. He'd already heard about Jeremy, but David mentioned a few others he'd been out with. Somehow Rob was left with the feeling that none of them had been serious.

In turn, David had asked him about his previous girlfriends. Rob told him about two or three girls he'd gone out with when he was at school. "What about Sally?" David asked, keeping his voice neutral. "Is that serious?"

"Just friends." He sounded wistful. "Anyway," he said resolutely, "we're both too young to be thinking of settling down."

He hadn't meant it to sound so hurtful, it just came out that way. He cursed himself for his tactlessness.

SEVEN

One Sunday evening, Rob said he didn't feel well. He'd been quiet all day and looked pale. "I think it must be flu," he said through a sore throat. "Sally was off last week with it."

"Why don't you phone Ian and tell him you'll be off sick?"

"No. I'll wait and see how I feel tomorrow."

The next day he knocked on David's bedroom door. "You look awful," David commented as he opened the door. "Look, go back to bed. I'll get you something to eat before I leave."

"Thanks. I feel lousy," Rob said, his voice heavy with cold. He turned, his legs feeling shaky, steadying himself with his hand against the wall. Then he turned back. "Could you phone Ian for me? Say I'll give them a ring at work later." His voice tailed off weakly, and he made his way back to bed.

David let Ian know that Rob wasn't well, and then he made tea and toast which, along with a glass of orange juice, he took upstairs.

Rob thanked him for making him breakfast but looked as if he just wanted to go back to sleep.

"I'll get you some Paracetamol – I think there's some in the bathroom cabinet. Is there anything else you want? I'll leave the heating on."

"I could do with some more tissues." He was already half-way through the box on the bedside cabinet.

"I think there's another box downstairs. I'll have a look." He came back a minute later with it. "I'll get some more on my way home."

"You're going to be late aren't you?"

"Hell!" said David, glancing at his watch. "I've got a meeting at nine." He looked at Rob. "Are you sure you're all right? You don't want me to phone the doctor?"

"No, I'm OK."

"Shall I ring at lunchtime to see how you are?"

"No – the way I'm feeling now, I'll probably be asleep." He smiled wanly. "Thanks, though."

David was loath to go. "Look, I'll leave my number by the phone. If you want anything or you feel worse, give me a ring at work. They can manage without me for an hour or two."

"OK."

"Well, I'd better go. Oh, Ian said they'd expect you when they see you and you weren't to rush back. He said not to phone today. Leave it till you're feeling a bit better." He could see Rob was fighting a losing battle to stay awake. "Take care," he whispered. "Bye."

Rob half nodded.

On the way home, David bought two boxes of tissues, some lemon-flavoured medicine which was supposed to be good for colds, some other remedy which the pharmacist had assured him would help someone with a bad cold or the flu to get a good night's sleep, and a newspaper.

He knocked on Rob's door and, after a pause, went in. Rob was awake but the toast was untouched and only the orange juice drunk. David put everything on the bedside cabinet, feeling awkward at being in Rob's room. He noticed an old sixpence on the shelf of the cabinet and a photograph, presumably of Rob's parents, propped up by a couple of books. "How are you feeling?" he asked gently.

"Pretty awful," admitted Rob. "Sorry about breakfast. I didn't get round to it."

"Oh, don't worry about that. D'you want something else? How about some soup?"

Rob shook his head. What was it? Feed a cold and starve a fever? He supposed flu was a fever. He couldn't really concentrate at the moment.

"Coffee?"

"No, nothing sugary. Could I have some toast and Marmite?"

"Have we got any?" David meant the Marmite.

"Yes. In the same cupboard as the coffee."

"I'll find it. Anything else?"

"Some more orange juice if there is any."

"OK."

David returned bringing the toast and orange juice, and a glass of water.

"Thanks." Rob took a piece of toast and started eating it slowly.

"Is there anything else you want? A book to read?"

Rob shook his head. He found swallowing the toast painful, so took a sip of orange.

"Are you warm enough?"

"Mmm."

"Shall I open the window to let some air in? It's not too cold out." He realised he was fussing.

"Please."

"I'll come back before I go to bed to see if you want it closed. D'you want the radio on?"

"No, thanks. I keep falling asleep."

"You're sure you don't want me to call a doctor?"

Rob shook his head again. "It's just flu. I'll be fine in a day or two."

"OK." David could see that Rob was once more finding it hard to keep his eyes open. "I'll be up later to see how you are."

When he went up again, Rob was in a restless sleep. He probably wouldn't need the night-time medicine after all. David put some fruit and a jug of iced water on the bedside table, then closed the window. He collected one of the empty glasses, but left the plate with the toast in case Rob still wanted it. Finally, he emptied the wastepaper basket.

The next day, he looked in on Rob, but found him asleep. He appeared hot, so David opened the window. The sound of the door shutting behind David woke Rob, who noticed the freshly-made toast and the fruit, which David had placed there the previous evening, before he dozed off again.

He kept waking and then sleeping, and eventually he woke up towards four o'clock and ate something. He felt worn out. He knew his bladder was full but he kept putting off getting out of bed. Eventually he made his way to the bathroom, every step seeming to take far more time and effort than usual. He hated not brushing his teeth, but he couldn't summon up enough energy to do so. He went back to his room, climbed into bed, and lay there exhausted and breathing heavily as if he had just run a race. He wondered if David had been on time for his meeting.

Had the meeting been today or yesterday? It was Tuesday, wasn't it? He'd only been ill since Sunday and already he didn't know what day of the week it was. It was strange being ill. It made him remember days when he'd been off school. Why did he always feel guilty about being away? After all, you couldn't help being ill and even if you went in people would complain that you were spreading germs. Maybe you were afraid of missing things and never being able to catch up and other people taking your place. Perhaps he'd be better tomorrow.

David was kind, he thought. He really deserved someone special. He'd get over whatever it was he felt for Rob. Perhaps it was all in Rob's own imagination anyway. Making the common mistake that, just because David was homosexual, he fancied any and every man. He looked at the bowl of fruit, the empty plate where the toast had been, the orange juice, and couldn't help thinking that he hadn't jumped to conclusions: David's feelings ran deeper than just friendship. It certainly wasn't a case of simple lust, either, these last couple of days he'd been ... What? Attentive. Gentle. As if he really cared. Hell, he didn't want that complication, Rob thought tiredly. What made it worse was that he liked David and didn't want to hurt him. Perhaps he ought to leave when he'd recovered from the flu. It was beginning to feel claustrophobic, as it had just before he'd left home. Oh, to hell with it! he thought wretchedly before he dozed off.

The sound of the front door opening woke him. He listened to David moving about downstairs, putting the kettle on, turning on the radio. After a few minutes, he heard footsteps on the stairs and a soft knock on his bedroom door. "Come in," he called.

"Hello. How are you feeling today?"

"A bit better. I ate breakfast." He sat up.

"What would you like for supper?"

"I'm still not really hungry. I can always eat some of the fruit."

"Anything to drink?"

"Have we got any more orange juice?"

"I bought some today." He took Rob's empty glass and went downstairs, reappearing a few minutes later with another glass and a small jug of orange juice. "Oh, I bought this, too." He held out a music magazine which Rob got each week. Rob stared at it strangely, as if he'd never seen it before. "It is the one you get, isn't it?"

Rob was engulfed in a wave of despair. David was startled to see his eyes suddenly fill with tears. "Are you feeling worse?" he asked anxiously, as Rob felt under his pillow, without success, for a handkerchief. David just stood there feeling inadequate as Rob struggled not to cry. "Oh, love, what's the matter?" he asked, his confusion at Rob's misery overriding his natural caution, his words only serving to make matters worse.

"Just go away," Rob gulped, grabbing a tissue from the box. The magazine had been the last straw. He could see David was completely bewildered by events but Rob's words got through to him and his face showed first hurt and then resignation.

"What is it?" David tried one last time.

"Nothing. I'm OK. Just leave me alone, won't you?" Rob tried to smile, to take the sting out of his words, but he was just too worn out.

They looked at each other uncertainly. Rob looked so young and defenceless and so utterly miserable that David wished he could help but he couldn't think of anything that wouldn't upset him even more.

"Please, David."

David hesitated, then turned and went out of the room, closing the door quietly behind him.

He went downstairs. He felt both rejected and dejected. He'd wanted to stay and find out what was bothering Rob; he'd wanted to put his arm around him. Illogical, he thought: if it had been anyone but Rob that's what he would have done. But he couldn't touch Rob, he couldn't allow himself to. He was afraid he'd end up by telling Rob how he felt. He'd been paralysed in the face of Rob's tears. Odd how loving someone could make you act as if you didn't care.

He pushed his food around his plate, wondering if he should phone the doctor or even Rob's parents. It might be that having the flu had upset him, or that things at home might not be going as smoothly as Rob had said. He'd just had what must have been one of the quietest twenty-first birthdays on record – David had respected Rob's wishes not to make a fuss about it and knew that nowadays an eighteenth was sometimes more of an occasion – but maybe that's what he'd really wanted: the chance to celebrate with his family whom he hadn't seen for a year.

He hoped Rob hadn't noticed his slip of the tongue or, if he had, that he'd put it down to sympathy. Jeremy might be able to get away with calling people 'love' without their taking a blind bit of notice, but it was the first time he could remember using the word himself.

At about half past ten, he went upstairs again and opened Rob's door. He stood in the doorway, wanting to make sure Rob wasn't any worse, but not wanting to wake him if he was asleep. He had just considered and dismissed the idea of going in – he didn't want Rob, in his present state of mind, to wake to find him creeping around his room in the dark – when Rob said: "It's all right, I'm awake."

David smiled sheepishly and came into the room, leaving the door open so that the light from the landing spilled in. "You OK?" he asked quietly.

Rob nodded. "Yes. I think I was just feeling sorry for myself."

"Flu can make you a bit depressed," David agreed, having no idea that he was one of the contributory factors to that depression. "Can I get you anything?"

"No, thanks. David?"

"Yes?"

"Thanks for putting up with me." He sounded rather down.

"You can't help having flu," David said, resolutely cheerful.

"Goodnight."

"Goodnight. Hope you sleep well." He shut the door softly as he went out.

David delayed going in to work the next day as he didn't want to wake Rob, but he did want to make sure that he wasn't as depressed as he had been the previous evening. At twenty past eight, he knocked at his door, and went in.

"Hello," Rob said, obviously feeling brighter. He sat up in bed.

"Hello. Marmite on toast?"

Rob laughed, then caught sight of the time. "You'll be late. I'll get up in a minute and make something."

"I am late – I'll make it up another time. What would you like for breakfast?"

"Could I have cheese on toast? And some coffee?" he asked after a moment's thought.

"I thought you were off sweet things."

"I feel like drinking something other than orange juice," Rob said feelingly.

"All right, I won't be long."

Rob was glad that his ingratitude of the previous night seemed to be forgotten.

David returned with breakfast – and a packet of biscuits – on a tray. "As you sounded a bit better, I thought you might as well have the biscuits up here!" Rob nursed a fondness for most types of biscuit. While Rob ate, David fetched the small television set from his parents' room and put it on the chest of drawers near the door. "I think this'll work off an indoor aerial," he said, plugging it in. "It's only black and white, but it'll give you something to watch if you get bored just lying in bed. It's about time this room was decorated," he went on, looking around, although to Rob the room seemed fine. "Dad and I keep saying we must get around to it, but we never seem to." He grinned. "Perhaps if you're going to be home all day, you could do a bit of painting."

Rob laughed. "That sounds like a sure way to suffer a relapse!"

"I'd stay in bed if I were you," David advised. "I mean, you've been pretty groggy the last couple of days and you haven't eaten much. Oh, Ian phoned last night to see how you were. I told him not to expect you this week – Sally's back, though, so they're managing. Would you like me to phone her and ask her to drop round tonight?"

"No, don't bother. Thanks for offering, though. I'll probably get up and make something for lunch – I think my appetite's coming back – so maybe I'll give her a ring at work."

"Well, don't overdo it. Graham came back too soon last year after a bout of flu and was then off for another week. Jill reckoned if he'd listened to her and stayed off a bit longer in the first place he'd have recovered sooner."

"Let's hope I haven't passed it on to you."

"If you have, I'll expect the full five-star treatment," David joked. He glanced at his watch and raised his eyebrows. He'd better be going if he was to do any work this morning. "Give me a ring if you need anything."

"OK." He wondered if he was still infectious. Or did he mean contagious? He'd have to look it up.

When David went upstairs that evening, he found Rob watching television. "Hello. How are you?"

"Back in the land of the living! Although perhaps after a day spent watching Australian soaps that's a contradiction in terms." He grinned.

"D'you want some coffee? I'm just making some."

"Thanks."

"Do you fancy supper tonight?"

"Yes, please."

"Anything in particular?"

"No. Whatever you're having."

"OK."

He took up Rob's coffee and later, took up a tray with some fish in a cream sauce, broccoli and potatoes, and a banana yoghurt.

Towards nine o'clock, he went back to collect the tray.

"What have you been doing? I mean, apart from waiting on me."

"I've just finished writing to my parents," David answered, taking the tray from Rob.

The theme tune to M.A.S.H. caught his attention.

"Why don't you stay and watch?" It sounded as if Rob wanted some company, so David took the tray downstairs and then came back.

He was glad things seemed to be back to normal. Obviously Rob either had not heard him when he'd called him 'love' or had ignored it.

He wondered what his own parents had thought when he'd first written to them saying that Rob was staying there. In his recent letters, he'd been careful not to mention him too often, but he thought they might have noticed something. He and his father had always been very good at knowing each other's feelings. His mother wanted him happily – well, whatever the equivalent of married was – too, having long given up any thoughts she'd ever entertained of white weddings and grandchildren. She'd never said she'd expected him to marry but it was something that was just taken for granted. Until he'd broken the news to them.

They'd been good about it. He'd never feared telling them in the first place – he knew what to expect – and telling them had brought them closer. He knew the arguments and recriminations Jeremy had had to suffer from his parents and was grateful that his own were so understanding. Even when he'd visited them in the summer, they hadn't asked him any searching questions about Rob.

They sat in companionable silence, and when the programme ended David got up. "Tea?"

"Could I have some hot milk? With sugar?"

"I don't see why not. I see you've got a few biscuits left!"

Rob looked guiltily at the nearly empty packet which, that morning, had been unopened.

"You're obviously on the mend." David went downstairs, made tea for himself and hot milk for Rob, and then took both mugs upstairs.

"Thanks," said Rob, taking the mug in his right hand, and indicating with his left that David should sit on the bed. "I promise I won't get you running about like this tomorrow."

"Oh, don't worry. It's keeping me fit. Did you manage to cook lunch?"

"Yes. Well, I took something out of the freezer and put it in the microwave. Chicken, I think. You get on well with your parents, don't you?" he said, catching David off-guard by his intuition.

"Yes, I suppose I do."

"I do miss them, you know. My parents." He sipped his drink, looking thoughtful. "Reminds me of when I was young. Drinking hot milk in bed, that is," he went on. "How old were you when you realised ...?"

"Oh, about thirteen or fourteen. Quite late, I think. A lot of people realise when they're very young. I suppose I was lucky in that everyone assumed I felt like they did. I probably assumed, too. You know the sort of thing – if a girl wanted to play football, they'd tell her she couldn't, she was just a girl. I'm afraid I probably went along with it, even though it was unfair. We hadn't heard of sexism then. I was always accepted. And then I grew up. I gave it a couple of years, just in case it was a phase I was going through – although you never think it is at the time – and then I told Mum and Dad. Or rather I told Dad and then I told Mum. And then we all had a talk and they said it was all right. By then they knew that if I was set on something, they wouldn't be able to change my mind. My mother still tells the story of me trying to ride my first bike – and those were the days when hardly anyone wore cycle helmets. Apparently I was black and blue because I'd fallen off so often, but I still wouldn't give up. Anyway, it's not something where you have any choice." He smiled at Rob, thinking he'd happily tell him his life story if he'd let him. Apart from one detail. Something that he didn't seem to have any choice over, either.

"Look," David went on, "any time you want to phone your parents, just go right ahead. Don't worry about the phone bill, there are enough international calls on it to make an inland call unnoticeable. And if it's private, just tell me to clear off for a while!"

Rob stared at him and David couldn't read the expression in his eyes. Perhaps he shouldn't have mentioned the subject after all.

Suddenly Rob smiled, the smile lighting up his face and reminding David how much he loved him.

"Sally phoned, by the way," Rob said. He wondered whether David had, after all, telephoned her.

Maybe that was why Rob was more cheerful. "How is she?"

"Much better, but she said she still felt a bit tired. She apologised."

"What for?"

"Giving me flu. I told her I was over the worst. In fact, I think I'll get up tomorrow."

"I've been saving the housework for you," David said.

"How considerate!"

"You don't have to do it all at once. Take it easy, just do the washing and ironing and the dusting and Hoovering, and have a rest in the afternoon."

"The whole house or just my room?"

"I thought you could do the whole house, you know, a bit of spring-cleaning."

"But it's not spring."

"It doesn't matter if you're a bit behind as long as you catch up in the next few days."

"And I thought you were being considerate bringing me meals in bed. You just wanted me fit to do some work about the house!"

"Well, they say a change is as good as a rest. That reminds me, if you do get the chance could you repair that loose tile? Especially if it starts raining. Just get the ladder out and make sure there isn't any water getting in."

Rob muttered something rude and David grinned.

"Seriously, we should do something about that tile before the spring, otherwise we might have starlings nesting. And having seen how kind-hearted you are with dandelions, I can't imagine you letting me throw a nestful of baby starlings out of the loft!"

"You wouldn't anyway."

"No," David admitted, smiling. "But I'd be bloody fed-up if they woke me at dawn each day."

"OK, I'll give you a hand with the tile."

"I just need someone to hold the ladder."

"That's all I was thinking of doing. You'd have to reduce the rent if you want me to go up ladders. I forgot I was on a step ladder once, and fell off. I was meant to be giving Dad a hand at the time, and he wasn't very pleased when he had to clear up the tin of paint I spilled. He swears I did it on purpose just to get out of helping him."

"Have you always been accident-prone?"

"I do seem to be gifted that way, especially when it comes to kitchens," Rob agreed, drinking the last of the milk.

"You mean the time you opened the washing machine when there was still water in it?"

"Oh, no, that was planned. A case of killing two birds with one stone. The kitchen floor needed cleaning, too."

"Well, next time," said David, "remember not to turn it off at the mains. It overrides the safety mechanism."

"All right. Well, I'd better brush my teeth, I suppose." He started to get out of bed and David, suddenly embarrassed at their proximity, got hurriedly to his feet.

"I'll say goodnight, then," David said from the doorway.

Why does life have to be so complicated? wondered Rob, who couldn't see any way to avoid hurting David. He couldn't stay there forever. The trouble was, he liked being there. It felt more like home than home did.

The next day when he got home, David was pleased to find Rob, admittedly clad in his pyjamas and dressing-gown, downstairs. It had seemed quiet without him. And even when Rob fell asleep after supper, David was glad of his presence.

David read until eleven o'clock and then decided to go to bed. Rob was still fast asleep, so David sat on the edge of the sofa and gently shook his shoulder.

"Rob, it's nearly eleven. I'm going to bed now."

Rob turned lazily over onto his back and smiled sleepily up at him. "I must have been more tired than I thought," he said.

David looked at him, at the high cheekbones, the pale blue eyes softened by sleep, the light brown hair. He felt very close somehow. He longed to reach out and ruffle Rob's hair but he restrained the impulse. I love you, he thought.

Then he started, realising he'd been sitting there for a minute or so, his hand still resting on Rob's shoulder.

He stood up. "Goodnight," he said softly.

" 'Night. I'll be up soon."

In bed, David lay awake. He heard Rob turn the lights off and then come upstairs and go into the bathroom. A few minutes later, he heard him close his bedroom door.

He stared up at the ceiling. He felt at peace. He felt happy. He couldn't explain why. There was no reason to it: he knew Rob would eventually leave; he knew Rob didn't care for him the way he cared for Rob. He half wondered if he loved him for that very reason, as if part of him didn't want to get involved, but then he remembered how he'd felt looking into Rob's eyes and wanting him.

Wanting him.

He wondered what it would be like to hold someone and actually say, 'I love you'. Would he ever know?

Yet, strangely, he felt complete. Things were simple. They'd given each other what each was able to give. Love and friendship. He didn't expect anything more.

He didn't dream of anything more, either: it would have seemed an abuse of trust. He supposed you could live without sex – well, he'd done it for long enough and some people did so throughout their entire lives – but he found it strange that he'd lived so much of his life without being affected by strong emotions. Perhaps that was why he felt so deeply now. He'd never been in love before, never felt elated at someone else's nearness, never been quietly happy that they cared a little for him. He'd always thought his head ruled his heart but now he had his doubts.

He smiled, thinking of the sleepy expression on Rob's face. David had always been fascinated by his face, the eyes especially. These windows of the soul.

David's eyes betrayed his secret. Rob's did not.

EIGHT

One Sunday morning towards the end of November, when Rob had been there just over a year, David was in the kitchen when he heard the phone ring. Rob answered it. It would be Sally, perhaps to say she couldn't go swimming that morning and could they leave it till next week.

"David!" called Rob. "It's your Dad."

David returned to the lounge, a puzzled frown on his face. It was the middle of the night where his parents were. He hoped nothing was wrong. "Thanks," he said as he took the receiver from Rob. "Hello, Dad. How are you?"

Afterwards, he put the phone down slowly.

"That'll be nice," Rob said. He'd been in the room while David was speaking to his father. "They'll be home for Christmas."

"Yes," David agreed hollowly, not turning round. "Yes, it will." His parents had been to a party and not got back till late, so late in fact that his father had decided to phone David and tell him their news. In just over a month they would be home for what would be a long stay – at least a year – until David's father returned to the States on a final contract.

Until his parents came back, that's what they'd both said. Rob would stay until his parents came back.

He felt numb. Christmas was only a few weeks away. He'd been looking forward to spending it with Rob. And now?

He went back to the kitchen and sat down. Sunlight streamed

through the window but he didn't notice it. He was dimly aware of Rob calling out: "Goodbye," as he presumably went off to the swimming pool.

He hadn't thought it would be this soon. He wasn't ready. He wouldn't ever be ready.

He didn't know what to do. There wasn't anything to do. He felt empty and alone. He'd always known Rob would go eventually. He had no hold on him. What use was love to someone who had no need of it, who didn't want it and to whom it could be only an embarrassment? If only they could have had Christmas, he thought, and then dismissed the idea as he knew it still wouldn't have been enough.

He swallowed.

At least he was now able to say he'd loved someone. And he had been happy the past seven or eight months. He'd simply fallen in love with the wrong person.

Next time – he shied away from the utter disbelief that there could ever be a next time – he'd be more careful.

He tipped his undrunk tea down the sink and started to wash up the breakfast things. He and Rob had never got round to using the dishwasher, it had been one of their standing jokes. Unless it was the weekend or they'd got the day off, they'd usually leave the breakfast things till the evening and then together they'd do all the dishes at the same time, taking it in turns to wash or dry.

Then he got something out of the freezer, ironed a couple of shirts and vacuumed the upstairs landing. All the time he was conscious of a dull, empty feeling.

Then he remembered Rob had told him he'd be having lunch at Sally's parents', so he wouldn't be back until the evening. Funny how David had never been jealous of Sally, not in the conventional sense; only now he envied her the time she spent with Rob.

He remembered that day in March when he'd first been aware of being in love. Brighton, the walk by the sea, Rob not wanting his photo taken. No photos. He had no photos of Rob.

It was Tuesday when Rob said he thought he'd found somewhere to stay.

"Ian's brother's friend, Chris, shares a house, and one of the girls has just been offered a job in Nottingham, so she'll be starting work there in January. Chris thinks she'll move out before then. He's going to ask Jane if it's OK for me to have a look at the room tomorrow evening."

David feigned enthusiasm. "That's good. I wouldn't like to think of you walking the streets at Christmas." The words sounded false, even to him, and he'd unintentionally reminded both of them how they'd met. Perhaps that was his subconscious bringing together beginnings and endings.

Rob saw the room, and liked it, the house and the other occupants. They liked him. The rent was affordable. David's parents said they'd be home the Monday before Christmas; Rob said he'd move out on the Sunday. It was all happening so fast.

The evenings were different now. David kept getting the feeling that there was something he should say, explain. If only he could put the clock back.

Rob knew.

He wanted to tell David he understood, that he hadn't meant this to happen, that he was sorry. But what could he say that would help? There was nothing special about him, and David had always known he wasn't interested. It made it worse for Rob, watching David pretend everything was fine. He felt it was all his fault. He'd known where David's inclinations lay and he'd never given it a second thought. He'd always relied on David's strength of character. And he'd been right, but oh so unfair, expecting David's emotions to be controllable at will. It was ironic: when he'd moved in, Rob was afraid of being hurt. Now he was the one causing the pain. He'd stayed too long: it was time to go.

"Saturday, you know, your last Saturday here, we could go out for a meal, if you like," David said as off-handedly as he could manage, having finally plucked up the courage to ask.

"Yes, all right." It didn't sound like a good idea to Rob, but if that was what David wanted then it was the least he could do.

David felt a surge of relief. He'd been afraid Rob might have been going out somewhere.

He looked towards the window, although the curtain was drawn. "I think I'll go for a walk," he said, getting to his feet.

"Are you going to the White Hart?" A couple of times, in the summer, they'd gone to the pub or walked down to the river.

"No," David said rather abruptly. "I'm not feeling very sociable tonight," he added, in case Rob had thought of joining him. The mood he was in, he was afraid he'd say things he didn't want Rob to know. He couldn't bear to stay in. There was so little time left, and it felt as if he was wasting it, but he had to get out of the house.

It was mild outside and it was quiet. Rain fell gently. He walked for nearly two hours, not conscious of his surroundings, not aware of thinking at all, but not surprised when, at last, he found himself back outside his parents' house.

Rob was in the kitchen. "Do you want some tea?" he called, on hearing David come in.

"No, thanks," David shouted from the hall. "I think I'll go straight to bed. Goodnight."

Rob stared at the kettle and sighed.

Upstairs, David undressed, got into bed, turned off the light and lay staring up at the ceiling. He hadn't been able to face Rob. His mind was still confused. All he was aware of was a pain deep inside. He forced himself to breathe deeply and steadily and to concentrate on relaxing his body. Eventually, he found he was no longer tense and could think clearly. There was one simple piece of logic to which he sought to cling: Rob didn't love him, therefore Rob was not right for him. His head readily accepted this. There was just the little matter of persuading his heart that the equation was correct. But by the time he fell asleep, he thought he was at least part way there.

The evening out was a mistake.

David couldn't think of anything to say. Already it felt as if Rob had gone. He'd lost his temper with the waiter, too, after Rob had remarked in passing that his main course wasn't very hot. David, despite Rob's saying that he didn't mind as he wasn't very hungry, had demanded that they change it. Rob was embarrassed and he didn't eat all of it when it was changed – or reheated and returned, as David, in his black mood, surmised.

The conversation was stilted and half-hearted.

David looked at Rob and it was as if he was looking at a stranger. He didn't feel broken-hearted. He didn't feel anything. He mechanically put food into his mouth, chewed and swallowed, and didn't know what he was eating.

They didn't have dessert or even coffee.

They drove home in silence.

It was only when David had switched off the engine and Rob had said uncomfortably: "Sorry, I wasn't really hungry tonight," that the bubble which had seemed to enclose David burst and he felt human again.

"No, I wasn't in the mood for eating out, either." He looked at

Rob, and Rob was flesh and blood and no longer a stranger. He smiled. "Sorry. I shouldn't have been rude to the waiter like that. I don't know what came over me."

"We all have off days."

They sat, silent, in the intimacy of the car. David, realising that he had a strong desire to put his arms around Rob, made an effort to pull himself together. "Come on." He nodded towards the house. "This place does a decent cup of coffee."

"The service isn't bad, either," Rob said gently.

As they sat drinking their coffee in the lounge, David felt a deep sense of peace. Now that everything was so nearly over, the agony of counting off the days, the hours, left had gone. There was acceptance within him. There was also an overwhelming sadness. He allowed himself to watch Rob, committing his face, the way he smiled, the way he moved, to memory.

They talked. David thought he sounded drunk as the words spilled out of him. He was no longer afraid that he'd tell Rob how much he cared. There were so many other things he wanted to say, he wanted to talk all night, if he talked all night then tomorrow wouldn't come and Rob wouldn't leave and everything would be all right.

"I suppose you're first person I've told," David said. "Apart from my family. I mean, it's not that I'm ashamed of what I am, it's just that I'm not sure people will know how to deal with it. Not that there should need to be a way of dealing with it. To me, it's fundamental yet somehow unimportant. It should be like saying that you wear contact lenses. A sort of, 'Oh, I didn't realise that!' and then it's forgotten. I know that's not always what happens.

"When I've been out with Jeremy, people tend to guess that I'm homosexual, too. You can see their curiosity. I can understand that. But sometimes they've treated us differently. They've never acted offensively towards me, but some get angry with Jeremy as if he's offended them. Well, sometimes he does," he admitted. "He goes a bit too far. They don't seem to realise he's only joking. I think he does it as a form of protection, you know, attack being the best form of defence. He told me that once some bloke in a café told the owner he ought to ban Jeremy, he'd probably got AIDS. The owner was apologetic but Jeremy was furious. Not just because the man had been abusive, but also because there was no medical evidence to support the theory that it could be spread through ordinary, everyday contact. I mean, why do people think you're promiscuous, just because you're gay?" He stopped short, conscious of having lost the thread of his argument. He supposed Rob knew he wasn't promiscuous – he'd never stayed out all night and hadn't brought anyone home while Rob had been there. He wasn't even sure whether he found anything morally objectionable in promiscuity, although you obviously had to take care nowadays. He'd felt desire for people he scarcely knew; and, although he wasn't interested in casual relationships himself, who was he to judge other people?

He swallowed. "I suppose I'm just looking for someone to love, just like all the rest of us." He didn't say he'd found him.

"And someone who loves you."

"Mmm." How much greater was the need to love than the need to be loved? "I'll miss you." And then, because that sounded too stark, David added: "You've always understood. I mean, I think you have. You've always acted as if you did. And that's all we've got to go on – our perceptions of other people's actions." Somewhere along the line, he realised he was past the point of no return, telling Rob everything he considered important, knowing he would never see him again.

Rob shrugged. "You never lied about it. And I did keep my door locked for the first few months," he reminded David, smiling.

"Well, we didn't know each other. I thought you were going to steal the contents of the house. When I got home, the first thing I did was to look for the television set to see if it was still there."

They laughed. That had been just over a year earlier. One year, and his whole life had been transformed. "Do you want some more coffee?"

"OK." He could see David wanted to talk.

When he came back, David continued. "Sometimes I wonder what it would be like to be married. Not seriously. I mean, I don't dislike women. I can imagine that marriage would have its good points. But then I think how could you ask someone to take you on, knowing that they would be making do with second best? It wouldn't be fair on them."

"It wouldn't be fair on you, either."

"No, I know." He smiled. "Take no notice of what I'm saying. I feel a bit drunk for some reason." He sipped his coffee.

"You and Jeremy ...?" Rob started to say.

"Just friends."

"You never wanted something more?"

David shook his head. Not from Jeremy, not from anyone else. Not till now.

"Do you mind the thought of never having children?" Rob asked, curious. It was something he'd not discussed with David, but in his present mood he thought David would be less reserved than usual.

"Only in a general way, I suppose. I mean, we're all brought up to believe that when we grow up we'll get a job, buy a house, get married, have children. And you still wonder what a child of yours would be like. It must be the most creative thing most of us ever do." He looked at Rob and it hurt him to think of his being part of a family he'd never meet.

"I remember Jeremy telling me he'd got really fed-up at work one day with all the innuendo about not turning your back on him, so much so that he lost his temper and said something like, 'I wouldn't mind but most of you I wouldn't touch with a bargepole and as for the rest I'm not such a sod that I wouldn't ask first!' "

"What happened?"

David laughed. "Well, what Jeremy hadn't appreciated was that the boss had walked in just before his outburst. Jeremy said his boss had stood there, quite straight-faced, and asked him which category did he fall into? Which reduced even Jeremy to speechlessness."

Rob smiled. David was obviously fond of Jeremy, whatever he said.

He talked about other things, too. About his time at university. Things he'd done when he was young. The time when he and his cousin had gone tobogganing.

Eventually he saw that Rob could scarcely keep his eyes open. "Go on, go to bed."

"I think I will," Rob said sleepily. He stood up and stretched, then he waited, thinking David would be going up, too. But David remained where he was. "Well, goodnight."

"Goodnight, Rob."

He sat there in the quiet and knew it was all over. Tomorrow would be rushed and tense, and they wouldn't know what to say to each other.

Tomorrow? He looked at the clock.

Today.

When he woke, it was late and the house was quiet. For one dreadful moment he thought Rob must have left, that he'd missed him, but then he reminded himself that Rob was both polite and considerate and wouldn't have gone without saying something.

He dressed quickly and went downstairs to find that Rob had made them both breakfast.

"What time do you have to go?" he asked, although he knew the answer.

"Eleven. Chris said he'd pick me up then."

"You don't need a hand with anything?"

Rob shook his head.

"Where will you be spending Christmas?"

"Sally's parents are going abroad for a week, so she said I could spend Christmas Day round there and help her to cook the dinner."

David smiled. Rob's cooking was still for the most part confined to following the instructions on packets and tins.

Rob looked sheepish. "All right, peel a few vegetables and help with the washing-up," he conceded.

"What about the rest of the holidays?"

"Well, I'm working between the 28th and New Year's Eve, so there's not really much holiday. Not everyone in the house is going home for Christmas, so I won't be on my own."

"You're not staying at Sally's?"

Rob grinned. "No. Her grandmother will be there while Sally's parents are away. And then there's a party on New Year's Eve. That should be fun."

"And you're going home on New Year's Day?"

"Yes. Dad said he'd drive down and pick me up. I warned him I might still be in bed when he arrives!"

"Nervous?"

Rob nodded. "It'll be just me and Mum and Dad. I didn't want them to make a big thing of it. You know, the return of the prodigal son."

"I hope everything goes all right."

"Thanks." He drank his tea. "David?"

"Mmm?" David was eating a piece of toast.

"Thanks for everything. You helped me when I needed it. It meant a lot to me." He smiled.

"That's OK. I've enjoyed having company. Are you all packed?"

Rob nodded. "Is it just you and your parents for Christmas?"

"Yes. Dad hopes we can visit my uncle and aunt and cousin early in the New Year. He thought it would be a bit hectic trying to see them any earlier."

"Well, have a happy Christmas."

"You, too."

"Say 'thank you' to your parents for me."

"I'll get Dad to send you the bill if we find there are any structural repairs we need to have done following your stay!"

"Sorry about the saucepan." He'd burnt it the other week, and it had had to be thrown away.

"I don't think it held any sentimental value for my mother. Besides, it'll give her a chance to get Dad to buy her another!" David smiled at the table. "At least the smoke alarm will have a rest. You do realise you don't have to wait till it goes off before rescuing food from the grill?" He wondered how he could joke when it might be the last time he'd ever see Rob. "You have told your parents you're moving?"

"Yes, I told them last week in case they were about to send a Christmas card. And I didn't want Dad turning up here by mistake on New Year's Day. I think everything is going to be OK. I've got things in perspective now. "

"I'm glad." David fixed his gaze on the window, sure that at any moment a car or van would draw up. "Well, if you ever need anything ..."

"I will," Rob assured him. He knew he should ask David to visit, but, under the circumstances, perhaps a clean break was best.

"I only hope they realise in your new place that cooking isn't one of your skills."

"I think they've got a rota. I expect on my night, the local take-away'll experience a sudden upturn in business!" A blue car just pulling up outside caught his attention. "That must be Chris. Time to go." He stood up and avoided looking at David. "I'd better get my things." He went into the hall, followed by David. "Goodbye.

And thanks for everything."

"Goodbye."

They stared at each other, and then Rob turned towards the door.

"Rob!"

Rob looked round.

"Take care."

He nodded. "And you. Bye, David." As he closed the door behind him, Rob was conscious of a feeling of relief as if a weight had been lifted from his shoulders. It hadn't been as bad as he'd feared.

David stared, unseeing, at the front door for a while. It had already begun, the litany of time. Soon it would be an hour ago that Rob was here; then this time yesterday; and then this time last week.

Then he went into the kitchen and washed-up the breakfast things.

In the lounge, he was aware of the gaps in the stack of records – all Rob's records had gone.

Upstairs, he paused outside Rob's room, now the spare room once more. It felt odd opening the door, as if he was trespassing.

The room looked somehow larger than when he had last seen it. He looked around. There was no forgotten handkerchief under the pillow, no sock gone unnoticed at the back of a drawer. Even the sheets and pillowcase had been taken off and left downstairs next to the washing-machine.

And when David had cleaned the room and opened the window to let in some fresh air there was nothing left at all.

It was as if Rob had never been.

The next day, a potted plant arrived.

"To say 'thank you' to your mother. Rob," the note, in a florist's hand, read.

NINE

His parents didn't notice at first. Even Christmas Day, the day he'd feared, passed without his being unbearably conscious of Rob's absence.

It hit him only on Boxing Day – the anti-climax, all the presents given and received, the food eaten, the world unchanged – the realisation that it was all over. He'd been watching Top of the Pops. Rob had always watched it and the thought that he might be watching it now was somehow comforting.

His father had been about to turn it off as lunch was ready and David had long since stopped being interested in the sort of music they usually played.

"Would you mind leaving it on, please!" David said, more sharply than he'd intended.

"No, of course not. I didn't realise you were watching." He looked curiously at David, but his son avoided his eyes. "Are you feeling all right?"

"Yes, I'm OK."

"You look a little pale."

"I'm fine."

Philip Rees knew his son well and could see that something was bothering him. He also knew that David would get round to telling them in his own good time. "Well, lunch is ready now."

Afterwards, David said, "I think I'll go out for a walk."

"I thought you wanted to see the film?" His father looked

puzzled.

"I expect it'll be on again."

His mother said: "It's raining. Why don't you leave it for half an hour? It might have stopped by then."

"It's only drizzle. I'll be all right."

Like Rob just over a week earlier, he was relieved to get out of the house. He actually breathed a sigh of relief as he closed the front door.

He felt guilt at his anger against his parents, anger that they had precipitated Rob's departure, that they were there instead of him.

He walked where he and Rob had walked on those summer evenings which seemed so long ago. Down to the river where he sat on a damp bench and watched the cold, dark water for a long time. The towpath was muddy and he hadn't thought to put on boots, so he turned away from the river and walked to the park. The rain had stopped and there were a few children riding shiny new bicycles, and families by the pond throwing stale bread and leftover Christmas pudding to the ducks.

He stopped to watch and, for the first time in his life, he felt like an outsider, a spectator rather than a participant, even though several people, cheered by the season, nodded 'hello' to him. He found himself looking at the nearest family with something bordering on envy – a young couple with an excited little girl who was throwing pieces of bread as if they were missiles and a shy little boy who was torn between holding his mother's hand and joining in with his sister. If his train had not been cancelled that day, he'd never have met Rob. The last few months had been unimaginably happy. He just had to get through the next few months somehow ...

He left the park. Rob lived not very far away.

All I want, he said to himself, is to see him. To talk to him. To sit down and have a cup of coffee with him. Is that too much to ask? He breathed deeply and tried to remind himself that feeling sorry for himself wouldn't do any good as he turned left, away from the magnetic pull of the house.

Anyway, it wouldn't have worked out like that. If he had gone, Rob probably wouldn't have been in. Or one of the others would be there, too, and after David had left he'd have told Rob that his friend had the hots for him. Rob would be embarrassed or, worse, would pity him. And he had too much self-pity as it was.

It grew dark.

David realised he was cold.

He went home.

He wasn't aware of the anxious look his parents exchanged when he returned, his face strained, his eyes dull, only half interested in what they said to him. Barbara Rees wondered if he was coming down with something. There was always a lot of flu about at this time of the year. Philip Rees thought it wasn't anything like that. He believed their son was deeply unhappy, and hoped David would confide in them soon. Even if they couldn't be of much help, at least they could listen.

Later that evening, Mrs Rees wondered why her son was sitting in the dark of the spare room, his forehead against the cool window-pane.

He told his mother about a week later.

He'd come downstairs, unable to sleep, and made some tea. His mother had heard him, and got up, too. She made her way down to the kitchen, where she found David sitting at the table, staring at the cup he held between both hands.

"There's enough for a second cup," David said, having dragged his mind back from wherever it had been.

"Are you having trouble sleeping?"

He nodded. "The last couple of nights. I can't seem to drop off."

"You've looked a bit peaky ever since we got back."

"I'm all right." He smiled at the old-fashioned adjective his mother had used.

"But you're upset about something. We've both noticed."

He didn't reply.

She grew alarmed. David had always been open with them. What on earth had happened to change that? "Is it something to do with the boy who was staying here?"

"Rob?" He found it difficult to say his name. "Yes."

"You know all your friends are welcome here," his mother said at last.

"Oh, Mum, it wasn't like that!"

His mother waited for him to continue, worried at the despair in his voice.

"He's not gay. I just allowed myself to get very fond of him. And now he's gone and I don't suppose I'll ever see him again. He's everything I've ever wanted. I don't know what to do," he blurted out, becoming confused at the naked pain of his words.

His mother's eyes filled with tears. "Oh, David, I'm sorry!"

"I'll survive." He smiled at her.

And Mrs Rees wished she knew what to do. "Would it help to invite him here one evening?"

He shook his head. "A clean break's best. There'd be no point ..."

They sat, the silence broken only by one or other of them sipping tea.

"David, I know you've got to be careful, but we don't expect you to live like a monk now you're over twenty-one."

"Yes, Mum, I know." He smiled, but his eyes were still bleak.

"That boy you used to see a lot of when you were at university – didn't you say he'd been to see you recently? Your father and I liked him."

"Oh, Mum, I hadn't seen him for ages! He was passing, so he dropped in. It was never serious, anyway."

"Yes, but if there's ever anyone you want to bring home ..." The despair on her son's face stopped her from finishing. "Oh, David, we just want you to be happy!"

"I know." He looked unseeingly at the kitchen clock. "I thought he'd still be here for Christmas. We'd agreed, you see, that he could stay while you were away."

"We thought it would be a nice surprise if we were back in time for Christmas. Instead we drove Rob away. We didn't realise we'd ruin it for you!"

"You didn't ruin it. He would have gone sometime." He wanted to say he had been pleased to see them, but he couldn't manage to. He picked up his cup, but found he'd drunk all the tea. He didn't really want any more, anyway.

"What was he like?" his mother asked gently.

"Just ordinary." He smiled to show he wasn't being sarcastic. Just ordinary. With the same hopes and fears and dreams and faults as the rest of us.

He stood up. "I think I'll go back to bed now. Will you tell Dad for me?" He couldn't face telling his father, being aware of his sympathy.

Barbara Rees nodded. "Of course I will. I hope you manage to get to sleep." She watched David leave the kitchen, and then she boiled the kettle again and made some more tea. She thought David's father would need it. Even if he didn't, she certainly did.

Oh, why couldn't you protect your children from pain?

TEN

Graham got married at the start of January. The irony of it was not lost on David, who felt like the spectre at the feast.

"Cheer up!" someone said. "Your turn next!"

He'd been invited to both the wedding and the evening reception. Stephanie was there, too. When he arrived at the hotel towards eight o'clock, David caught sight of her sitting by herself, the others who'd been at the same table having got up to dance at the start of a Sixties record.

They talked easily. They agreed that the bride looked lovely; that music today couldn't compete with that of the Beatles, Stones and Simon and Garfunkel decade, not that either David or Stephanie had been very old at the time; and that organising a wedding must be a nightmare. They wondered what had happened to teenage rebellion, free love and kipper ties. Stephanie said she didn't know much about kipper ties. David said she hadn't missed much.

Later, when the bride and groom had departed, together with the customary paraphernalia – romantic, practical or plain crude – associated with such send-offs, the music slowed, and David asked Stephanie if she'd like to dance.

And because he was lonely and because it was easy to close his eyes and imagine, he held her tight and only reluctantly let her go when the music changed.

Back at their table, he became abrupt, afraid that he might have given her the wrong impression. Then he realised he was being unfair, and possibly even hurtful.

"I'm sorry," he said.

Stephanie wasn't offended. "It's all right. Sometimes slow dances make me feel like that, too," she sympathised. "And weddings make you take stock of your own life. My mother keeps asking when I'm going to get married, as if there's someone just waiting to sweep me off my feet. The trouble is I find I'm asking myself the same question nowadays."

"There's plenty of time," David reassured her.

"That's what I always used to think. Now I'm not so sure. I'm nearly thirty."

"So am I."

"Well, it's different for men." She smiled ruefully. "So much for women's lib when it comes to the crunch, huh? Don't get me wrong, I like my work and I wouldn't rush to marry the first man that came along, it's just ..." She shrugged. "It would be nice to get married and have children. And women have a biological clock that ticks away faster than a man's. Not that I'd feel a failure if I didn't get married, but I'd feel ... as if I'd missed out on something." She stopped, thinking she'd said too much.

"I know what you mean." He smiled, recognising another lonely soul. "It's not much different for me. Maybe my mother doesn't keep asking when I'm going to get married, but I know she'd be happier if I was settled." And that was what he now knew he wanted.

She smiled, too, glad he understood. She'd always found him pleasant and easy to talk to even though she didn't know him that well. Tonight, for reasons neither fully understood, they had gravitated towards each other and had trusted the other enough to exchange small confidences. Neither was exactly in a party mood.

Towards midnight, they both decided it was time to leave. It seemed natural for David to ask her back for coffee. She'd invited him on several earlier occasions, but he'd always declined, wishing to avoid any misunderstandings. Tonight, however, he thought his constant refusal had been both childish and churlish.

She accepted his invitation and followed him home in her car.

If Stephanie was surprised to see his parents, or they were surprised to see her, they didn't say.

At least Graham's absence – a two week honeymoon in Barbados – meant that David had plenty of work to keep him occupied.

His mother surprised. him one day by asking if he still saw Jeremy.

"Yes, we keep in touch. I haven't seen him for nearly a year, though." He had in fact avoided him, sure that Jeremy would have noticed his growing fondness for Rob.

"Why don't you ask him round?"

"I thought you didn't like him?"

"Well, I can't say I took to him, but it's your home as much as ours and you can invite who you like." Anything, she thought, to bring her son out of this depression.

"Maybe I'll give him a ring."

"You've not really talked to us," his mother began uncertainly. "We thought it might be easier for you to talk to Jeremy."

"I'm sorry. I'm not sure I want to talk to anyone at the moment."

"Well, if you change your mind, Jeremy's welcome to come over."

David might not have phoned had his parents' concern not made him realise that perhaps they had a point. Of late, he had been neglecting his friends.

"Hell, it's been ages! I've been meaning to phone you but then you beat me to it! Come in!" Jeremy held the door open and David entered the flat.

"How are you? You look as if you're wearing better than me, but then I'm sure I've led a much more dissolute life than you!"

David smiled at the barrage: Jeremy never changed. "It's good to see you," he said.

"Well, come in! What the hell are we doing standing in the hall?" Jeremy's eyes roamed over David, but David was used to this customary appraisal. "I can't see any sign of middle-age spread or grey hairs. Still, perhaps they wouldn't be visible in places I'm privy to, more's the pity." He grinned.

"Hey, I'm only a month older than you and neither of us is thirty yet."

"We will be before the year's out. Remind me to tell you about our party later. And I swear my brother's got a beer-gut and he's four years younger than me."

"How is your family?" David asked as they sat down in the small lounge.

Jeremy grimaced. "Don't ask! Mum and Dad are just the same, so's John. I thought he'd mature with age but he's still the uncouth lout he always was. Ellie's well. You know they've had another daughter?" John was Jeremy's brother, and Ellie his sister.

"I remember she was pregnant the last time I saw you."

"Christ, was it that long ago! I suppose it must be. Well, Lindsay's three and Kate's eight months. I keep telling them they've got another two to go to balance the statistics. I mean, I'm not planning on producing two point whatever-it-is children, so they can have my allocation. I suppose it's one, though, not two. One per person, two per couple. Funny, Ellie didn't seem to think much of the idea. I go round there a couple of times a month. I take them lots of toys and play with them myself – it's a great excuse. Ellie's said I mustn't buy any sexist toys – can you believe it, she said that to me! – so I have to get things like teddy bears and

Lego.

"It's hell trying to stifle my natural inclination to buy dolls. I always wanted one of those they advertised when we were young – what were they, Sindy or Barbie? The ones where they claimed 'Her hair grows'. No, I'm a liar. I really wanted an Action Man, at least for a while. My brother caught me undressing his one day and told Mum who told Dad who threw it out. John wouldn't speak to me for days. Even when I bought him a new one out of my pocket money, he still wouldn't let me borrow it. Still, by then I'd found out that Action Man wasn't anatomically correct, so I wasn't too bothered!"

David had long since given up trying to sift fact from fiction, and just listened patiently. "You get on all right with Ellie's husband, then?" he asked when Jeremy paused for breath.

"Oh, yes. Roger's OK. He's decided I'm harmless. I think Ellie took him to one side and told him he shouldn't take what I say seriously. Mind you, I can't understand why she should say that. I consider myself perfectly serious." He'd put a cushion on his head as he was speaking.

David burst out laughing. "I suppose it's better than telling him you're a certifiable lunatic!"

Jeremy pretended to look hurt. "Huh! And you call yourself a friend? Not only burdened with the curse of Oscar Wilde, but branded insane, to boot. Actually, I think Roger likes me because I can understand Lindsay. Ellie says we've got the same mental age. That doesn't stop me sometimes from wishing to gag my sweet little niece. Ellie and I took her shopping and Ellie stopped to talk to one of her neighbours, and the next thing I knew was that Lindsay was introducing me, as cool as you please, as 'Uncle Jeremy and Daddy says he's gay'. Ellie didn't help. All she did was to clarify that Lindsay didn't mean Daddy was gay! Just as I thought we'd all be dragged to the nearest police station and be charged under Section 28, the neighbour remarked to me that she'd got three kids and you couldn't keep anything a secret with them around. And it's not as if she doesn't know what it means. She keeps asking me if I'm going to have to wear a dress when I get married. You should have seen Ellie and Roger's faces when she came out with that one. The child must think I'm some kind of transvestite. I've never been so insulted!"

David gave up trying to keep a straight face. "Your sister must have the patience of a saint to put up with you!"

"I think she got used to it early on. She'd usually stick up for me if Dad was angry. Even now." He stopped, and then decided to go on. "Well, we were all round at my sister's and Lindsay was clambering all over me, the way kids do, and Dad said didn't I think I went round there too often? You know, as if I didn't leave Ellie and Roger any time on their own. What I knew he meant – and Ellie did, too – was that he thought I was a bad influence on the children. Roger told me not to take any notice of what my father said. They didn't. Anyway, as I told him, it's not easy to influence someone. I mean, if we took after our parents, we wouldn't be gay!"

"Still fighting battles, then?"

"I still have to. What about you?"

"No battles." He thought of Rob. Perhaps a war he'd lost.

"You're not really into the gay scene, are you?"

"I went to Brighton."

Jeremy raised his eyebrows at the fact that David even knew there was a big gay scene there. "So, what were we doing? Cruising the gay clubs? Or trawling the local bookshops?" he added, hitting the nail on the head. "You still a virgin, then?"

"You still interested?" David countered.

Jeremy shrugged. "Well, I thought if you were, we could do something about it. I've got some bondage stuff – oh, nothing heavy," he added hastily. "The dressing-up's the fun part. A friend and I used to amuse ourselves. Actually, the worst moment was when we thought we couldn't undo the knots and we'd have to call the fire-brigade!" He laughed. "In fact we decided to call it a day when we realised we were more excited by the prospect of six burly firemen bursting in on us than we were by each other. No, I suppose that's not really for beginners and I remember how shocked you were when you read my copy of Gay Times. By the way, why are men always referred to as 'guys' in the ads? We could try a bit of safe sex, if you like. You go into the bedroom and I'll stay here, and we just describe it to one another! No?"

"You're impossible, you know that?"

"Oh, most people say I'm quite easy!" He paused. "Would you like some coffee, by the way? I'm dreadful as a host. I offer you my body, and forget the niceties like offering you a drink. Priorites adroites." Would the French have understood his attempt at humour?

"Thanks."

"I take it you mean the coffee." When David didn't contradict him, he sighed and went into the kitchen, returning after a few minutes with two cups. He gave one to David and then sat down again. "We could go to bed, you know," he said. "Just as friends, I mean. No strings. No declarations of undying love."

"Your attempts to broaden my sexual horizons do you credit," David said, grinning.

"Ah, it's the challenge, like Everest. Or the thrill of the chase. Maybe it's because I know you'll say 'no'. But then you always do," he added pointedly.

"Why do you assume I've never slept with anyone?"

"Why do you never deny it, then?" Jeremy parried.

David stared at Jeremy, who met his gaze. Jeremy was nobody's fool. "Nice coffee," David said, wondering if Jeremy would see something Freudian in the fact that he'd fallen in love with someone he would never sleep with. Odd how Rob had always been trying to get him to improve his romantic life, while

Jeremy seemed intent on furthering his sexual education.

"OK. Point taken." Jeremy drank some coffee, then fetched a tin of biscuits which he offered to David. "So, have you been out with anyone lately?"

" 'Fraid not."

"Chastity's the in thing now. Even I practise it six days a week. I give myself a day off most Saturdays. I do look forward to my days off!"

"You are being careful, aren't you?"

"You sound like my sister. Yes, I'm being careful." They were both aware that he had said 'sister' and not 'mother'.

"Are you still going out with Paul?"

Jeremy gave a mock sigh. "Water under the bridge. He was getting a bit too serious. You know, dropping hints about moving in. That's usually enough to make me run a mile!"

"But you've lived with people before," David said, puzzled.

"Well, sort of. I always made sure they didn't give up their own flat or tell their parents they could let their room. And I always made certain that they took their washing home to mother. Or to father. Who am I, of all people, to be sexist? Can you imagine having to put other people's underwear into your washing machine? Ugh! Or, even worse, them loading your stuff? Oh, mortification!"

"You make life very hard for yourself. We're only human. We all have failings."

"Speak for yourself! I haven't got any. I liked Paul. It was just he seemed to want a lifetime commitment and I didn't. I didn't think I could be faithful. I was still scanning the Lonely Hearts columns in case there was anyone who took my fancy. Maybe when I'm hit by the *grand amour* I'll happily forsake all others." He laughed. "Maybe I do need someone with the patience of a saint. With Paul, I might have been all right for a year or two, but then I'd have got bored. That's the way it's been with everyone else I've been in love with. I haven't got much staying power when it comes to the day to day grind. You know, doing the shopping, mowing the lawn, that sort of thing. Maybe my parents put me off. I envy Ellie."

Briefly, David was reminded of the family he'd watched at the duck pond. And, then, of Rob mowing the lawn that day in April the previous year.

"You know, Roger, the kids, the house. They're happy. That's one of the reasons I go round there. Just to remind myself it can all work out. I sometimes wonder if we all had the same parents, Ellie, John and myself. We're so different. John takes after Dad, whereas I'm the opposite – at least I do my best – and Ellie's spent her life trying to keep the peace." Ellie was on his side really, even if she did keep telling him he could behave more responsibly. She must have known by now that, in the face of opposition or prejudice, he would only become even more outrageous.

"When did you split up?"

"About five months ago. I've been seeing Gary occasionally. D'you remember Gary?"

"Didn't you go out together a few years ago?"

Jeremy nodded. "That's him. It's nothing serious. Just someone to go out with."

David knew exactly what he meant.

"I haven't seen much of you for a while."

"No, I'm sorry." David didn't give the main reason why he hadn't been in touch.

"Well, it's my fault, too. Have you eaten?" David hadn't. "Shall we eat something here and then decide where to go? I've got a couple of pizzas – pizze? – in the fridge. Is that all right?"

"That's fine."

"I'll just shove them in the oven, then." He went out into the kitchen, and returned a couple of minutes later. "So how are your parents? Are they back?"

"They're both well. They came back just before Christmas."

"You had a row or something?" Jeremy's antennae had obviously picked up some nuance in David's tone.

"No."

Jeremy let it drop. David had always been a hopeless liar but, whatever it was, he didn't want to talk about it. Yet. But Jeremy was puzzled, as David's relationship with his parents had, to him, at any rate, always seemed highly enviable. "They must have been away a long while this time."

"Mmm. Just over a year. They came back last Christmas for a few days, and I went out there for a fortnight in the summer and we visited a few places. They're glad to be home."

"Your Dad must be nearing retirement now."

"He reckons a couple of years, then he hopes to retire."

"What'll they do, your parents?"

"They've always talked about buying somewhere smaller when they retire, but I get the impression they'll stay where they are."

"What about you?"

"Oh, I expect I'll move out once Dad no longer has to go to the States. But I'll stay in the area. I like it here, and anyway there's my job."

Then the pizzas were ready, and they ate.

David found himself gradually relaxing. He hadn't realised he'd been tense. He liked being with Jeremy. He could say what he felt and knew it would be understood. It was an easy relationship, despite Jeremy's ritualised attempts to get David into bed, and one which they could pick up again even after they hadn't seen each other for a while.

Afterwards, when they'd washed up, they sat down again in Jeremy's lounge. "Well," Jeremy said, "what now? The local disco? Girls don't seem to mind it when I say I'm gay. I think they all believe they'll be the one to convert me. Or we could go to a pub I know. See if we can meet Mr Right." He'd been joking, but one look at David's face made him instantly serious. "Looks like you already have," he said perceptively. His voice softened. "Are you going to tell me about it?"

"That's one reason I came here," David admitted. Then, after a while, "I met someone. He needed somewhere to stay. I said he could stay at my parents' house while they were away. You spoke to him on the phone once, do you remember? I never thought ... I mean, I never meant any of this to happen. I shouldn't have asked him in the first place. Once I realised I was starting to feel like I did, I should have asked him to leave. He wasn't gay. I just didn't think I could be so stupid as to fall in love with him." He stopped because he was starting to lose control and he wanted to explain it properly.

"Then, of course, I didn't want him to go. It was so nice having him around. I suppose it felt a bit like marriage must. Without the sex." He paused, but Jeremy didn't seem inclined to say 'Just like marriage' as David thought he might. Then he went on.

"You know, someone to care about. Someone that made everything seem more worthwhile. It was nice to come home and know there'd be someone there. And if he was late, then I'd look forward to hearing his key in the door. I liked talking to him. I liked listening to him. I liked knowing he was in the house. There was suddenly a reason for doing things." He stopped again.

Jeremy asked: "He didn't know how you felt?"

"No." Then he corrected himself. "Well, I never told him." He wondered for a moment whether Rob had ever suspected ... No, surely not. His reaction to David would have changed if he had.

"And then, just before Christmas, my parents phoned to say they were coming back. Rob had been there over a year, and I'd been in love with him since last March. Not long, I suppose. I knew he'd go eventually, I knew he couldn't stay forever, but I still wasn't prepared for it. When you want something so much, when it seems so right, you find it hard to believe it can't happen.

"He left just before Christmas.

"I told myself it was all right. I'd get over it. I will, I know.

"I've never been in love before. That's why it hurts so much now. I keep telling myself it's stupid, that nothing could ever have come of it. I even tell myself that it's worth feeling the way I do, because at least I was happy for eight months. And I was happy, it didn't seem important that it was so one-sided. I consoled myself with the thought that he liked me. I mean, he knew I was gay, and it didn't seem to bother him.

"And the trouble is I still want him. I just want it to be like it was. And I don't know what to do." The longing and the pain of the last few weeks were plain to see.

Jeremy moved from his chair and sat on the sofa beside David. "Come on," he whispered, putting his arms around him. "It's all right." So that was what it was all about, he thought.

"That's why I didn't invite you over," David said haltingly. "I knew you'd see how I felt. I didn't want Rob to find out."

"It's OK." Oh David, he thought, your face must have given you away. He must have known. Had he been using David, or had he just been kind? Knowing David, most likely the latter.

They sat for a while like that, Jeremy marvelling at how little we really know people. Was this really David, calm, unflappable, self-possessed David? It wasn't the only surprise he was to get, for he suddenly found he was being kissed fiercely on the mouth.

They drew apart a little and looked at each other. Jeremy knew that at that moment David would willingly have gone to bed with him. "Well," Jeremy said, swallowing, "it's a good job you made it clear earlier that you weren't interested in sleeping with me. What a mess!" he continued, his right forefinger touching David's face. He smiled gently, and David smiled back half-heartedly. "Well, I think the disco's out as far as tonight's concerned. Looks like you'll have to settle for tea and sympathy."

He leaned his forehead against David's, and they sat like that for a few minutes. "Sorry, kid," Jeremy said. "There's me prattling on about nothing in particular while you're sitting there contemplating throwing yourself under a No.9 bus."

"It's not that bad." They both smiled as they knew it wasn't far off.

"Do your parents know?"

"Yes. They kept asking if I was feeling all right, so I had to tell them something. They got the abridged version. I'm afraid you got the whole thing."

"You've listened to me often enough. The highs and lows, and there were enough of those. So do you think you'll see him again?"

"I don't suppose so. I won't try to see him at any rate. And if he wants to come and see me, I suppose I'll have to put him off. It just seems so stupid, falling in love with someone who's heterosexual."

"No, it's not. If we only fell in love with people who could love us too, there'd be no agony aunts, no divorces. And you and I are in a Catch 22 situation. It's like Quentin Crisp said – or am I thinking of Groucho Marx? – we don't want the sort of men who could want us because they're not macho enough!" He grinned.

David managed a slight smile. Macho wasn't the first word which sprang to mind when he thought of Rob.

"Or was it a sweet face and a sweet nature you fell for?" He saw he was right. "So what's he like, Rob?"

It was a relief to have told someone. Maybe now he could think of Rob without despairing of the future.

They were sitting in front of the television, David on the sofa, Jeremy on the floor. David had been absently running the fingers of his right hand through Jeremy's hair, much as if he was stroking a cat.

When the programme ended, Jeremy said, "Do you want to watch the other side? There's a film on." He looked up.

"What?" David asked.

Towards twelve o'clock, Jeremy had made more coffee. David came out of his reverie.

"Better?"

"Mmm. A bit." He sounded a little surprised at his admission. "Thanks for listening."

"What are friends for? You should have given me a ring earlier. No need to suffer in silence. It makes a change me lending the shoulder to cry on."

"I didn't want to spoil your Christmas, too. Where did you spend it, by the way?"

"Oh, I had Christmas dinner with the family, then I went round to Gary's parents' in the evening. I couldn't stick the whole day at my parents' house – didn't have enough valium with me. His parents are OK. Well, as much as anyone who has a wolf for a pet can be considered OK. They said it was a German Shepherd but I didn't let that fool me. I think they realised I was terrified when I nearly fainted as it started licking my hand. I thought it was going to have my arm off, although Gary assured me it was only being friendly. Then they put it out in the hall, which was fine until I wanted a piss. I asked Gary if he'd come with me but at first he thought I was joking, then he got annoyed because he thought I was suggesting a quickie in the bathroom. By the time he realised I was serious I'd nearly made myself *persona non grata*!"

"Why didn't you just say you hate dogs!"

"You know how some people are. If you say you don't like Fido, they think there's something wrong with you."

David grinned. "What about the New Year?"

"I spent it baby-sitting."

"No party?"

Jeremy shook his head. "Well, there was one I could have gone to but I didn't really feel in the mood. Then Roger phoned and said his mother wasn't well and could I baby-sit for them. Just Lindsay, they were taking the baby with them. So I went round there and got a little tipsy. Only a little. I didn't want Lindsay to come downstairs and find her uncle passed out in a drunken stupor. Not to mention what Ellie would have to say to me if she caught me in that sort of state when I was looking after Lindsay. Then, when Roger and Ellie came home, I got a bit more tipsy. In fact we all did, and I had to stay the night. Of course, what I'd forgotten was that children wake up at the crack of dawn, full of energy, and refuse to let you sleep any longer. It's very difficult trying to nurse a hangover when a three year old is intent on showing you what Father Christmas brought her. Why the hell there isn't a law banning toy shops from selling trumpets I don't know!"

Eventually David stood up. "I'd better be off."

Jeremy accompanied him to the door. "Let's go out somewhere next Saturday."

"You're not seeing Gary?"

"No, he's in Germany."

"All right. I'd like that."

"The cinema or something. You choose. I'll give you a ring later in the week."

"OK. And thanks."

"All part of the service. Look, I may not be the ideal candidate for the Samaritans and I know that at times I come across as being selfish and a bit flippant, but I do understand." He looked sympathetically at David.

"Why d'you think I came?"

"I thought you were just after my body."

"I'm not that desperate!"

"Sod!"

They smiled at each other, David reluctant to leave. "Bye," he said at last.

"Bye. See you next week."

Jeremy sighed as he closed the door. What had he been thinking of? All these years of trying in vain to tempt David into bed and, when he stood the best chance ever, he balked at it.

Even worse, David now knew he had principles! Oh, well.

He went to bed.

ELEVEN

"Thank you! They're lovely!" Ellie accepted the flowers David had brought. "Come in. It's a long time since anyone bought me flowers," she said accusingly to Jeremy.

"You don't bring your own sister flowers," he remonstrated.

"You certainly don't! Anyway, go through and sit down. Lunch won't be long."

Inviting David to his sister's was a nice gesture on Jeremy's part, thought David , and he was made to feel welcome by Ellie and her husband, Roger. The two little girls were there, Kate still too young to do much more than stare at them all, but Lindsay, once she'd overcome her initial shyness, turned out to be a chatterbox. She dropped her first bombshell as they were halfway through the main course.

"Are you and Uncle Jeremy getting married?"

David, not entirely sure that he'd heard right, looked at Jeremy, wondering what he'd said to his niece to make her ask such a question.

Uncle Jeremy, apparently used to dealing with this sort of remark, replied calmly that only men and women married each other.

She thought about this for a while, and then asked David if they were having a baby.

David had unfortunately chosen this moment to take a sip of the wine Roger had poured for them. He choked. When he'd recovered sufficiently, he looked round the table. Ellie was biting her lip in an attempt not to laugh; Roger was grinning in a 'Kids, who'd have them?' sort of way; and Jeremy was looking exceedingly amused at David's discomfiture.

"When I was young," Ellie said, "I thought you had to be married first before you could have children."

"That's nothing," Jeremy retorted, in an obvious attempt to cap what his sister had said. "When I was young, I thought I'd end up married, with three or four kids!" When the adults had stopped laughing, Lindsay patiently repeated her question, and Jeremy carefully explained that only men and women could have children. Like Mummy and Daddy? He nodded.

The little girl stared thoughtfully at David, then, as if she'd made up her mind about something, smiled. David smiled back. She reminded him of someone. He looked at Jeremy. There was definitely a family resemblance, the same glint in their eyes. Ellie had her hands full there, he thought.

After lunch, Lindsay proudly displayed her collection of dolls and teddy bears.

"Bit sexist, isn't it?" Jeremy said, eyeing the numerous blue-eyed, blonde-haired female dolls. Obviously someone hadn't obeyed Ellie's strictures.

Ellie shrugged. "I think the teddy bears are all addressed as 'he'."

Roger looked up from his newspaper. "As far as I can gather, it just means we have to buy her dolls and train sets to prove we're not giving her an unbalanced view of life. And it means Ellie makes me do the housework at the weekends." He grinned affectionately at his wife, who didn't mention that he'd always done his share of the housework even before Lindsay and Kate were born. He might be a New Man, but he didn't want it broadcast.

"This one's good," Lindsay went on.

"Yes," David agreed, as the china blue eyes of a doll blinked at him when Lindsay tilted her forward and back. "She's very nice."

"Her name's Clara, and if you put water in her she wets herself."

"Very lifelike," he ventured.

"Or d'you like this one more?" she asked dubiously, holding up another doll for his inspection.

"Oh, no, Clara's very nice."

Having commented on all the other dolls, she said wasn't it sad that he couldn't have children.

"Come on, Big Ears, let David have a bit of peace." Roger looked up at David apologetically. "I'm afraid we still haven't found the volume control on them," he said, meaning his daughters. Kate was now yelling because she couldn't get one of Lindsay's toys that had, for safety's sake, been placed out of her reach. "Go and pester your Uncle Jeremy," he told Lindsay, who immediately demanded to know why he'd called her 'Big Ears'.

It was only as they were leaving a couple of hours later – Jeremy had gone upstairs in search of their coats – that David found out why Lindsay had been so persistent about finding out which doll he preferred. Solemnly she presented him with Clara, and said he could keep her.

"Thank you." He escaped into the kitchen after Ellie, and sheepishly held out the doll.

"So that's what all that was about! The little minx!" Her tone, however, belied her words. She was evidently touched by the gesture, as David had been. "She's been going through a weddings-and-babies stage ever since Roger's sister got married. I'll tell her you thought it needed its mother, shall I?"

"Thanks."

"I hope you weren't too embarrassed. We've always tried to be open about things, so Lindsay knows a lot of things that most kids of her age don't. Even if she does tend to get it a bit muddled!"

"No, I didn't mind. She seems to treat it in a very matter of fact way."

"Kids usually do if you don't make an issue of it."

"Just as long as I didn't drop any clangers. I don't have much contact with kids."

"Compared to Jeremy, you are the soul of discretion."

The same thought – that that wasn't saying very much – went through both their minds and they smiled at each other.

"We think she takes after Jeremy when it comes to saying embarrassing things. We're dreading it when she goes to school. You can just imagine it – her worried teacher taking us to one side at the parent-teacher meeting and asking us whether Lindsay's essay about her family was fictitious or not. She's devious just like him, too." She cast a jaundiced eye at Clara, who was now sitting next to the kettle. "She gave you her least favourite doll!" Suddenly she became serious. "How are things? Jeremy told us."

"OK. He may be devious, but he's not all bad, your brother."

"I'm really very fond of him although he can drive me to distraction sometimes. You've known each other a long time, haven't you?"

David nodded.

There was a short silence, then David asked curiously: "Did your brother – John, that is – ever have an Action Man?" But Ellie didn't get a chance to answer.

"Talking behind my back?" Jeremy demanded, putting his head round the kitchen door. "Aren't you ready yet?" He jingled his car keys impatiently, even though it had been he who'd kept David waiting.

Ellie gave a long-suffering sigh and looked sympathetically at David.

TWELVE

"David!"

David swung round from the display of pullovers to find Mike and Carol grinning delightedly at him. He and Jeremy had come into the department store as Jeremy wanted to get a sweater. So far, he had asked David's advice on what to buy and then promptly ignored it, which was par for the course, and then he would wander off as something else caught his eye. David remembered other shopping expeditions and wondered why he'd agreed to come on this one. Shopping with Jeremy should carry a government health warning. He'd already remarked that he hadn't realised Jeremy intended doing his Christmas shopping so early, but it was like water off a duck's back. It was, therefore, with undisguised relief that he'd seen Mike and Carol.

After they'd established why they were there, and that they were all well, Carol said they'd been on their way to the restaurant when they'd spotted him. "Come and have a cup of coffee, too," she suggested.

David, sorely tempted, glanced at Jeremy, who waved him away. "I'll come and join you when I've made up my mind here," he said, indicating what might have been just the sweaters or the whole of the floor.

"OK. I'll see you later." David made his escape.

It was ten minutes before Jeremy reappeared. "Have I got time for a coffee?" he asked, noticing that everyone else had almost finished. David nodded. "Anyone want another?"

"No, thanks."

"Can you look after these, love?" he asked, depositing several carrier bags onto the vacant seat beside David, and then walking off towards the counter.

Thank you, Jeremy, thought David mutinously. Land me in it, and then abandon me. He looked up to find Mike and Carol staring at him.

"Is he er ...?" asked Mike.

"Yes."

Mike and Carol exchanged glances, then looked at David with undisguised curiosity, too polite to ask direct.

"So am I." Realising what they'd make of that, David added, "We're just friends." Although at the moment, he felt as if he could cheerfully have strangled Jeremy.

The object of his murderous designs returned, put his cup of coffee on the table and sat down next to David. "Salmon pink," he announced, opening one of the bags so they could see inside.

"Very nice," Carol said dutifully.

"I could never take seriously someone who buys salmon pink sweaters," David remarked.

"Now he tells me. If I'd known earlier, I'd have bought the navy!" He sipped his coffee. "I never realised you were colour-prejudiced before."

David found himself starting to smile. Damn Jeremy! David always found it hard to remain annoyed with him for long.

"Your friends look as if they could do with a stiff drink."

Mike and Carol, sitting opposite them, did indeed look as if they'd found the last five minutes confusing. "I'd have thought you'd have grown used to this sort of reaction," David said.

"I used to carry a hip flask for just this kind of eventuality, but people kept making Mae West-like remarks. Anyway," he said, suddenly becoming serious, "I don't think it's that. I think it's you they're surprised at."

Mike was disconcerted at Jeremy's perception, and by the

somewhat icy stare directed at him through extremely intelligent eyes. Like many people, he'd taken Jeremy at face-value, and found he'd misjudged him. Jeremy was not someone to be taken lightly.

"Some people," Jeremy continued in a deceptively casual manner, "think that they can come out of the closet and their friends will simply accept them as if nothing's really changed. I'm under no such illusion." He looked at Mike and Carol.

For a while there was silence.

Then Carol spoke. "You really ought to bring Jeremy along to one of our parties." To Jeremy's surprise, it sounded as if she meant it.

"It certainly wouldn't be dull," her husband agreed.

David admired the loyalty behind Jeremy's outburst, even if it had been misguided.

Jeremy looked from one to the other and shifted uncomfortably in his seat as he realised that David's friends, far from being put out, were smiling at his performance. "D'you ever wish the ground would open and swallow you up?" he asked after a while of no one in particular. "Or d'you ever realise that you've jumped to the wrong conclusion and made a complete idiot of yourself?"

"Not very often, no," David said. To Mike and Carol he added, "I'm sorry I never got round to telling you. I thought it wasn't important."

"It isn't," Carol assured him. "We've known each other too long for it to make a difference. Not," she added pointedly, looking at Jeremy, "that how long we'd known someone would influence the way we felt."

"Look, I'm sorry if I was rude. I really thought ... I think I'll just go home quietly and stick my head in the oven." Jeremy made as if to stand up. Despite his flippancy, he was genuinely contrite. He didn't mean to 'out' anyone who didn't want it; despite thinking that, if everyone who was gay spoke up, society would be forced to give them the equal rights which had been denied them for so long.

"Your penitence would be more convincing if I didn't know you had an electric oven!"

"You've heard of burnt offerings, haven't you? Well, then." Jeremy turned to Mike and Carol. "I really am sorry. I honestly thought you were having second thoughts about being seen with us."

Mike looked a little guiltily at his wife. "I suppose we were wondering why you'd never told us," Mike said hesitantly to David. "At least, I was." It had crossed their minds, as David had never brought anyone to any of the parties to which they'd invited him, that perhaps he wasn't attracted to women; but they'd never seriously thought they'd guessed correctly.

"He believes in the army's motto: never volunteer." Jeremy said. "Mind you, I don't have to tell people. Somehow they just seem to guess."

"I haven't told many people," David confirmed. "Not that I mind you knowing. If I did, I'd have gagged Jeremy. He tends to give the game away." He grinned at Jeremy, who was the picture of hurt innocence.

"And you told me you weren't interested in bondage," he said in an aggrieved tone of voice.

"See what I mean?" said David.

After a while, Mike said, tongue firmly in cheek, "I like the sweater."

"Liar!"

"No, honestly. It suits you."

For some reason inexplicable to the others, Jeremy found this hilarious. "I'd better buy another one, then." Everyone else looked puzzled. "Well, this one's far too small. It's only a ladies' size. I bought it for my sister – it's her birthday next week."

David groaned and closed his eyes, pained. Slowly he said,

"Never ask me to come shopping with you again. I just can't take it."

Jeremy smiled sweetly. "Never mind. As a 'thank you', I'll ask Ellie to save you a piece of birthday cake."

Carol glanced at her watch. "We'd better be going. We've only got five minutes left." They'd parked in one of the town's multi-storey car parks. She stood up.

"Nice meeting you," Mike said. "We meant it about the party. You're welcome to bring Jeremy."

"I'll send him along by himself, then. A couple of hours' shopping is enough for me. A whole evening in his company and I think I'd be able to plead manslaughter on the grounds of diminished responsibility!"

Mike and Carol laughed, while the object of David's sarcasm muttered something about it being the last time he'd invite David to go shopping with him, anyway.

They said goodbye.

Jeremy looked enquiringly at David. "Am I forgiven? For dropping you in it like that?"

"I suppose so. Just promise me one thing."

"What's that?"

"That you meant what you said. About never going shopping with me again!"

THIRTEEN

When he got home from work, his mother was in the hall. "There's a parcel come for you," she said, smiling.

David went into the lounge to find a flat, square package marked 'Do not bend'. The shape of it, together with the handwriting, made his eyes light up. Mrs Rees, watching, noticed and wondered who it was from. Probably Jeremy, she thought.

David was reading the card inside.

'I hope this arrives on your birthday. I wasn't sure what to get you, and I thought this was something you'd never have bought for yourself. You said you liked it.

'I'll give you a ring tonight (Wednesday). If you're out celebrating when I phone, I'll try again later in the week.

'Happy Birthday.

'Rob.'

David smiled delightedly. Rob had phoned once before, a couple of months earlier, and they'd talked for a long while, David asking him how his trip home had been, and thanking him for the flowers Rob had sent his mother.

"What is it?" Barbara Rees asked, as David undid the inner wrapping.

"A record."

"From Jeremy?"

"Rob sent it." He tried to keep his voice neutral, but his mother was not deceived. It was funny, he hadn't expected anything and yet here was something tangible even if he failed to recognise the name of the song or the group. He hadn't thought that Rob would remember his birthday, let alone some remark he must have made about the record.

"That was nice of him. Have you seen him at all?" his mother asked carefully, hoping, for her son's sake, that he hadn't. From the little David had said, Rob sounded much more suitable than Jeremy, and yet she found herself thinking more affectionately of the latter. He'd managed to cheer David up where she and his father had failed.

"No, I haven't seen him since before Christmas."

"But he still lives near here?"

David nodded. "Looks like he's still working at the same place." He put the card alongside others he'd received, and then picked up the record. "I think I'll go and change."

Upstairs, he played the record while he took off his suit and put on a pair of jeans, but he was only half-listening, the rest of his mind rehearsing what he'd say when Rob phoned.

It was after his father had come home and they'd eaten that the phone rang.

"I think it's for me," he said, getting up hastily. He lifted the phone off the hook and gave the number, his mouth suddenly dry.

"Hello. David?" It was Rob.

"Hang on a minute." David put the receiver down, and told his parents he'd take it upstairs. A minute later, he said: "Hello. I thought I'd use the phone in my parents' room." He was breathless, yet he doubted it was the run upstairs which had caused it.

"Happy Birthday!"

"Thanks. And thanks for the present. I didn't expect anything."

"Well, thirty's quite a landmark. It hadn't got broken or scratched?"

"No, it was fine. I played it earlier this evening."

"I remember you saying you liked it. I hoped you'd be able to play it on your gramophone. I expect your arm's aching, what with all that winding up."

"I'm not the only one doing a bit of winding up. These slurs on my age do not pass unnoticed."

"Sorry, I was forgetting it's your birthday, and that it's only polite to show a bit of respect for your elders."

"I'm collecting my free bus pass tomorrow. After that, I'll take you down the park and you can play on the swings."

"Last time I use my staff discount on you! Are you going out tonight?"

"I'm going out for a meal with my parents at the weekend. Then there's the party in a couple of weeks."

"Party?"

"Nothing special, really." He wished he could invite Rob, but it was out of the question. "Jeremy – he's thirty later this month – suggested having a joint party at his flat. Actually, by 'joint', I gather he meant he invites all his friends and I pay all the expenses!" He heard Rob laugh.

"D'you see much of him, then?"

"I've seen quite a lot of him just lately."

"And?"

"And what?"

"Are you going out with him or what?"

"No."

"I'd do better trying to get blood out of a stone!" Rob complained jokingly. "Are you going out with anyone?"

"Not at the moment. I've been out with Graham and Jill a couple of times." Jeremy had been on at him, telling him he should get out more, but he hadn't sounded too impressed, either, when told about the occasional game of badminton followed by a meal in the company of a colleague, his wife and her friend. Not when he'd discovered that the friend was female, anyway.

"I miss you," David said simply, and then hoped that Rob hadn't followed his train of thought.

"I miss the peace and quiet," Rob said after an almost imperceptible pause. "It's like a madhouse here sometimes." He told David about the house and its occupants. "By the way, I'm taking driving lessons."

"Tell me when you have them, and I'll make sure I keep off the roads."

"I'm not that bad!" Rob retorted. "Well, I haven't hit anything yet."

"Must be dual control."

Rob said something rude and David laughed.

"At least I can operate the car stereo."

"That should ensure the examiner passes you first time. Have you got a test arranged?"

"Next month. Angela says she'll let me use her car nearer the time to get in some more practice."

"After the insurance money, is she?"

"No," Rob said, laughing. "She said she'd give me free lessons if I promised to cook for her."

"At least your cooking's improved, then," David said.

There was a brief pause and then Rob owned up. "She wants to lose weight before she goes on holiday and thinks my cooking's just the incentive she needs!"

"People can be so cruel," David said sympathetically.

"You know, they actually make me clean any saucepans I've burnt myself."

"You must have had plenty of practice by now."

"I don't do it as often as I used to. Well, not since the others suggested I stick to doing the washing-up."

Oh God, how he missed him.

"Are you going away on holiday this year?" Rob asked.

"I haven't booked anything. Jeremy suggested we go to Lesbos, but I think that was meant to be a joke. What about you?"

"Nothing planned. Sally keeps on at me to join her in Corfu –

there's a whole crowd going – but I'm not sure whether my finances will stretch to it. I might go and stay with Mum and Dad for a few days. Your parents are still home, then?"

"Yes. Dad's got to go abroad again early next year, and that should be the last time."

"He's retiring?"

"In about two years' time. How are your parents?"

"Fine. I think they've accepted that I had to get away for a bit. Mum says she misses her little chats with you."

They talked about work for a while. David asked what Simon was doing the following weekend.

"Angie and me were thinking of going to see a film."

"Which one?"

Rob told him.

"Jeremy and I saw it. I managed to enjoy it despite the company."

"Sometimes I think you complain too much about Jeremy. He can't be that bad!"

"I exaggerate sometimes. Well, have a nice time."

"You, too. I suppose I'd better go."

"OK. Thanks for phoning. And for the present."

"Drop in if you're passing the shop."

"Yes," David said, knowing that he had no intention of doing so.

"Bye."

"Bye, Rob."

He sat looking at the phone for several minutes after replacing the receiver. Then he stood up, left his parents' room, and went into his own.

He put the record on again. It was a song called 'Alone', and he remembered hearing it on Top of the Pops and commenting that it was better than most of the other stuff they played. Rob had grinned, and said he sounded like his father.

He hadn't really listened to the words the first time he'd played it, and he wasn't conscious of having taken them in before, but this time he did. It was uncanny. It was as if someone had read his mind.

You don't know how long I have wanted to touch your lips and hold you tight.

You don't know how long I have waited ...

For the secret is still my own

And my love for you is still unknown.

Alone.

Till now, I always got by on my own,

I never really cared until I met you...

It was a long time before he went downstairs.

His mother took one look at his face and wished Rob a million miles away. She briefly considered whether to go to the shop where he worked and tell him how much his phone calls unsettled David, but dismissed the idea. She had the feeling that her son might never forgive her for interfering if he found out.

Perhaps Jeremy was right, David thought. Perhaps he should make more of an effort to get Rob out of his system.

He wondered how he should start.

FOURTEEN

That Christmas he received a card from Rob, so he sent him one in return, conscious that his own feelings prevented him from making the first move.

It had been over a year since he'd last seen him, despite the fact that they lived within a few miles of each other.

Time had helped dull his sense of loss.

For a couple of months he'd gone out with someone he'd met at Jeremy's party. Neil was kind, gentle, thoughtful and perceptive. He had dark hair, eyes that were somewhere between green and brown, and he shared David's love of books. He taught music at one of the local sixth form colleges.

"I think we should call it a day," Neil said one evening after they'd been to see a film.

David had looked at him in surprise.

"We're not going anywhere." This caused them both to smile since they were sitting in David's car outside Neil's house.

"But I enjoy going out with you," David said, still puzzled. They got on well together.

Neil had looked at him pensively. "You enjoy going out. You enjoy having someone to go out with. It just happened to be me. It could have been anybody."

David stared at the windscreen unwilling to acknowledge the truth of what Neil had said.

At last he said, "I'm sorry." It sounded inadequate even to his own ears.

"It's not your fault. Jeremy warned me you were still carrying a torch for someone."

Good old Jeremy.

"I didn't realise it was quite so obvious." David paused for a while, then added, "I suppose I thought if I went out with someone else it might help. I'm sorry," he said again.

"So am I," Neil said regretfully. They sat in silence, both wondering if things might have been different had they met a couple of years earlier.

"Never mind," Neil said finally. "It's just one of those things. I expect we'll see each other around."

David watched him get out of the car, walk up the front path, and let himself in to the house.

He sighed, and then turned the ignition key before signalling to pull out.

New Year's Eve arrived after somewhat muted Christmas celebrations, natural and made-made disasters being very much in mind. David received three invitations: one from Graham and Jill who, now they had a house of their own, were anxious to repay friends' hospitality; the second from Mike and Carol who usually held a party at this time of year; and another from Jeremy. Not that it was his party, but he told David he was sure it would be all right. He said he'd heard from Neil that they weren't seeing each other any longer. "I thought you two would get on all right," he sighed.

"We did," David assured him.

"So what went wrong?"

Jeremy, being Jeremy, pretty quickly worked it out for himself. "Look, don't spend New Year's Eve on your own. Why don't you come with us? The more the merrier. Pat won't mind."

In the end, he went to Mike and Carol's party. He'd toyed with the idea of giving Neil a ring and asking him if he'd like to come, but eventually he decided to go alone. There was a mixture of relief and disappointment on his hosts' faces when they found he hadn't brought Jeremy with him. "He's gone to another party," he explained, "although he'd have liked this one. I didn't know it was going to be fancy dress!"

"It isn't," sighed the six foot tall, fifteen stone rugby player, wearing a dress and bright red lipstick who was on his way to the kitchen to get another beer.

"We only talked about having one," Carol said guiltily.

"I might be able to lend you an old tracksuit," her husband added.

But the sorrowful transvestite looked at Mike, who was considerably smaller than him, and shook his head. "I don't suppose you've seen Lesley, have you?"

"What's she look like?"

"A parrot. I mean she's dressed as a parrot. When she realised it wasn't fancy dress, she locked herself in the bathroom. She won't let anyone in. They're having to use the downstairs cloakroom. I don't think she's talking to me actually." He sighed again. "I expect she's still there," he said as he wandered off.

It was an extremely good party. Even Lesley, once they convinced her that there were worse things than being dressed as a parrot, enjoyed herself.

FIFTEEN

One Thursday in January, towards nine o'clock, the doorbell rang. David had been reading, and wasn't expecting anyone. It was probably someone collecting for charity or perhaps one of their neighbours, he thought. Mrs Stevens occasionally brought him a cake she'd baked and came to make sure that the house wasn't falling down about his ears.

He picked up a couple of coins from the table just in case it was someone asking for a donation. It might even be the milkman. He didn't seem to have any particular day on which he collected money or, if he did, David was usually out at work then. That was something he needed to get sorted out. While his parents had been home, his mother had been there to pay the milkman. The last time they'd been away, the milkman would leave a bill once a month, and David would leave out a cheque the following day. There was a new milkman now, and David hadn't yet had a chance to speak to him.

He turned on the outside light as the doorbell sounded again, and, keeping it on the chain, opened the door. Quickly he closed it, released the chain, and opened it again.

"Hello," Rob said.

David stood there, not knowing what to say. Eventually he said: "Come in," and moved aside to let Rob by.

They went into the lounge and stood looking at each other.

"It's been quite a while," Rob said.

"Yes." David knew he was grinning like an idiot but couldn't help it. The surprise and the sudden rush of affection had overwhelmed him. He'd thought he'd got over Rob or at least had things in perspective, but looking at him he knew he still felt the way he had a year earlier. "Would you like some coffee?" he said at last, wondering why Rob was there.

"Thanks."

David escaped to the kitchen, aware that his emotions were about to betray him. He breathed deeply to steady himself, and when he went back into the lounge, he was once more in control.

"Sit down," he invited, finding that Rob was still standing and was looking about him as if to see whether anything in the room had changed since he was last there.

Rob sat down, shrugging off his jacket. "Thanks," he said again, a little shyly, accepting the cup of coffee. "How've you been?"

"Fine. And you?"

"Oh, fine."

They noticed each other's awkwardness and smiled. For a while there was silence.

"Thanks for the record," David said at last.

"Well, there's no point working in a record shop if you don't take advantage of it."

"It's good to see you." An understatement.

"You too." Rob put his cup down. "How long have your parents been away?"

"A couple of weeks." David looked puzzled, having forgotten he'd told Rob they were likely to be going away again early in the New Year. "How did you know?"

Rob hesitated briefly. "I've phoned a couple of times and got no reply so I guessed they weren't here." He didn't explain why he'd been phoning. That would have to wait until he was sure of something. "How long have they gone for this time?" He leaned back in his chair, looking more relaxed.

David cradled his cup in his hands. "Dad thinks it'll be the best part of a year. Still, they were home for longer than usual, and this'll be the last trip." He took a sip of the coffee.

"Are you seeing anyone?" Rob asked.

"Only Jeremy, and that doesn't count." Perhaps he'd tell him about Neil later.

"I missed you."

At Rob's words, David looked up. It was as if he'd never been away and yet David wasn't sure what to say to him. There was silence for a few minutes.

"Could I move back while your parents are away?" Rob asked carefully.

David hesitated. It was what he wanted, wasn't it? What he'd said to Jeremy. But you could never go back, and the thought of Rob leaving a second time was unbearable. "Are you finding it harder to manage than you thought?" he asked, stalling for time. If the rent had gone up, Rob might be finding it difficult; and then driving lessons weren't cheap. "Did you pass your test, by the way?" he asked, grateful to find a neutral subject.

"Second go." Rob grinned. "I hit a few things the first time. Only the kerb!" he added, catching sight of David's expression.

"Are you thinking of getting a car?"

"I don't think I can really afford one just yet. But I'm managing OK," he said, changing the subject back. "It's just that one of the people I share the house with has a sister who's fed up living at home. If she moved into the house then at least Angie would be there to keep an eye on her. I thought if I came back here, she could have my room." He looked expectantly at David.

"I thought you were happy there?"

"I am."

"So why give it up? You may find that you won't be able to move back when the time comes. And if you have to go somewhere else, you mightn't like it as much." It was ironic, when you thought about it: here he was, putting forward reasons for Rob not to move out and come to stay with him.

"I'm willing to risk it. I don't suppose I'd have stayed there forever, anyway. Would you mind if I came back?" he asked again.

"I don't think it's a good idea," David said slowly.

"Why not?"

David racked his brains for a convincing answer and came up with nothing. Eventually he was forced to the conclusion that the only way of dissuading Rob was to tell him the truth.

"Because I love you," he said quietly. "And because I want you," he added more quietly still in case Rob thought his feelings more altruistic than they were. He avoided looking at Rob. He'd burnt his boats now. Rob would tactfully change the subject, stay for another five or ten minutes, and then leave. They hadn't even had a proper chance to talk.

Lost in his own thoughts, he almost missed what Rob said.

"That's not a problem."

"For me it is," said David simply.

"What I mean is, I wouldn't mind sleeping with you."

"If you need somewhere to stay, of course you can come here. You don't have to …"

"Sleep with you?" Rob completed for him, smiling. "No, I know I don't have to. But I think I might enjoy it."

David looked at him, bewildered.

Rob tried hard to suppress a smile. "I never said I was heterosexual."

They stared at each other for a long while.

"But – I'd no idea – Are you sure?" David floundered.

"I'm sure."

"I never knew. You never said a word." There were so many questions, he couldn't think what to ask.

"I thought about telling you, but I was afraid things would get too complicated. I needed to get it sorted out in my own mind first." Rob paused, then went on. "I don't think I love you, but I do care about you. I don't know if that's enough for you to be going on with." His face was serious as he looked at David.

"It's enough," David said softly. "You knew," he said softly. "You knew how I felt. All this time."

Rob nodded. "You never mentioned it, so I didn't either."

"It was the one thing I never told you." David shook his head, still finding it hard to believe. "I missed you so much."

"I know."

They smiled at each other.

"Can you stay tonight?"

"No, I've borrowed Angela's car and she needs it for work tomorrow. I'll come tomorrow – I can collect my things at the weekend – if you don't mind me moving back in."

Mind? David was overjoyed.

They grinned at each other.

"Talking of which," Rob said, glancing at his watch, "I'd better go. Angela'll want to make sure I've got the car back in one piece. Thanks for the coffee," he added, aware that it sounded rather formal under the circumstances. "I'll come round about half past seven."

"I could come and collect you," David offered.

"No, it's all right. I haven't got much. Just a few clothes and some CDs." He looked at the depleted record cabinet and smiled. "I bet you haven't bought a single record since I moved out."

"No," David admitted. "But someone sent me one." They exchanged looks. "Half past seven, then."

"About then."

"OK." They went into the hall, and David opened the front door. "See you tomorrow."

"Yes. Bye."

David closed the door slowly and went back to the lounge. He could scarcely believe it. An hour had changed his life completely. He felt relief, surprise, but, most of all, an overwhelming sense of happiness. He was complete. Rob was coming back. What he had dreamt of was now a possibility. He'd said he cared for him, too, maybe not as deeply as David cared but enough to want to hold him and be held by him. And love could grow.

And David wanted him. Those months without him had made him realise that, in the darkness, his body ached for Rob.

When he went to bed, he couldn't sleep. He kept smiling to himself, wondering whether Rob was awake, too, and thinking that this would be his last night alone. How had he never guessed? After all, Rob had realised how David had felt, while he hadn't even suspected that Rob was gay. Had he been so wrapped up in his own thoughts, trying to preserve his own innocent deception, that he hadn't observed Rob's reactions?

He didn't know how he was going to wait. He allowed himself the luxury, taboo for so long, of thinking about making love with Rob. To be able to reach out and touch him, to kiss him, to caress ... to be caressed. To feel Rob's hands on his body.

Tomorrow, he thought, this time tomorrow ...

SIXTEEN

He awoke still feeling euphoric. He arranged to take the afternoon off and, because of this, worked harder than usual during the morning, despite the feeling of anticipation which gripped him.

It was only when he stopped at half past twelve that the doubts and uncertainties began to assail him.

Had last night simply been a dream, a product of wishful thinking? Had Rob really said those things? Could David have mistaken his meaning?

He stopped at the supermarket on the way home to buy chicken, broccoli, fresh fruit and wine. And a packet of contraceptives. Ten years ago he thought he'd never need them.

Once home, he tidied the lounge and then went into the kitchen to prepare the evening meal. He tried some of the wine, which tasted good and helped him to relax.

What if Rob didn't come? David wouldn't blame him if he'd changed his mind, he was only young, perhaps too young to know what he really wanted. At his age, David had been occupied with exams, deciding what sort of job he wanted; not taking on commitments.

Idiot! he told himself as he chopped up carrots. Rob came to you. He made the decision. You accepted it. Why should the difference in our ages matter now? There was a similar difference between his own uncle's age and that of his aunt, and they'd been happily married for nearly thirty years.

He swept the carrots off the board and into the casserole dish, and started on the potatoes.

You're just nervous because it's the first time, he told himself. You're not quite sure what to expect. You're afraid that it won't be as good as you want it to be, as you've imagined it can be. You've waited so long and now you think you'll be no good at it, not at first. Hell, did you expect to get behind the wheel of a car and be able to drive it perfectly without any practice? Why should sex be any different? It takes time to find out what someone else enjoys – and what you enjoy. We're both in the same boat, we've never slept together. He looked up from peeling the potatoes. I wonder if Rob's slept with anyone before? On balance, probably not. Not that it would matter. I'm not going to mind if he has, although I suppose it would mean he'd be comparing me with whoever it was. Still, at least one of us would know what he was doing.

He had another sip of wine and then added the potatoes to the casserole. He got an onion from the fridge and took the outer layer off, removed the root and shoot, and started dicing it.

It couldn't be that bad, he reasoned, otherwise no one would do it. Anyway, how could you know you didn't like something if you hadn't tried it? If that was what Rob wanted, then he wouldn't object.

He finished chopping the onion, his eyes stinging, and swallowed a mouthful of wine to take away the pervading taste and smell.

I wonder if it hurts?

Then he added the chicken and some of the wine and put the casserole in the fridge. The wine was quite acceptable, he thought, carrying his glass back into the lounge and resolving not to drink any more until they sat down to eat. If they sat down to eat, a little voice inside his head added.

The small square packet of contraceptives on the table caught his attention. Reluctantly he opened it and then one of the three smaller packets inside. The first time he'd seen a condom was when he'd been in his early teens, and curiosity had got the better of some of his classmates. They'd drawn lots to see who'd be the one to go into the chemist's and buy a packet of Durex. He supposed the name of the brand he'd just bought had been chosen for its ambivalence: equally suited to partners of different sexes or of the same sex.

He regarded the oddly-shaped item with a mixture of disbelief, disappointment and resignation. In an age that has seen Man land on the moon, it was strange that methods of contraception had progressed no further than a sticky, balloon-shaped piece of Clingfilm.

Oh hell, he thought. Did you have to use a lubricant? Why had he never asked Jeremy when he'd had the chance? There was some Vaseline somewhere; failing that, there was always the bottle of olive oil in the kitchen cupboard.

Upstairs, while the bath was filling with water, he studied his reflection in the mirror. What did Rob see, he wondered, when he looked at him? Reasonable, he thought, trying to be objective. He'd always been fairly happy with his appearance, neither over- nor under-weight, fit from his games of squash, a face that was pleasantly ordinary. Perhaps modern technology could provide him with a more attractive nose than Nature had, but it seemed to suit his face.

His eyes travelled down the mirror. He'd seen enough nakedness after games lessons when he'd been at school or after games of squash since he'd been working to know that other parts of his body were fairly normal too. Not, he smiled to himself, that much could be done if they weren't. He wondered whether similar thoughts were going through Rob's head.

The water was warm and relaxed him. He hadn't slept much the night before and the combination of warmth, wine and lack of sleep overcame him.

When he awoke, the water had cooled. He got out of the bath feeling cold and tense.

After dressing, he got some clean sheets from the airing cupboard and put them on the bed in Rob's room. Hell, he hadn't Hoovered in there yet. It was another half an hour before he was satisfied with the room. He had opened the window to let some air in and turned the radiator on so that it wouldn't get too cold. He hoped the cyclamen wouldn't mind the unaccustomed heat. Perhaps he'd better move it tomorrow.

His throat had become dry and a little irritated by the dust, so he went downstairs for something to drink.

Absentmindedly he poured out some more wine, realised his mistake but decided to drink it anyway. He'd already drunk too much on an empty stomach, so a little more couldn't make much difference. What else did he have to do? The packet of contraceptives stared mockingly up at him from the table. Not exactly the most romantic or subtle thing for Rob to see as soon as he walked through the door. He threw away the opened one and took the others up to Rob's room. He glanced indecisively at the bedside cabinets, realised he'd no idea which side of the bed he'd be sleeping on, and left the packet in the bathroom. A thought struck him: hadn't he read somewhere that you couldn't use an oil-based substance with a condom? He sighed and went downstairs.

Next he did the washing-up and cleaned the kitchen floor, wondering why he hadn't cleaned the floor before he'd had a bath. He told himself he was being stupid: Rob had seen the kitchen looking untidy before and he wasn't coming to inspect it.

So why was he coming? Why had he never said anything before? Until yesterday he'd never given David the slightest encouragement. How long did he mean to stay?

In the lounge, he looked for suitable records or tapes to play that evening. Standard seduction setting: low lights, soft music, good wine. Rob was right about his record collection, he thought, rejecting most of them immediately. What had he got that Rob liked? There was always the Dire Straits album. Well, that was all right, then, they could just listen to Dire Straits the whole evening! Stop panicking, he told himself.

Pyjamas! Clean pyjamas. He got a pair from the airing cupboard and took them into his own room. To take them into Rob's would be tempting fate. Did you need pyjamas for an evening of passion? he wondered.

He made another cup of coffee and some toast, and sat down in front of the television, trying to relax again. For a while he succeeded, and then at a quarter to seven, just as he was about to shave and change, he realised he'd forgotten to turn the oven on.

It was going to be a disaster.

Rob wouldn't come.

He drank some more wine and pretended he didn't care.

Then he went to get changed because he did.

Rob was on time, smiling happily when David answered the door and carrying a bottle of wine and a holdall. At least David's fear that he wouldn't turn up had proved groundless. They greeted each other awkwardly, a formal kiss without any sign of passion on the part of either of them, and David put the bottle of wine on the table. A good job Rob brought some, he thought grimly, as he'd already worked his way through most of what he'd bought earlier.

He didn't remember talking very much at first, content to listen to Rob. He watched his face and thought how beautiful it was. A gentle face. Eyes that shone with a mixture of shyness and openness and understanding. A smile that made you think you were special. He watched Rob's hands holding his knife and fork, cradling the wine glass – he was somehow pleased to discover that Rob still wasn't really very keen on wine – and toying with the salt cellar.

It was after the main course and while he was taking the dishes out to the kitchen that he realised he was drunk. It didn't seem to matter. He just felt relaxed and suddenly talkative. Everything was fine. He needn't have worried after all. He brought the dessert into the dining room and poured some more wine for himself and lager for Rob. He talked about work and what had happened since they last met, not yesterday, he meant since Rob had moved out. He told him he'd gone out with Jeremy quite a bit, and then he mentioned Neil. Neil was different, not like Jeremy, he didn't mean he wasn't gay, he was, just that he'd really been going out with him but it hadn't been important, he hadn't minded when Neil had given him the push. He and his father had decorated the spare room, Rob's room, their room, well, given it a lick of paint. It looked nice, well, Rob would see for himself. He stopped abruptly. Rob was looking at him and smiling. David smiled back.

"I've been playing squash quite a bit. You know, Graham at work. We're both about the same standard. And I saw Mike and Carol a couple of weeks ago. They had a New Year's Eve party. They said I could bring someone if I wanted to. They know I'm gay. I bumped into them once when I was with Jeremy, so I thought I might as well make it official. And we've been to a couple of concerts. Mike and Carol, that is. And a play. A local production of Alan Ayckbourn's 'Bedroom Farce'." He swallowed. "It was quite funny. I sometimes even watch Top of the Pops, not that I know any of the groups now unless they've been going for at least fifteen years. Sometimes I watched it because I thought you might be watching it, too."

He picked up his glass, found that it was empty, saw that the bottle was empty, and felt lost.

His words seemed to have dried up.

Eventually he asked Rob if he'd like some coffee, and, when Rob said yes, he went into the kitchen and very carefully made two cups that he took back into the dining-room.

He sipped the coffee, feeling remote. At last he looked up. "I'm sorry. I'm drunk."

Rob had realised that David was nervous and had been drinking more than usual. "But you haven't had that much," he protested.

"I was drinking before you came. And I didn't have any lunch."

"But why?"

David shrugged. It was laughable, he knew. Jeremy would definitely see something Freudian in it: falling in love with someone you think is straight; then getting drunk as soon as you discover he isn't. "I wasn't sure you'd come. And if you did, I thought it would be a fiasco. Which is what I've turned it into anyway."

Rob said, puzzled: "But it's only me and it's only sex."

"I know." If David had been sober, he might have picked up some of the insecurities that lay behind those simple words. "But I love you and I wanted it to be special and now I've ruined it all by drinking too much."

"What exactly are you worried about?"

David stared at the cup of coffee he was holding as if it might contain the answer. "Mainly that you wouldn't turn up. I was beginning to think I'd imagined yesterday. I remembered when you first came here – you remember, you said you were going to get your belongings and you'd be back later that day but you weren't?"

"I came back the following day."

"And then yesterday you didn't sound very sure about what you wanted."

"I'm sure it's worth seeing if it will work."

"And when I told myself I was being silly and of course you'd come, that made me worry nearly as much."

Rob waited for him to continue.

"It's just ... I haven't ... I mean I've never ... I haven't been out with many people. We never ... I've never slept with anyone, you see. There was always plenty of time. Then I wanted to wait until I was sure I was in love. And, just as I was beginning to think that was a bit too idealistic, along came AIDS and it wasn't worth going in for one-night stands just to see what it was like. So I was afraid tonight might be a disaster. And I didn't want that because I love you too much."

"And would you love me less if I was no good in bed?" Rob asked, moved.

"Of course not."

"I came back because I like you, not just because I wanted to sleep with you."

"Have you slept with anyone before?" David asked hesitantly.

Rob nodded. "Safe sex, I suppose you could call it."

"I'm sorry. I shouldn't have asked. I didn't mean to pry. I know I'm behaving like an idiot. I never planned to be drunk the first time I made love."

"I must admit I didn't think you'd have to get drunk in order to face making love with me," Rob said, his eyes dancing.

"That's not all," David said, getting up from the table and going into the lounge, where he sat on the sofa. Rob followed him, but took a seat in one of the armchairs opposite. "Oh hell!" David whispered.

"I'm listening."

David wanted to hold Rob and not to have to talk, but now he'd started he thought he might as well get it off his chest. The Dutch courage wouldn't last indefinitely.

"I'm not very keen on the idea of ..." he searched desperately for the right word but gave up. "Perhaps that was the true reason why I've never slept with anyone before. This afternoon I kept telling myself that it would be all right, after all, I love you." He paused. "So, basically, as far as sex goes, I've never done it, I'm not sure I want to do it, and, even if I did, I'm too drunk to do it."

David looked up to find Rob trying hard to keep a straight face.

"You don't mind?"

Rob shook his head. "Look, everyone's been in the same boat – not having slept with anyone before – at some stage, and most people manage somehow. If something in particular bothers you, we don't have to do it. There are plenty of other ways of making love, I don't mind what we do. And as for being drunk, well, I can wait. I assume you've not turned into an alcoholic since I went away?"

"No, only since you came back," David replied, not intending to be funny but making both of them smile at his words.

Rob got up, went over to the sofa and sat down next to David. "Idiot," he said, affectionately.

Suddenly they were holding each other and David was whispering Rob's name in between tentative kisses. His head had begun to spin from all the wine he'd had and he found his eyes beginning to close. "Oh hell! I think I'm falling asleep," he said despairingly.

"You must be the only man who falls asleep before making love!" Rob laughed. "Go on, go to bed. I'll wash up."

"But I put clean sheets on the bed, I had a bath. I even cleaned the kitchen floor!" David wailed. He knew from Rob's expression that he must have said something comic but he couldn't quite work out what.

"Go to bed!" Rob ordered.

"Are you sure you don't mind?"

"I'm sure. Don't worry, I'll still be here tomorrow."

They both stood up and David drew Rob close. They stood, body pressed against body. "I love you," David whispered.

"I know."

"I'm sorry."

"It's all right. Don't worry about it."

"If I'm still awake?"

"If you're still awake," Rob promised.

"Goodnight, then." And, still thinking about the way their bodies had touched, David went to bed.

After David had gone upstairs, Rob carried the dishes out to the kitchen and started on the washing-up. He smiled. He'd never expected the evening to end quite this way. He'd never known David to be out of his depth before. He wasn't sure he wanted to be loved that much. There was so much David didn't know about him. What would he say if he ever found out?

He was glad to be back. It still felt like home. Although he'd visited his parents, he was aware that he no longer had any plans to move back in. They'd been good when he'd told them he was gay. His mother had cried a little at first and had asked anxiously why he'd felt he had to run away. His father didn't quite know what to say. They'd never had anything like this in the family. But he wasn't to worry. They'd stand by him. He looked at the bowl of suds. He could have told them, they understood and didn't mind. They'd thought it was the pressure of exams.

He tipped the water into the sink, rinsed out the bowl and dried his hands. He'd let the crockery drain. He dried and put away the cutlery.

In the lounge, he turned off the stereo, which had long since finished playing a Dire Straits CD. He smiled as he caught sight of the record he'd bought for David's last birthday. 'Alone.' An apt title for tonight.

Upstairs there was no promise to keep. David was sound asleep and Rob undressed and got into bed without waking him. He looked at David tenderly for a moment, whispered "Goodnight", and turned off the light.

SEVENTEEN

Rob was the first to wake. He looked at David who seemed restless and, who, indeed, woke up a few minutes later.

"You look awful." David was very pale and yet there was a slight sheen to his forehead.

His eyes half-closed, David said: "I feel awful. It must be a hangover."

"Never mind. I expect it'll soon go. Do you want anything to eat?"

"No, thanks."

"I'll bring you some orange juice and Paracetamol." He leant over and kissed David, who tried to focus.

"I'm sorry, Rob."

"It's all right. Try and sleep it off."

David closed his eyes and even the knowledge that Rob was getting dressed within a few feet of him didn't make him open them again.

Opening the bathroom cabinet, Rob placed a packet of contraceptives alongside the one David had bought and grinned as he realised they weren't likely to be used. He found a bottle of Paracetamol tablets, and, humming cheerfully to himself, took it in to David.

"I thought I might go out – if Angie will let me borrow her car, I can move some of my things."

"I was going to give you a hand."

"You're in no fit state to at the moment. Don't worry, I'll manage."

Towards five o'clock, David felt a bit better and decided to get up even though his head still ached. He found Rob on the floor by the record cabinet, putting his own records back. Rob looked up. "Hello. How are you feeling?"

"So-so. The headache's not so bad but I still feel a bit fragile."

"Shall I get you something to eat?"

"No, not yet. Maybe later."

"Perhaps it was a migraine. Red wine's notorious for causing them."

"Maybe. Whether it's that or just a good old-fashioned hangover, I've no one but myself to blame." He went over to Rob, and ruffled his hair. "Thanks. I know I've made a complete fool of myself. Did you collect all your stuff?"

"Yes, I've got everything now. I've left my clothes in your room. I didn't want to disturb you."

David managed to eat something for supper but he still didn't feel particularly well when they went to bed.

"How's your head?" asked Rob, starting to undress.

"It still aches. I'm sorry."

"There's no hurry." Rob smiled, and David undressed too. Rob was beautiful. And he was unaware of it. David gazed at him.

He found that his penis was no respecter of headaches; but when he looked at Rob he felt disappointed that Rob didn't have an erection as well. He couldn't help staring. He wondered why – after all, he couldn't claim unfamiliarity with the male body. Was it because it was the most obvious symbol of masculinity? Well, maleness, he corrected himself. Maybe it was the idea of pleasure given and received.

Curiosity must be a common reaction, he thought, noticing the direction of Rob's eyes.

They grinned at each other as they got into bed.

"Oh God, why did I do it?" David asked. "Why did I go and get drunk?"

Rob smiled at his frustration. "I'd have stayed Thursday night if I'd realised ..."

"That I was going to get in such a state? Oh, it's not your fault. I'm just sorry."

"Don't be. Anticipation's half the fun."

David pulled Rob's face down, kissed him fiercely and then winced. "Looks like I'm going to have make do with that for a bit longer." He stared into Rob's eyes. "I love you," he said quietly. "You don't know how often I've wanted to say that."

"Maybe I do," Rob said.

David thought he understood Rob's remark; it was several months before he learnt what Rob had meant.

EIGHTEEN

David's headache had gone by the time he woke up the following morning. He lay in bed savouring his sense of well-being and the feeling of contentment at Rob's closeness. He felt whole. He felt alive. He felt happy.

He watched Rob as he slept, seeing the duvet rise and fall with each breath. It was difficult to believe it was real apart from the gentle sound of Rob's regular breathing. He could reach out his hand and touch him, but he didn't; he wanted just to watch. He smiled, wondering if he snored. He'd have to ask Rob. Suddenly he found that he was staring into Rob's wide-open eyes.

"Hello."

"Hello. Have you been awake long?" Rob asked, yawning.

"About a quarter of an hour. Do I snore?"

Rob laughed. "I don't think so. I didn't notice if you did. Why – do I?"

"A little."

"Do you want to go back to your own room then, if you can't stand it here with me?"

"I think I can cope. I'll just put a pillow over your mouth if it gets too bad!"

"How's your head?"

"I feel fine now. The headache's gone."

"I knew you'd run out of excuses eventually. Perhaps you could manage to fall downstairs on your way to get me a cup of tea and break your leg."

"I'd have to be in traction before that would stop me. Anyway, what's wrong with getting your own tea?"

"It's your turn today – I got yours yesterday. Well, a glass of orange which you didn't drink and a couple of Paracetamol."

"Just getting my own back for that time you had flu," David reminded him. This fencing, flirting with each other prolonged the delicious sense of anticipation David was experiencing.

Eye contact, David thought. If you stared hard at someone for more than a few seconds, it usually meant that you were about to fight them or make love to them.

"I …"

"What?" they began together. "You first," Rob said.

"I was just going to say I'm glad you're here. What were you going to say?"

"Oh, nothing important. I wondered what was for breakfast, that's all."

"Are you hungry?" David asked, thinking that food was the last thing on his mind.

Rob grinned at the dismay in David's voice. "I dare say I could be distracted."

"D'you mind if I have a shower first?" After a day spent mostly in bed, he felt in need of one, especially if they were to make love.

"Can I join you?"

"What, at the same time?" David said, conscious of how naïve it sounded.

"Yes."

"I suppose so." His nervousness made him sound ungracious. The thought of taking a shower together aroused him even more. Oh God, he thought, as he got out of bed, please don't let me come before we reach the bathroom.

The water was warm on their backs as they held each other close. David's skin tingled, the nerve endings crying out for more.

After a while, Rob moved away and picked up the shower gel

that, until then, had been just another unopened Christmas present. He ran some into his right hand and began rubbing it over David's body. Oh God, David thought again.

A minute later, Rob laughed and asked him to turn the shower off. "Whose bright idea was this anyway?" he complained as he blew a drop of water from off the end of his nose. "I feel like a drowned rat."

Somehow David managed to turn off the shower. "That better?"

"Yes." His hands, still soapy, moved down David's body. David was aware that his breathing was becoming erratic. As Rob's caresses aroused him more and more he found himself unable to concentrate on anything but the pleasure he felt. His body seemed to be a mass of sensations, and he no longer knew where he was or what he was doing. "Oh God, that's nice," he moaned, hardly believing that he could experience so much pleasure. He wanted it to last forever. But it didn't, of course.

Suddenly he was aware of his surroundings again, and found he was breathing deeply as if he'd just run a race. He smiled sheepishly at Rob, who kissed him lightly on the mouth, a welcome back kind of kiss, totally different from the hunger with which David had been kissing him.

"You're taller," David said, remembering how, when Rob first arrived, he'd borrowed a pair of David's trousers that had been too long for him. Now he and David were the same height.

"Am I?" Rob turned the shower on, using his left hand, and held his right under the water to wash the stickiness away.

"Sorry," David said without thinking.

Rob turned off the shower, and suddenly they were falling about, giggling like a couple of kids at the idiocy of David's remark. As they hugged each other, David said: "You're cold."

"I am a bit."

"Let's go back to bed."

The bed was warm and snug and David felt happy and relaxed. After a few minutes, he fell asleep.

Rob watched him, conscious of a feeling of detachment. It had been nice, being in the arms of someone who really cared for him, feeling cut off from the outside world. He'd enjoyed making David happy. He was aware how much power he wielded over David's emotions and he wished that he cared as much for David as David obviously did for him. The first time. That was always special. Rob still remembered his first time.

It was ten minutes before David stretched and opened his eyes, surprised to find he'd dozed off. "Hello," he whispered, his hand reaching out to touch Rob's face.

"Hello. OK?"

"Yes," David replied although 'OK' hardly summed up the glorious sense of release he felt and which was written all over his face.

They lay contentedly in each other's arms and David thought he'd never been so happy. Gradually, though, he became aware that Rob's mood had changed. Well, he thought philosophically, there was no hurry; and since it had been David that had ruined Friday evening he could hardly mind if Rob wasn't in the mood now. He remembered that Rob had asked about breakfast. "Starving?"

"So-so," replied Rob.

David started to get out of bed. "What would you like then?" he asked, putting on his dressing-gown.

"You're getting breakfast now?"

"It's gone ten," David answered, failing to notice anything odd in Rob's expressionless voice. "What do you want? Toast? Cereal? Bacon and eggs or something like that?" He'd have cooked a ten-course banquet if that was what Rob wanted. "Or we could go out for lunch. Just have a cup of coffee now. I don't mind, whatever you want." He searched for his slippers and put them on. Rob still hadn't said anything. "Rob? What would …" He stopped, realising something was wrong. Rob had turned away and was very still. David walked round to the other side of the bed. "Rob?"

Rob wouldn't meet his gaze. David was shocked at how pale he looked. "Rob, what is it? What's wrong? What have I done?"

"What have you done?" Rob repeated hollowly, stressing the last word, his eyes narrowed. "Is that the going rate then? Breakfast in bed in return for a hand job?" Suddenly he looked up, knowing he'd gone too far. "I'm sorry. But what am I supposed to do, play with myself?" he asked wearily.

David sat down on the edge of the bed, shaken. "No, of course not."

"It feels like you don't care," Rob continued, trying to keep his voice steady. His face felt stiff.

"Oh, Rob, you know I do." He'd thought Rob had been angry; now he realised he was intensely hurt.

"Then why didn't you touch me? Why didn't you want to make love to me?"

"I did. I do. I don't know, I thought you weren't in the mood any longer." He sighed. "Perhaps it was just my imagination. Maybe I was afraid to try in case you'd reject me."

"So how do you think it feels when you do just that to me? Why didn't you ask?"

David looked at floor. One minute he'd been feeling on top of the world; the next he felt utterly wretched. "I suppose I'd got so used to trying not to think what it would be like to touch you that when it came to it I was afraid to. I'm sorry. I didn't mean to spoil it for you." He couldn't have made a worse job of everything, he realised unhappily: first, getting drunk; then having the hangover; now, not making love to Rob or even bothering to find out what Rob wanted. He felt clumsy and selfish and insensitive.

There was silence for a while, and then Rob took a deep breath and said: "Come back to bed."

They held each other.

Tentatively they looked into each other's eyes, afraid of finding that what they'd said had been unforgivable.

"I'm sorry," David said again.

"It's OK." Rob tried to smile, and David was reminded how fragile things were.

And awkwardly, for it was the first time he'd ever done this, David reached out and began to make love. He wasn't sure how well things went but vowed to himself the next time would be better.

Afterwards, he kissed Rob's nose and eyelids and ears until Rob laughed and said he thought David had intended getting up.

"Oh, all right." David grinned. Touching Rob and watching him climax had given him an erection again. "As long as you'll drive me to the hospital if I do myself a mischief zipping up my jeans!"

It took Rob a couple of seconds to work out what he meant, and then he grinned mischievously back.

David's eyes widened and then closed as he felt Rob's hand move to his penis. "Oh God!" he whispered.

NINETEEN

They went for a walk by the river that afternoon. To David's relief, Rob seemed to have forgotten or forgiven him for the upset earlier in the day. When they got home, they moved some of the furniture and belongings from David's old room into the one they now shared.

It wasn't a dream: Rob had come back.

They ate early and then Rob had a bath. When he came downstairs, David smiled as he joined him on the sofa.

"What is it?" Rob asked.

"I was just remembering," David replied. There was a pleasant, soapy smell as he drew Rob close. "That first night you ever spent here. Remember? We'd just met at Waterloo." Rob nodded, and David said: "When you came downstairs just now, it reminded me of that. There I'd been, swearing my motives were altruistic and my intentions honourable, when you came into the kitchen and for a moment I really wanted you. I wondered what it would be like, making love with someone I hardly knew. And then I thought I'd better stop thinking things like that or you'd be even more frightened than you were."

"You knew I was frightened?"

"Mmm."

Rob laughed. "I knew you'd been staring at me. But you looked so embarrassed by what you were thinking that I decided you were harmless."

"I fell in love with you that day we went to Brighton. When we were in the restaurant."

"So that's why you were so quiet on the way home. I was afraid I'd upset you."

"What made you think that? I know you'd been taking the Mickey but I hadn't minded that, you did it often enough!"

"I thought ... oh, it's stupid, now I look back on it. I thought you were upset about the photograph."

David looked puzzled. "What photograph?"

"The one I wouldn't let you take. I thought you thought I didn't want you to have a picture of me. You know, because you were homosexual. You'd been so good to me, letting me stay, offering to take me to Brighton, and then I thought I'd ruined your day just because I hate having my photo taken."

So that was it. "When did you realise I was fond of you?"

"Just after you came back from America, you know, when we went down to the coast. It never crossed your mind that I'd guessed?"

"Jeremy asked me that. I thought you'd have treated me differently if you'd found out. Sometimes you seemed to understand how I felt. I just thought it was because you were more empathetic than most people. Funny – you read me like an open book and I didn't even realise you were gay." For a while, they sat in silence. "What would you have done if I'd said I'd been going out with someone?" he asked, curious.

"I'm not sure. If I'd thought it was serious, maybe I wouldn't have said anything."

"If I'd caught the train I'd intended to, we'd never even have met." Suddenly David was serious. "I am sorry about this morning. I haven't done a thing right since you came back."

"And I'm sorry about what I said. You weren't the only one who was nervous. I just didn't expect you to be. It's not like you. You're usually so level-headed. Perhaps we should have taken things more slowly."

"I don't think I could have waited." He'd waited so long as it was, he thought. "Besides, we know each other pretty well and we're both over twenty-one." After a minute, he asked diffidently, "Do you think we could we have an early night tonight?"

"Tired?" Rob asked, tongue-in-cheek. "Yes, all right."

David's finger traced the outline of Rob's lips. "We could make love in the shower if you like. Can I ask you something? You don't have to answer." He failed to notice Rob tense. "Did you love him?" he asked hesitantly. "The person you slept with, I mean."

"Yes. But I found out he didn't really love me. Maybe that's why I overreacted this morning." His face was serious, then he smiled. "You remember when I had flu?" David nodded. "I nearly told you then. You remember – when you woke me up to tell me it was late?"

"What stopped you?"

"I didn't want to complicate things. I wasn't sure how I felt."

"You feel very nice," David said, swallowing. "This morning …"

"It was my fault as much as yours."

"I didn't mean that. I was going to say how much it meant to me." They looked at each other, then David took Rob's face in his hands and tenderly kissed him on the lips.

In the bedroom, he undid the buttons on Rob's shirt, and slid it off his shoulders. Beautiful shoulders. He kissed them slowly, aware of Rob's vulnerability. David's touch was gentle and tentative at first, gradually becoming more confident. Palm against palm, fingers entwining, chin rough against smooth, warm skin. Tongue sought tongue, hands touched face, chest, back. Pupils became dilated, lips swollen, bodies hard, until Rob stopped thinking, existed only through his senses. Quick, shallow breaths, then a series of shudders, and finally stillness.

He knew it had been better for Rob than it had been that morning. He was glad.

He'd thought he would come as soon as Rob touched him, but Rob brought him close to climaxing and then took him back from the edge several times as time itself became an infinite split second. Each touch made him feel more alert, more alive. His body reacted automatically, screamed with pleasure, cried out for more. He could scarcely believe he could feel any more intensely, and then his whole being seemed to explode in a shower of white light, and it was over.

They lay hot and spent, David's arm around Rob's shoulders, Rob's head on David's chest. After a while, Rob rolled over onto his back. David turned and propped himself on one elbow. "Was it all right?"

"Mmm, it was good. What about you?"

David laughed self-consciously. "Very good. I love you," he said softly, looking down at Rob.

Rob started to say something.

"No lies," David said, putting one finger over Rob's lips before he could say anything. He didn't want to be told that he was loved unless it was true.

"No lies," Rob agreed, the words having a curious finality about them. "I do care, you know."

"Why didn't you tell me? I'd have understood. I'd have waited."

"I don't know. Sometimes I thought you deserved better."

"But why, for goodness' sake?"

"Oh, you know me," Rob said flippantly. "Full of self doubts."

After a while, David said: "If I'd known it was as good as this, I don't think I could have waited this long. But I'm glad I did. It wouldn't have been the same with anyone else." His hand brushed Rob's cheek.

Rob stared at David, his eyes clouded. Don't love me too much, he thought, but he merely said: "Did you set the alarm?"

It didn't matter anyway, as David was awake before the alarm, and switched it off.

Rob stirred. "What's the time?"

"Nearly seven." He gave Rob a bear-hug, then released him, his face so full of happiness that Rob couldn't help but smile back, conscious that David had recovered his natural confidence. David touched the light stubble on Rob's face, and became aware that Rob was sexually aroused. Delighted, he found his own body responding.

He sighed in mock exasperation, while Rob laughed as David wondered aloud why it was so much harder to take off someone else's clothes than it was to take off your own.

"It all adds to the fun," said Rob, grinning at David's difficulties.

It felt so right, being with him, thought David.

Eventually they lay together, skin touching skin.

Afterwards, Rob looked at David.

"What is it?"

"Nothing," Rob said, thinking it was strange how sometimes he felt the older of the two. No lies, David had said last night. And he'd promised. There had already been one lie, though, not a recent one, but he'd allowed David to go on believing it. His glance fell on the alarm clock. "Christ. We're going to be late!"

David was late. They'd had a hurried breakfast and then he'd driven Rob to work. "I can get the bus," Rob had said when David offered to collect him after work too, but when David's face fell he gave in and accepted a lift home.

David felt strange entering the office he shared with Graham. He felt as if it must be written all over his face. Hell, it must be obvious why he was late, but Graham seemed to accept the only slightly bent truth of the alarm not going off. He was sure he must be grinning like a Cheshire cat, but the only time Graham raised his eyebrows was when David had to admit that he'd forgotten his squash kit so they wouldn't be able to play. Still, he'd already had quite enough exercise for one day.

He smiled. If this sort of thing was going to happen on a regular basis, he'd have to set his alarm clock for half an hour earlier.

At least.

TWENTY

The next few months were, to David, idyllic. He loved being with Rob, being able to hold him close. In the morning, he felt content listening to Rob's breathing, knowing that at night he could touch him and tell him things he'd never told anyone else. When Rob made love to him, he was lost; he could never have imagined an experience so arousing and so moving. It was as if a door, hitherto closed to him, was now open, revealing things he hadn't known even existed. Until they'd made love, he'd always assumed that sex wouldn't be very important to him; he'd done without it after all; but he had been proved wrong. Not that he minded. And even though David knew he loved Rob more than Rob loved him, it didn't matter. To David, Rob's actions and words showed that he did care.

He thought everything was all right.

June came. Rob was out when his mother rang. David had spoken to her several times, and had noticed that she greeted him differently nowadays. Before, when Rob was just staying there, she'd ask almost immediately if she could have a word with him and would keep to topics such as the weather; now, she asked after David's health, whether his father's work was going well, how his own job was going, and whether Rob had remembered to go to the dentist.

On this occasion, she proceeded to give David details for him to pass on to Rob about the anniversary party being held in a couple of weeks. She and her husband were celebrating their silver wedding. "It's such a pity you've got to work that weekend," she said. "We've both been looking forward to meeting you."

David only half-heard the rest of what she said. He felt cold. Rob had never mentioned that his parents had invited him too, and David never worked at the weekend.

There were, of course, several reasons why Rob might have thought it a bad idea for David to go. Perhaps it wasn't the right occasion to meet Rob's parents for the first time; it would be better if they were on their own rather than surrounded by friends and relatives and with time to talk. Perhaps he was embarrassed at bringing someone home because he didn't know how his parents would deal with the situation of a sexually active son. He might be worried that his parents would object to the age difference or have more in common with David than he did. He could be ashamed of the house or concerned that his parents would treat him like a child in front of David. Maybe he even wanted to meet David's parents first.

But there seemed to David only one reason why Rob hadn't told him: Rob simply hadn't wanted him to go. That their relationship wasn't as strong or as important to him as it was to David.

When Rob came in, David didn't say anything straightaway. It was only as they were finishing their meal that he casually remarked: "Your mother rang."

"Oh?"

"Yes. She wanted to know whether you'd be coming on the Saturday, or whether you'd be there on the Friday night." He paused, then added: "She also said it was a pity I couldn't come too." He watched Rob for his reaction, still hoping that there'd been some mistake, but Rob said nothing in denial or explanation and, after a second, looked away, his face impassive.

David waited a minute, then stood up, collected their plates, and went out into the kitchen.

A couple of minutes later, Rob followed him.

"I thought I'd put everything in the dishwasher," David said. He knew he was being petty, but he couldn't help it. He was hurt and he wanted to make Rob feel as unwanted as he felt. Rob looked at him, then, as there was no washing-up or drying to be done, turned and slowly went back to the dining room.

They were deliberately polite to each other over the next few days. Rob put his shoes neatly together under the small table instead of abandoning them in the hall when he came in. David would ask Rob if he minded if he watched the television news. Each was waiting either to be asked or to be told why. Both remained stubbornly quiet, however.

When it got to Saturday, David tried to resolve whether he wanted to make love that evening. Part of him longed for the physical and emotional zenith and comfort and release; while part of him was still hurt and wanted to hurt Rob. In the end, his usual reasonable self told him this wordless argument was stupid and should be stopped, so that when Rob naturally reached out for him, as if nothing was the matter, David responded, willing to suspend disbelief and consign the misunderstanding to the past.

At least it hadn't affected their love-making, he thought afterwards, as, propped up on one elbow, he looked down at Rob. It was perhaps the unaccustomed tension of the past few days that made him more willing than usual to talk about his emotions. Maybe, if he spoke about things, it would help break down the barrier between them. "It's like ... seeing stars," he said, a little shyly. "When we make love. You know, like watching fireworks explode. You can't believe it's real. You wonder how anything can be so exciting, and then a rocket goes off and it's even more spectacular."

Rob smiled, his eyes tender. "I'm glad," he whispered.

"How do you feel when ..." The question he should never have asked.

"Warm. Comfortable. Secure."

He could have been describing a blanket. "Even when you come?"

"It's nice."

"Nice? Only nice? I thought ..." David broke off. "I thought things were all right. More than just nice." He was lost. It had never crossed his mind that Rob felt that way. "You never said anything. Is it something I'm doing wrong? Something I'm doing or not doing?" He swallowed.

"No, everything's fine," Rob assured him.

"But how can it be if ..."

"Honestly, it's all right."

"You would tell me? If there was some way I could make it better for you?"

"Yes, of course. David, it's fine."

"I just want it to be as good for you as it is for me."

"It's fine. Really. Anyway," he added, so quietly David wasn't sure if he'd been meant to hear, "I didn't expect much."

Deeply hurt, David turned away.

After a minute, Rob said: "I'm sorry. I didn't mean it like it sounded." He leant over but David refused to look at him. "It is all right, I do like it when we make love, really I do. It's not the sex, it's just that I don't love you." As soon as the words were out of his mouth, he cursed himself for saying them. "David, I'm sorry. I do care. I care about you more than I do about anyone else. Forget what I just said. Sometimes I say things without thinking or I put them badly. Nothing's changed. I still care. David?" He swallowed. "Please?"

David said nothing. I don't love you. It had been like a slap in the face. He hurt too much inside to forgive Rob just yet.

Eventually Rob gave up.

He'd really thought everything was all right. Oh, Rob never said he loved him, but his actions had given David hope. Had it all been just a sham? And sex? He hadn't expected much, he'd said.

Had David been foolish enough to believe that Rob, having slept with someone else, would have been content with their own love-making? David had thought about his own wants, not about Rob's needs.

Nothing's changed, Rob had said. That was true. They were back where they'd started in January. That wasn't so bad really. Maybe they just needed a bit more time. Perhaps it would be all right. Perhaps Rob thought that David had been pushing too much for a commitment from him. This business with his parents' anniversary party, for instance. Rob needn't have lied. David could be patient.

He realised that Rob had been very quiet.

He turned towards him.

In the glow cast by the landing light – they usually left it on while they made love – David could see Rob was lying as far away from him as possible; any further, and he'd have fallen out of bed. He was perfectly still, his back towards David, and his whole body radiated unhappiness.

"Come on, Rob, I'm not angry," David said, his voice tired.

Rob rolled over, and buried his head against David's chest, taking care to make sure David couldn't see his face.

"It's all right," David whispered reassuringly, stroking Rob's hair. "It doesn't matter." They lay together, David comforting Rob until he felt him relax. When he thought Rob was ready to talk, he said gently: "Won't you tell me what's wrong? There is something wrong, isn't there? Something you've not told me?"

For a moment, Rob was still. Then he rolled over, away from David, and once again lay rigidly at the edge of the bed. He hadn't spoken a word.

David congratulated himself on his patience. How long had it lasted? Five minutes? He stared up at the ceiling. He hated knowing Rob was miserable, but didn't know how he could help since Rob wouldn't say what was bothering him.

Eventually he turned his head. "Rob?" he said quietly.

There was no reply. He must be asleep. David carefully got out of bed, went silently to the landing and turned out the light.

Rob stared at the wall. He didn't see it, though. Even when the light had been on, he hadn't seen it. He was caught between a rock and a hard place. What did they call it nowadays? A no-win situation. Catch 22.

The next day, he told David that he'd phoned his parents to say David would be coming too.

TWENTY ONE

"I must be getting old!" Rob joked, as they took their ploughman's lunches over to an empty table in the sunny back garden of the pub they'd stopped at.

David had decided to take Wednesday, Rob's day off, as holiday, and they'd got up early and spent the morning walking. The air had been fresh, the sun had shone, and the countryside was pleasing to the eye. They'd been relaxed and had talked easily together, and David was relieved at that. Ever since Rob had told him that they would both go to his parents' silver wedding celebrations, Rob had been on the quiet side. David hadn't noticed at first; he'd just been pleased that it seemed their argument was finally settled; but gradually he'd become aware that Rob had lost his natural enthusiasm and avoided the subject of visiting his parents. More and more his face wore a defeated look, but he maintained the fiction that nothing was wrong.

David smiled. "Come on, I'm nearly ten years older and I'm not dropping from exhaustion!"

"You've got proper walking boots!"

"That's hardly my fault. Besides, today was just a short stroll."

"And you play squash regularly. I think I'll have to start up Sunday morning swims with Sally. You can come too." He wondered what Sally would say if she knew. She'd had an ear infection and then Rob had caught a cold so they missed several Sundays at the pool and had then let things drift, Rob happy to spend his Sundays lazing in bed.

"I'll stick to squash, thank you."

It was peaceful in the garden. Although it was still quite early for lunch, there were a few people besides them: shop or office workers who'd driven out to the country pub to enjoy the mild, bright weather. It had been a good day for a walk: too early in the season for the paths to be crowded, and not too hot; although, sitting there in the still, sunlit quiet after their exertions, David felt warm.

He grinned at Rob and helped himself to a radish from Rob's plate. Rob didn't like them and would have left it anyway, despite his protests at David's action. "D'you want the onion too?" he asked and, as David pretended interest, he speared the pickled onion with his fork and put it into his own mouth.

"Well, that puts a spanner in this afternoon's planned activities!"

"So you'd got this afternoon mapped out, too, had you?" asked Rob who knew full well what David was implying and was grinning because of it. "I thought I'd have a nice, relaxing day off, you know, a lie-in this morning, potter about this afternoon."

"Well, you can have a lie-in this afternoon."

"Shush!" Rob looked towards the next table in case the people sitting there had overheard their conversation. David was obviously in a good mood; usually he was discretion itself.

When they got home, Rob made some coffee and they sat on the sofa, drinking it. "Oh, I don't want to get up," he groaned, happily. He wondered if David would object to massaging his feet for him.

"You don't have to. I'm not fussy. For what I had in mind, the sofa will do just as well."

Rob smiled. "No, I'd better Hoover the bedroom. It could do with it."

"You might as well leave it. After all, we won't be here this weekend." It was as if he'd pressed a switch: one minute, Rob had been relaxed and smiling; the next, he was tense. The look of defeat had reappeared. "Come on, love, it won't be that bad," David said, putting his arm round Rob.

"How do you know?" Rob said, getting up from the sofa and going to sit in an armchair.

"I don't understand," said David, attempting once again to pierce this wall that Rob erected whenever the subject was mentioned. "You keep telling me your parents are reasonable people, and yet you get into a state every time I talk about seeing them."

"Just leave it. Please."

"That's just not good enough, Rob." David wanted to clear the air once and for all.

"So you have no faith in my judgement?" Rob sounded hostile.

"Look, I'm sorry, I didn't put it very well. I only want to know because I care. I don't like seeing you upset."

"I'm not upset."

"You're certainly worried about something." For a minute, David could see some struggle going on in Rob's mind.

"You might not get on," Rob said eventually.

"That's always possible. But I've spoken to your mother and she sounds as if she's accepted the situation. They wouldn't have asked me now if they planned on having some sort of showdown. Anyway, that's not what's worrying you, is it?"

Rob stared back sullenly. "You don't own me."

"What the hell is it you can't tell me? Rob, I love you, for heaven's sake! There shouldn't be things we can't say to each other. We shouldn't have secrets."

"What is this, some kind of thought control? Do you really want me to tell you everything? Well, today I woke up thinking I was glad we'd both got the day off. Now I wish I'd gone in to work. Is that what you want to hear?"

"Sometimes I wonder if you mean it when you say you care."

The words hung in the air for a moment.

"Of course I care," Rob said very quietly.

"Then what on earth are we arguing about? I don't know what's wrong. Suddenly I can't do a thing right, and yet you keep denying that anything's wrong."

Rob just looked at the floor.

David felt anger welling up in him. "You can't just sit there and say nothing. If you don't tell me, I can't help!"

"So you're omnipotent, are you? You can solve anything? I'm sorry, I didn't realise," Rob said with as much sarcasm as he could muster.

"Of course I can't solve everything. But if something's bothering you, at least I can listen. You might actually feel better if you told me."

"I doubt that," Rob said grimly.

At least he'd acknowledged that something was wrong, thought David.

"You don't know until you try."

"Just because you gave me a roof over my head, it doesn't mean I owe you anything!" Rob retorted.

David was stunned by the bitterness in his voice. Their argument was escalating, but David didn't understand why. He tried to defuse the situation. "No, you don't owe me anything for that. I just thought that you owed something to me as a friend."

"I call that emotional blackmail."

"I call it love."

They glared at one other.

"We'll just have to agree to differ," Rob said in a voice that was too reasonable to be so.

"Anyone would think you're ashamed of me."

"That's nonsense."

"Well, what's so awful about introducing me to your parents?"

"Why should it be so important that my parents meet you?"

"If it doesn't matter, then why are you so against it?"

Rob took a deep breath. He was fed up of arguing and knew David had a point. "Perhaps you're right. Perhaps I am ashamed of you. Is that what you wanted? Are you satisfied now?"

"I don't believe you." He was sure Rob was on the verge of telling him. If he was angry enough, perhaps he'd come out with it, whatever it was.

"Why not? Does the truth hurt?"

"It's not me that's lying."

"I haven't lied." Rob looked away as he remembered he had.

"Maybe not, but you certainly haven't been telling the truth. Not the whole truth."

"You never made it easy for me." Damn! He hadn't meant to say that.

"What d'you mean?" Suddenly David was tired. He felt he was fighting a losing battle.

"You don't always like it when I tell you the truth." Rob knew he couldn't take much more of this.

"When?"

"When I told you ..." He stopped.

"Go on, I'm listening." David knew what Rob was driving at, but if he pushed just a little more, he was sure Rob would blurt out what was gnawing at him.

"When I admitted you didn't make the earth move for me," Rob said, his voice putting grim quotation marks around the last few words. Then, since David had asked and since he was losing control, he added: "And that I didn't love you." He was beginning to feel frightened at what they were doing to each other, but he didn't know how to stop.

"So what else could you tell me that could possibly be worse?" David asked, trying to ignore the pain caused by Rob's words.

"You don't know ..." Rob broke off. "You've put me on a pedestal. You don't know me," he said, the anger having turned to anguish.

"But I want to. What d'you think I've been trying to do for the last six months?"

"Screw me?" suggested Rob. "Oh, but I forgot, that's against your principles." He was close to breaking point.

"Love you," David said very quietly.

Rob looked at him. They were the wrong words. He stood up. "Maybe you'd better not come after all. Then you could go up to London and see if you can pick up someone else. Remember to make sure he's a virgin though – you wouldn't want someone demanding who'd want to fuck you, would you!"

They stared at each other. Rob turned as white as a sheet, then fled from the room. David heard the front door open and then close behind him.

David remained on the sofa as if frozen. What on earth had all that been about? Why had their argument become so acrimonious? He just wanted to understand and help. Was that so dreadful? He hadn't expected to be treated like the enemy.

He took the coffee mugs, Rob's coffee only half drunk and now cold, out to the kitchen and washed them up in a daze. The morning had been fine. What had changed? He didn't know. Oh God, what had he done? Why had he pushed Rob so hard? Did it really matter why Rob didn't want him at his parents' party? Rob had looked as if running straight out in front of a lorry would be a more pleasant experience than staying in the same house as David. Where had he gone? He hadn't taken the car, at any rate.

He put the mugs away and went into the lounge. He felt like he had done just after Rob had moved out, as if nothing would ever be right again. Some association drew him to the record cabinet where he picked out the record that Rob had bought him for his thirtieth birthday.

It was stuffy upstairs in his old room – the window hadn't been opened in months – but David didn't notice. He turned on the record player (too old to be called a stereo or hi-fi or stack system) and sat on the edge of the bed, which seemed smaller than he remembered it.

He was numb at first.

Gradually, as he played it for the second time, the record evoked the bitter-sweetness of unrequited love. His body began to relax. What had happened? he wondered. Why was it all going wrong?

It was obviously triggered by the coming weekend's visit to Rob's parents. First, Rob had concealed the fact that his parents had invited David; in fact, he'd lied to them. Now he seemed to be doing everything he could to forget about the weekend ahead and to put off David coming with him.

Rob didn't love him.

He didn't want commitment.

He wouldn't say what was bothering him.

David could guess. Rob wanted to leave but couldn't bear the thought of hurting him. He was being torn in two.

They'd got on better when Rob had just been staying there. They'd been friends, able to laugh, not hurting each other as they were now. Oh, he knew that the closer you got to someone, the more you were aware of their weaknesses, the more you were able to wound them, the more you were likely to take out on them all the petty day-to-day frustrations. This wasn't just an isolated argument, though: there was some undercurrent he'd been aware of for some time but which he didn't understand. He wished he'd just accepted Rob's decision that it was better for him not to go. He'd been tactless to keep mentioning the anniversary party when he'd known Rob had left home because of some misunderstanding with his parents.

They'd gone too far that afternoon. He didn't think he could stand any more of these scenes where they didn't even seem to like each other.

He swallowed. Perhaps sex was the problem. They hadn't argued like this before they'd started sleeping together. From what Rob had said, it sounded as if he had been disappointed. They'd tried, once, in fact. Rob had asked David to make love to him, and, afterwards, had asked if he could do the same. He hadn't. For some reason, although David had been willing – no, acquiescent was a better description – Rob had stopped and had not asked again. This afternoon's slanging match led David to think that Rob did mind. Perhaps it was because David held back physically that Rob, sub-consciously, held back emotionally. Was it better to be good friends than bad lovers? he wondered. For want of a nail ... For want of a screw, he thought in a moment of black humour.

Did Rob miss the person he'd been with before David? Did he still love him? He never mentioned him, a point that now seemed significant; and David had never asked, from an absence of jealousy and a deeply ingrained sense of respect for others' privacy.

He lay on the bed, staring up at the ceiling. He was afraid, if he said anything at all, that Rob would tell him it was over between them. That would be unbearable. To have known what it was like, being with Rob, and then to lose him. He couldn't raise the matter himself. He couldn't face the prospect of Rob leaving again. He remembered what it had been like, the last time. This time it would be far worse. Then, he'd accepted it, never imagining that it could be any different; now it would seem like a failure. He'd be constantly asking himself what he could have done differently to have altered the course of the outcome.

How could he live without Rob? He needed him. He wanted him.

He loved him.

He turned onto his side.

Was that how he saw love? Keeping someone with you at all costs, even when they were unhappy? After this afternoon's

200

outburst, he was in no doubt that Rob was unhappy.

Was that love?

He knew it wasn't. If Rob wasn't happy living with him, then David had to let him go. He had to want what was best for Rob. He had to find out what was wrong and try to put it right; if he couldn't, then he had to accept that Rob would leave.

He had to speak to Rob.

The decision taken, he closed his eyes. After a while, the mental release together with the physical exertion of the morning combined to make him fall asleep.

The place seemed quiet when he returned. The car was still there. Strangely enough, as soon as he had left the house, he felt calm. He promised himself that there'd be no more dreadful rows like the one they'd just had. He'd glanced at David's car, wished he'd let David contact the insurance company to arrange for the policy to cover him if he drove, and thought only he could have been stupid enough to storm out of the house when they'd only just come back from a six-mile walk.

He'd gone to the park. There were a few people there, enjoying the weather. Mothers on their way to collect their children from one of the local schools often came that way as it was a short cut or just somewhere pleasant to while away the time if they were early.

A heavily pregnant woman sat down next to him, her little boy staring at him in wonder. Then he turned back to his mother and said: "Mummy, I need a wee!"

"Oh, James, the toilets are on the other side of the park! We walked past them on our way in. I asked you if you wanted to go." Wearily, she started getting to her feet again, resigned to trudge all the way back to the far entrance.

"Why don't you take him behind that tree?" Rob suggested. "I don't suppose anyone would mind."

The woman looked more closely at Rob and smiled. There was something about him that was instantly likeable. It was true that they'd be out of sight and it was a long way back to the entrance. James was only three, after all.

She smiled conspiratorially at Rob, and led her son off. They returned a few minutes later.

"When's it due?" asked Rob politely. No one could fail to notice the fact the she was very large.

"About three weeks."

"Your second?"

"Third. We've got one of each already, so we don't mind which it is this time. As long as it's healthy. And quiet!" she added, as James' imitation of a racing car got louder. "Are you married?" He looked too young, she thought.

"No. I live with someone though." She frowned, and he realised he'd spoken less guardedly than he'd thought. "We've just had a row," he said in explanation.

"Take her some flowers when you go back," she said promptly. "It's always worked on me!"

Rob smiled, her assumption not rankling. "Maybe."

"Isn't it a lovely day? I haven't had time to notice it before. I hope it doesn't get any hotter, though. You get so uncomfortable when you're this pregnant."

"The weather forecast was for a few more days like this, then they said it would get hot and sticky and we could be in for a thunder storm."

"I know it's nice, but I just wish it was cooler."

"Mummy, who's that?" demanded the little boy, tugging at his mother's hand to gain her attention, and looking towards Rob.

"It's a gentleman!"

"What's his name?"

"I don't know, James."

"My name's James. What's yours?" the little boy asked Rob.

"Rob."

"Is he your friend, Mummy?"

"We're just passing the time of day."

"What time, Mummy? One o'clock? Two o'clock? Three o'clock? Four ..."

In an attempt to stem the flow, his mother hastily said: "Nearly three o'clock. Children take everything so literally," she added, turning to Rob.

"Is he Daddy's friend?" James continued doggedly.

"No, dear. I don't think Daddy knows him either."

"So why are you talking to him?" The child had obviously been given lectures on not talking to strangers. Perhaps this was the first taste he'd had of adults saying one thing and doing another.

The child's mother looked apologetically at Rob. "We're just being polite, James." She looked at her watch again. "Well, I suppose we'd better be going if we're to meet Clare when she comes out of school. It seems to take me ages to walk anywhere." She smiled at Rob as she got up awkwardly. "I'm sure things will be all right."

"I hope so."

"Bye, then."

"Goodbye."

"Bye-bye, Rob."

"Bye-bye, James." Rob watched as they walked off towards one of the park gates.

He paused outside the florist's and looked in. There were bouquets and wreaths, vases and pot holders, table ornaments and potted plants. A woman sat inside, making up a spray of flowers. On the table beside her were a selection of small greetings cards and an

Interflora catalogue. The woman glanced up, caught sight of Rob and smiled, and then resumed her work.

He wondered what David would say if he bought him flowers. Probably he'd be touched by the gesture. But not cut flowers, Rob couldn't bear the idea of buying cut flowers, and not a single red rose, which meant far more than just 'sorry'.

Poor David. Suddenly he felt an overwhelming feeling of compassion for this man who so wanted to believe that everything was all right and was so willing to think it his fault when he realised it wasn't.

Perhaps he should never have come back.

He turned, and walked away without going inside the shop.

Once home, he wondered where David was. The lounge was empty, as was their bedroom. The door to David's old room wasn't quite closed and Rob pushed it open, curious.

David was curled up on the bed, fast asleep.

Rob stood there, indecisive. The light from the record player caught his eye, and he went over to turn it off. He smiled tiredly when he saw what record David had been playing.

So he didn't love David? He didn't really know. But he didn't want to hurt him, which was what he seemed to be doing. He left the room, not closing the door in case it woke David.

Downstairs, he made himself some toast and ate it slowly. Not telling David didn't seem to be working, so perhaps he should tell him after all. Could it get any worse? Swallowing the last piece of toast, he made up his mind to tell him that night. But first, they'd make love.

After all, it might be the last time.

That evening they were both quiet and treated each other gently, each wishing to make amends for the afternoon, and each afraid of what he planned to do. Rob had apologised for his parting shot.

"I didn't mean it." He'd lashed out because he'd been in pain. "I just wanted to hurt you and make you stop. I shouldn't have said it." He searched David's face for signs of forgiveness.

David told Rob that it was all right and that he could go by himself to his parents' if that was what he wanted. Rob had wearily replied that it didn't matter. They were past the point of no return.

Once, David was about to ask what was wrong, but he got only as far as saying, "Rob ..." before Rob said, "Not now. Please, David." He'd sounded so drained that David hadn't the heart to pursue the matter. Oddly enough, they felt far closer to each other than they had done for the last couple of weeks. David allowed himself a measure of optimism. He knew Rob had decided to talk when he was ready. Maybe they could sort things out.

In bed, things hadn't gone smoothly. David had climaxed almost immediately, whereas Rob hadn't come after twenty minutes. "Oh, for Christ's sake, leave it!" he said irritably, and then closed his eyes wishing he'd said nothing. He sat up and pulled on his pyjama trousers.

"Sorry," David said. He sat up too. His earlier optimism had evaporated.

"Why do you always assume it's your fault? Why is it never mine?" Rob asked bitterly, looking at David as if he hated him. "Sometimes I think you love me too much!"

Sometimes I think you don't love me enough.

The unspoken retort hung between them.

Rob swallowed and looked miserably in front of him. He hadn't meant it to be like this. They both knew it was time to talk. Before Rob had time to say anything irrevocable, David summoned up his courage and said he had something to say. Rob remained silent, and at last David began, rather hesitantly, all the while trying to ignore an inner voice which cried at him to beg Rob not to go.

"Being with you has been everything I wanted it to be. I hoped I could make it the same for you. I know things haven't been right between us just lately and I know you're unhappy." He stopped, wishing Rob would contradict him, wishing he didn't have to go on. "Perhaps it's my fault. Maybe I don't satisfy you. I know I've always said I didn't want to ..."

He swallowed. He knew Rob knew what he meant. "Well, I don't mind trying. It's been unfair of me to expect you not to when you've been used to making love with someone else." He paused again, knowing that he had reached, for him, the hardest part. "And I know it must be difficult living with someone you don't love. I want you to stay, but if you feel you must go, then I'll try to make things easy for you." He took a deep breath, trying to steady himself. "All I'm trying to say," he finished, his voice breaking, "is that I love you very much and I just want you to be happy."

TWENTY TWO

Rob remained silent for so long that David began to wonder if he'd been listening.

At last, however, he said in an empty voice: "No, I don't want to leave."

"Then what is it?" David asked gently.

"You still think you can solve anything?" Rob said, harking back to their conversation of that afternoon. This time, however, there was no anger in his voice, only weariness. "Just wave your magic wand and everything'll be all right?"

"No. But if it upsets you so much, as it obviously does, why don't you just tell me?"

Rob smiled unhappily. Wasn't that exactly what he had planned to do? So why was he arguing?

"I never told you exactly why I left home."

To David, it sounded as if he was stalling for time. "You don't have to, if you don't want to."

"I don't want to. I just can't see any alternative." He stared in front of him. "Promise me one thing: that you'll just listen, that you won't interrupt until I've finished."

He paused, and David realised he expected a reply. "I promise."

Rob didn't say anything straightaway. It was hard to begin. When he did, there was no expression in his voice, as if he was simply reciting something that had happened to someone else. Unlike David, who'd had to struggle to put his thoughts into words, he didn't have to think much about what to say; after all, he'd rehearsed it scores of times to an imaginary audience. This time was hardly any different; if he kept looking at the wall opposite, he could forget that David was there. "One day when I came out of school, I found Mum and Dad waiting for me. My grandfather had been taken ill suddenly and they were going to visit him in hospital. They thought it better not to take me with them as it would only upset me and, as the hospital was quite a long way away, they decided to leave me at my uncle and aunt's. My aunt would go with them, of course – she's my mother's sister, and it was their father who was ill – and my uncle would look after me. He didn't know my grandfather so well as he and my aunt hadn't been married very long.

"So we went to my uncle and aunt's, and Dad drove my Mum and my aunt to the hospital. They were going to stay overnight at my grandfather's house, and come back the next day."

He halted and breathed deeply. If David hadn't already guessed what had happened, he'd soon know.

"I watched television, and had supper, and then it got late so I said I was going to bed. My uncle said he'd moved my things from the spare room. He said it was silly to put on clean sheets for just one night and it'd be warmer in the other room.

"I didn't think it was odd. I just accepted it, and went to bed.

"When I woke up, the nightmare had already started.

"I didn't know what was happening at first. I thought it was just a game, and then, when I realised it wasn't, I got frightened and asked him to stop. But he wouldn't.

"The next day, I told him I was going to tell my parents, but he said my aunt suffered from heart trouble too, like my grandfather, and any shock would be bad for her. When my parents returned, they told me that my grandfather had died.

"I was twelve."

He stopped again. Then he continued.

"Then one day, several years later, I found my mother in the kitchen, making a cake for my aunt's birthday. I watched her cracking eggs into a bowl, and said didn't it have too much cholesterol for my aunt. She looked puzzled, so I said what about my aunt's heart trouble. My mother said I was getting muddled up. Both she and my aunt were fine, they'd both had check-ups just after Grandad had died.

"He'd lied to me. That's what I couldn't understand.

"I was stunned. All those years when I'd told no one because I thought ...

"So after school the next day, I went round to my uncle's while he was still at work, and asked my aunt for the key to the shed. My uncle's a keen gardener and never let anyone in there unless he was there too, but I persuaded my aunt to give me the key. I think she thought I was helping my uncle prepare a surprise for her birthday.

"I didn't really have anything in mind. Then I noticed the plant my uncle had grown which he was going to give to my aunt as a present. It had a large white flower – some sort of lily, I think – that had just come into bloom. I cut the head off and nailed it to the inside of the door. I wished I hadn't done it afterwards, as my aunt liked flowers and I'd damaged the plant. I suppose, with hindsight, it seems a symbolic thing to have done, but I didn't intend it that way. I just wanted to hurt my uncle.

"The next few days were awful. Nothing seemed to have any point any more. I was questioning everything I'd based my life on. I blamed my parents for leaving me in my uncle's charge. I blamed my uncle, of course. But most of all I blamed myself for my own stupidity.

"So I left home and eventually I ended up in London. I don't really know what I intended to do, but I met you and you know the rest.

"I've been trying to put you off coming with me to my parents' anniversary party because my uncle will be there too and I didn't want you to meet each other. But that's not the only reason." He bit his lip. "When we met, I said I was nineteen. I was only seventeen. I'm still only twenty. I knew if we both went to my parents', everyone would be asking me what I wanted for my twenty-first, and I was afraid of what you'd say. I know it could cause a lot of trouble for you, me being underage." He looked at David anxiously. He'd never seen David angry and this time he had every reason to be: Rob had lied to him. And not just a little lie; he had caused David unwittingly to break the law. "I'm sorry."

"Don't worry about that," David said, bewildered that, despite everything, the only thing that seemed to concern Rob was the fact that he'd misled David. "Oh God, Rob, I'm sorry!" He put his arms round Rob, but Rob was tense and didn't respond. "Oh God!" David whispered again, leaning his head against Rob's. "How could anyone ..." His voice tailed off. "It must have been awful." He touched Rob's cheek, and gently turned Rob's face towards him, trying to read his expression, but there was none, none that he could read. Only a closed look that he might have expected from a stranger. But then how did you expect someone to look when they'd just told you something like that?

"I'm sorry, I really am," David said again.

"It's not your fault."

"Why didn't you tell me before?"

Rob shrugged. "I didn't want to upset you."

"Oh, Rob. Oh, love, I don't know what to say." He kissed him gently and then wondered if he'd done the right thing. He wanted to comfort him, but he didn't know what to say, and Rob seemed to have surrounded himself with an invisible wall which David didn't know how to breach. Perhaps it would be easier to talk downstairs. The bedroom wasn't the best place to discuss problems, even more so in this case, and David felt as if he was in shock. God knew how Rob felt.

"Can we talk downstairs?"

"OK. You want a cup of tea, don't you?" Rob asked perceptively.

"D'you mind?"

"I was going to go to sleep, but I dare say another half hour won't make much difference."

David realised he was perfectly serious.

In the kitchen, it was Rob who made the tea, and sat eating a biscuit as if nothing out of the ordinary had happened. He was polite and thoughtful and completely withdrawn.

"I must have said some terrible things," David said.

Rob looked puzzled.

"I mean, things that must have upset you." He rubbed his eyelid with one hand.

"It was all right. I knew you weren't doing it on purpose."

"I should have known."

"There was no reason why."

"But I should have guessed." David shook his head. "Things you've said. If I'd listened, if I'd thought ... I can see now why you said certain things, why you did certain things ... I should have known earlier." He looked down at the cup of tea he was holding and wondered why there were ripples on its surface and then he realised he was crying and his tears were falling into the tea.

"Oh, Rob!" he said in an anguished voice, not knowing whether he wanted to comfort or be comforted.

Rob regarded him through empty blue eyes from the other side of the kitchen table. "Your tea'll get cold," he advised. "I put sugar in it, by the way." David usually drank it without.

"I can't taste it."

"I'll put some more in, if you like."

"I can't even taste the tea." He smiled sadly at Rob. "Aren't you having any?"

"I won't be able to sleep if I do." He stared at David, who doubted that Rob would sleep at all that night. "I'll have a glass of milk," Rob compromised, and got up. He fetched a glass, went to the fridge, took out a nearly full bottle, and poured himself half a glass.

David wiped his eyes with the back of his hand. He swallowed, a vision of the twelve-year-old child Rob had been, standing by himself in the playground unable to tell anyone about his ordeal and watching the world through disillusioned eyes.

His eyes. David remembered that Rob's eyes were the first thing that had attracted him. They'd seemed so clear and direct and open. Oh God, he'd misunderstood so much! Why hadn't Rob told him before? They'd known each other for over two years, David felt as if he'd known Rob all his life. If only he had, he thought bitterly, if only he'd been able to stop this from happening. He hadn't known Rob at all. That's what Rob had said.

"I'm glad you told me," he said, his voice sounding strange to his own ears.

"I thought I owed you an explanation." He stared at David's cup of tea, wondering how long it was going to take him to drink it. He wanted to go to bed. "I think the fridge could do with being defrosted."

"What?" David asked uncomprehendingly, thinking his hearing must have been affected as well as his sense of taste.

Rob repeated what he'd said.

"I'll do it tomorrow. Today." It was always time that was most easily confused, distorted. Was it only Thursday? It seemed so long since they'd gone walking, their quarrel about the anniversary party so trivial now. But at least everything was out in the open. If only he could think what to say.

Rob waited with an expression that might have been boredom on his face.

"Sorry." David gulped down some of the tea. Was it hot? He couldn't tell. "Is there any more?"

"Mmm." Rob took the tea-cosy off, and poured some more tea

into David's cup. He sighed irritably at the delay. He wondered if David would mind if he went up to bed. He knew he ought to feel more charitable; after all, he'd never seen David so upset before. Well, it's not every day you find out that the person you're screwing was doing it before puberty.

He smiled. There were times when he thought he wasn't a very nice person. It must be pretty dreadful, really, finding out that the only previous sexual experience of the person you loved had been both illegal and unwanted. And it wasn't much better when you realised that when you'd made love it had been illegal, too. "I'm sorry."

"What?" David thought he'd missed part of the conversation.

"About being underage."

"It doesn't matter."

"I'll grow out of it, I suppose," he said, and wished he hadn't when he saw the pain in David's eyes.

"It doesn't matter, Rob."

For a second, Rob felt absolutely cold. It wouldn't matter to David if he were planning to tell him to go. Was that what he meant?

Something must have registered on his face, as David asked: "Are you all right?"

"A bit tired."

"Oh, love, I'm sorry. I can understand you not wanting to talk about it all now."

"I don't mind." Rob shrugged. Although he couldn't imagine what more there was to say.

"I don't know what to say. I can't seem to think straight at the moment." He looked at Rob, hoping for some encouragement, but finding only a cool, appraising stare.

"Can we go back to bed now?"

"Yes, of course." David glanced round the kitchen, as if seeking some sort of inspiration, but found none. He switched off the light, and followed Rob upstairs. He wanted to touch Rob, but Rob seemed to be avoiding him.

Rob just wanted to be left alone so that he could go to sleep. He wished David would stop looking at him like that, it wasn't as if the world was coming to an end. "Can you turn the light out, please?"

David did as Rob requested. He tried to put his arms round Rob, but Rob said: "Look, I just want to get some sleep."

David moved away, hurt, but then realised how unfair of him it was to expect Rob to cope with his distress as well as his own.

He didn't remember going to sleep. He remembered lying awake, made wretched by the thought that Rob had never slept with anyone he'd loved, tears running down his face as he tormented himself with what Rob had been through physically and mentally. All those years he'd bottled things up inside. What did he feel when he, David, touched him? Revulsion? Nothing? How could David ever make it up to him? What did love count for? Hadn't David felt the same desire that Rob's uncle must have felt?

Rob wasn't in bed. When David looked at the clock, he found it was quarter past eight. Had he set it? Or had he slept through it? It didn't really matter, he wasn't sure he would go to the office today, anyway.

Rob entered the room, fully dressed. He felt guilty about having let David sleep on.

"You're going to work?"

"Why not?" His eyes met David's. Again David had the feeling they could have been strangers.

"We need to talk," David said.

"There's nothing more to tell. It all happened a long time ago. Look, if I don't go now, I'll be late." He stared flatly at David, then turned and left.

After a while, David got up. He debated the merits of staying at home, and eventually decided to go to work. Perhaps he needed to be occupied. Maybe he'd be able to think more clearly if he was distracted for a few hours.

As soon as he got to the office, he realised he'd made a mistake. He brushed aside Graham's concern at his pallor by saying he hadn't slept well, but he found himself unable to concentrate on work. He tried to do as many routine things as possible first, hoping that this would clear his mind of the thoughts that occupied it. He got coffee for Graham and himself. He brought his attendance sheet up to date. He checked and signed some letters that he'd written on Tuesday. He read some circulars that had been on his desk for a week. He notified maintenance of a blind that wouldn't close properly and a file cabinet drawer that was off its runners. He replied to a message on his terminal asking him whether he was available for a meeting next month.

Then he tried to do some real work. He read the same document, on which Linda had asked him to comment, three times without being to able to make head nor tail of it. Graham brought him another cup of coffee, and he tried again. It was no use: it might as well have been written in Greek for all the sense it made.

Holding the cup in both hands, he stared unseeing at the calendar on the wall opposite. All he could think of was how awful it must have been for Rob.

When he'd drunk his coffee, he went into Linda's office, and told her he wasn't feeling well and was going home. He'd finish the report he was working on and his analysis of the document she'd given him next week. There was nothing else that couldn't wait until he got back.

Linda said she hoped he'd feel better soon. She was quite concerned. David was hardly ever ill. Odd how the more competent and indispensable the person, the better health they apparently enjoyed.

David returned to his own desk, and began putting away his work. "I think I'll go home after all," he said to Graham. "I've told Linda."

"I thought you looked rough when you came in."

"I'm all right. I've just had a bit of a shock."

"No one's ill, I hope?"

"No, nothing like that." He knew Graham was looking at him both curiously and sympathetically, inviting his confidence, but the secret wasn't his to tell. When he said nothing, Graham suggested: "If I were you, I'd take tomorrow as sick-leave too. Weren't you going away somewhere, though?"

The visit to Rob's parents had been driven clean out of his head. "Yes. I don't know if I will now." He sighed. "I'll take tomorrow as holiday. I should be OK by then." As he said the words, he wondered whether things would ever get back to normal.

He went home.

All afternoon, he tried to sort things out in his mind, but only two coherent thoughts kept surfacing: how could anyone do such a thing; and how could anyone do that to Rob? He lay on the sofa and tears came to his eyes and he cried for Rob, for himself and for the loss of innocence. He must have fallen asleep, for the next thing he was aware of was Rob watching him as he sipped a cup of coffee.

"Did you go to work?" Rob asked. He looked dispassionately at David's tear-stained face.

"Yes. I came home early. I couldn't concentrate." Rob's gaze disconcerted him. He felt he was being weighed and found wanting. He glanced at his watch. It was half past six. "Shall I get supper?"

"OK. By the way, I phoned my parents. I told them we wouldn't be coming after all. I said I'd got flu." His eyes rested on David. "You don't mind if we don't go, do you?"

"No, whatever you think's best."

"Sorry if I made you late for work today."

"I didn't do much while I was there anyway."

"I should have woken you though. I turned off your alarm before it went off."

"Don't worry. It meant I got a bit more sleep. Not that I got much."

Rob looked at the floor. "I'm afraid I did it deliberately. It was rather petty. I just didn't want to have to talk to you."

"It's all right." David wanted to say more, but Rob finished his coffee and went upstairs. He obviously still didn't want to talk.

TWENTY THREE

The next day, David woke when the alarm sounded. "Shall I pick you up from work?" he asked sleepily.

"If you like. You're not going in, then?"

"No. I thought I'd go for a walk." He wanted to think things over. "Shall I make breakfast?"

"No, go back to sleep," Rob said gently.

David was encouraged. "Can we talk tonight?"

Rob's face clouded over. "Maybe," he replied evasively and changed the subject.

David sighed. Perhaps he was rushing him.

Rob got out of bed and went into the bathroom. David listened to the familiar comforting sounds of an electric razor, followed by taps being turned on. When Rob returned, David watched him get dressed. He wanted him, but he knew his timing was bad. "I'll pick you up at half past."

"OK. Bye."

David stared at the door after it closed behind Rob, and then turned over and went back to sleep.

Rob ate the meal in silence. David talked about his day, and hoped that he wasn't irritating Rob.

Afterwards, he volunteered to wash up by himself, to which Rob said pointedly, "I'm not ill, David."

"No, of course not." They did the washing-up together as usual. While he waited for Rob to finish drying the last few items of cutlery, David said, "Rob?"

Rob looked round.

"It's all right." He hoped Rob knew what he meant. They looked at each other for a long moment and there was something in Rob's eyes as if he was ready to say how he felt. David wanted to put his arms round him, but he hesitated, unsure whether physical contact would be welcomed, and, as he hesitated, he saw the shutters come down again and the moment had passed.

"Thanks," Rob said, turning back to the draining board. "I've had an AIDS test, you know. So you've nothing to worry about. I didn't really think it was likely, but I'd never have forgiven myself if I'd passed it on to someone else."

Poor kid. All these years of silence and worry.

"You've never thought of telling the police?"

"No."

"You don't think ... well, he'd do it to someone else?"

There was a brief pause. "I don't think he would. I think he just made the most of the opportunity." Rob put away the last of the cutlery, hung up the tea-towel, and stared at David. "Wasn't there something on television you wanted to watch?"

TWENTY FOUR

Over the next few days, David noticed a pattern in their conversations. If he asked Rob directly about what had happened, Rob would give a terse reply and change the subject. If, however, David said nothing, then Rob would mention the subject himself, a bit like someone who couldn't leave a spot to heal but had to pick at it. Sometimes David had the feeling that Rob was challenging him.

The first occasion came when they were doing the washing-up.

"I used to blame my parents for leaving me there. And for not guessing what had happened. Funny, I must have been better than I thought at hiding it all. I didn't want to cause a family rift, I didn't want to upset anyone. That's why I never liked having my photo taken. I thought people could see it in my eyes if they looked hard enough. I didn't see how I could hide it." There it was again, the dig at David, David who'd loved him blindly. Then Rob had abruptly left the kitchen and David heard him go upstairs. He wondered if he should follow but decided Rob wanted to be alone.

Another occasion arose when they were loading their shopping into the back of David's car. Rob said, "I don't think about it all the time, you know. I don't actually think about it very much."

Was he blocking it out? David asked himself. And was that a good thing or not?

"You said you wanted me, you remember, when I came to see you back in January. There didn't seem much point in waiting till I was twenty-one. I didn't think about the implications for you until it was too late."

The fact that he was underage was obviously still preying on Rob's mind. David did his best to reassure him. Again, he had a feeling that Rob was expecting something else from him, waiting for him to do something, but David didn't know what.

In the car one day, Rob said: "I suppose I picked you up. At Waterloo."

"It was me that asked you to stay."

"Perhaps I wanted to be picked up, then."

David gently said, "That's why you looked so anxious when we got here? And why you demanded a key to your room?"

"Well, maybe part of me thought how could I possibly put myself at risk again. But the other part thought nothing worse could happen. Perhaps I even wanted ..." But even he couldn't bring himself to voice what he sometimes imagined when he saw David's expression. Why did he want to hurt David all of a sudden?

For a while, traffic was heavy and David had to concentrate on driving. When the road ahead became clear, David said he wasn't the best person to speak to as he couldn't be objective. Rob replied that he didn't want to talk to anyone else about it. "I didn't really want to tell you. Not now. I thought I could cope ..." He broke off. "You won't tell anyone?" he demanded. "Not your parents. Not mine. You promise?"

David promised.

"And if I refer to what happened, you won't just get angry or upset? I mean, if I can't mention it ever again, I might as well not have told you."

"I'll try not to."

One night, as they were getting ready for bed, Rob blurted out: "It didn't hurt. I always wondered about that, why it didn't hurt." He watched David carefully.

"I'm glad it didn't hurt," David said, not sure what Rob expected him to say.

"I didn't struggle. Not when I realised what he wanted."

"Don't feel guilty, Rob. You were only twelve, you couldn't have stopped him. It probably got it over with more quickly. Look, we could go away, if you like. Somewhere hot. You can choose where."

Rob shook his head. "It wouldn't be much of a holiday for you. Besides, it's not a good idea while I'm still only twenty. Anyway, I like it here." It was true: he felt safe there. He retreated to the bathroom, leaving David feeling that there was still a long way to go.

"I'm sorry." They'd been watching the news on television.

"It's not your fault."

"No, not that. About using you. I wanted to find out if sex could be enjoyable. I wanted someone I could trust. Someone to hold me and tell me they loved me. And you just happened to be there. I'm sorry I never cared enough." And, although something in his voice was near to breaking, his eyes were still calm and David didn't know what to do. It was as if Rob had built a wall around himself but, within, everything was starting to crumble.

"Christ, I hope it's not me that's upset you!" gasped Graham. He slumped to the floor and leant back against the squash court wall. Usually they were evenly matched, but this time David's aggressive play had overcome Graham easily and left him thoroughly exhausted.

"No, it wasn't you," David replied dully, his mind on other things.

Graham looked up at him closely. Rather than being elated at the easiness of his victory, he sounded depressed. But no confidences were forthcoming.

As he showered, David thought grimly that at least it hadn't affected his game. Not detrimentally. In fact, at this rate, he'd end up as the All-England squash champion.

That night was like the previous nights: David said 'goodnight' hoping that Rob would lean over and they'd kiss like they used to; and Rob waited in vain for David to hold him. He felt remote and abandoned, convinced that if David really loved him he'd know how he felt, each night that David just turned over and went to sleep making him feel more lonely and unloved than the last.

He lay there in his misery, feeling the tears come. He felt trapped, unable to understand himself: part of him didn't want David to realise he was upset, so his crying was silent and brought him no relief; part of him longed for David to hear and comfort him.

Tonight was worse. He got up quietly and went into the bathroom. In the mirror his face was white and pinched and streaked, his eyes swollen. He swallowed. It was all going wrong, everything he touched went wrong. He'd not stayed long enough at school to finish his 'A' levels, he'd upset his parents by leaving home, he'd got a dead-end job, and now he'd ruined things between David and himself. He couldn't blame David. He'd lied to him, well, perhaps not lied – apart from his age – but he'd certainly not told him everything from the start. It was all his fault. It had to be. There must be something about him, something that courted disaster and failure. How could he have been so stupid?

Why had he never told anyone before? He smiled grimly. Well, look where it had got him now.

He sank to the floor, his tears flowing unchecked, his sobs and hiccups louder now there was no one there to hear them.

David was only half-conscious of Rob getting up, but he awoke aware that he hadn't returned. He looked at the clock and found it was midnight. He turned over and closed his eyes. A few minutes passed, and he wondered whether Rob had gone downstairs – perhaps he couldn't sleep. Damn, he thought, feeling inadequate. He put on his slippers and dressing-gown and made his way towards the stairs. To his left, the light from the bathroom was visible, the door slightly ajar. "Rob, are you all right?" He pushed the door open slowly.

Rob was sitting on the floor, his back against the side of the bath, crying. Judging from his face, he had been doing so for some time. David thought his heart would break at the sight. "Come on, love," he whispered, sitting down beside Rob and putting his arms around him. "It's all right, it's all over. He can't hurt you now."

Rob swallowed and looked through tear-filled eyes at David. "That's not why I'm crying," he said, stumbling over the words, and blinking to try to clear his eyes.

"What is it then?"

Rob stared at him, gulped and continued to cry.

"Tell me, love. What's wrong?" His left hand stroked Rob's hair, pushing it back off his face. "Come on, you can tell me."

"I knew I should never have told you." Rob stopped, overwhelmed by a shuddering sob.

"I'm glad you did," David said softly. "I just want to help. What's wrong? What's making you cry like this?" He waited, praying that it was nothing too dreadful.

"You don't want me any more."

"Oh, Rob," David whispered, drawing him closer, "of course I still want you." He wiped away Rob's tears with his hand.

"Then why haven't we made love since I told you?" His anguish was unbearable to hear.

"Oh, love, I thought you didn't want to. You kept drawing away from me and I could understand you not wanting to be touched after all that had happened. "

"Well, I did," Rob said in a low voice. "I just wanted you to persevere." He clung to David, still crying. "I feel like someone dropped me and I broke."

"We'll put you together again."

"Like Humpty Dumpty?" Rob said and then he remembered the rest of the rhyme.

"It's all right, it's all right," David comforted, rocking him gently. "I'm sorry." Gradually his voice started to soothe Rob whose shudders and sudden gulps subsided. They sat there without moving for a while. "Better?" asked David gently.

"Mmm." Rob sniffed and tried to smile.

"I just thought you didn't want to make love, not yet," David said, his face buried in Rob's hair. "I should have asked you. I'm sorry." It was the second time he'd made such an assumption.

"It was my fault," Rob said jerkily. "It's not really fair expecting you to be a mind-reader."

David smiled, his face still hidden. "I'm obviously not very good at it. I didn't know what to do. Nothing I said seemed to help. I wanted to make it better, but you seemed ... frozen. I kept trying but I couldn't seem to reach you."

"I felt as if I was locked away inside myself. And you were outside and I wanted you but you weren't there." He started crying again, and reached out blindly for David.

"I'm here, it's OK," comforted David.

"It was like I wanted to see how far I could go before I provoked you into saying something."

"Shush, it's all right. You've bottled it up for so long, no wonder you feel so angry. If you want to take it out on someone, then I don't mind you taking it out on me." It's funny, he thought, how it seemed easier to talk to someone if you weren't facing them: the priest in the confessional, the psychiatrist in his consulting room, even the hairdresser seen only in reflection. It was as if you were just talking to yourself. Perhaps you were. Perhaps the important things we tell each other are just spoken aloud in order to clarify the issue in our own minds. Perhaps seeing the reaction on other people's faces would make us stop, aware we'd overstepped the bounds of ordinary conversation. His lips brushed the back of Rob's neck and he felt Rob's shoulders relax a little. There was still a long way to go.

"I've spoilt it all for you, haven't I? You were so happy when I moved in and now I've spoilt everything." Rob's shoulders heaved.

"It's all right, I'll survive. You don't have to protect me." If only he'd been able to protect Rob. David would have been what, twenty-two, when it had happened? Older than Rob was now. Old enough to have done something. But he hadn't known. And he hadn't guessed.

"I've been happy here, you know," Rob continued, looking around the bathroom through tear-stained eyes as if he'd never see it again. "Don't leave me," he whispered.

"No, I won't leave you." Not now, not ever, David thought, wishing he could ask Rob which he'd meant. They sat quietly, Rob's breathing still uneven. The middle finger of David's right hand gently traced circles on Rob's forearm.

"You used to do that just after I came back."

It seemed like a long time ago.

"It makes the odds better," Rob said at last. "When we sleep together. Before I came here, sex was all bad. Now it's just a bit that was bad. The odds get less ..." He ground to a halt, and hoped David had been able to piece together what he meant.

"I never thought of that," David said. Rob must have felt

himself deserted just when he'd laid his soul bare. No wonder he'd been so upset, afraid he'd made an error of judgement in telling David. He'd cried because he thought David didn't want him. He'd asked David not to leave. It might not be love, but it was a start. David could understand how Rob, emotionally battered and bruised, was unable to commit himself any further.

"I love you," David said, turning Rob's face gently towards him. "And I want you."

Rob's hand touched his. "You're good with people, you know."

"I don't seem to understand them, though, not the people I really care about." Not like Rob, who'd known all along how David had felt, while David had no inkling what was going on in Rob's mind. Not even like Jeremy, who'd notice the slightest nuance and would remind you of what you'd said five years earlier. "You always seem to know what I think, but I never know what you're thinking."

"That's because you love me. You've lost all objectivity. Along with quite a few hours' sleep," he said, attempting lightness.

"I'll catch up on it at work. They won't even notice the difference." He was rewarded with a shaky smile from Rob, even though his eyes remained serious.

"D'you think we could go and see my parents this weekend?" Rob asked.

"If you feel up to it."

"I'd like them to meet you. Besides, I feel guilty about not going to see them the other weekend."

"They'd understand if they knew. Don't worry about it. Shall we go back to bed?"

"Can we stay here a bit longer?"

"You're sure you're not cold?"

Rob shook his head. "No, I'm all right."

David smiled, and his arms tightened around Rob. After a few minutes, Rob looked up and asked, "What is it?"

"You get insomnia and I end up getting cramp!" David joked.

"I suppose it's not very comfortable here. Let's go to bed." They got to their feet and Rob caught sight of his face in the mirror. He looked dreadful. "You go on," he said to David. Rob held a cold flannel over his face for a few moments and breathed deeply. It didn't seem to have made much difference. Oh well. He followed David into the bedroom.

Oh God, it was good being held again. He felt safe and wanted. His tears had relaxed him and worn him out. He knew they were going to make love.

There was one thing David had to know. "Rob?"

"Yes?"

"You never think ... I mean, when I touch you, you're sure it doesn't remind you …"

"Don't ever think that!" Rob interrupted vehemently. "Promise me you'll never think that! Please!" His distress was obvious.

"I promise," David said quickly, wishing he'd kept his fears to himself. Fears that when they made love it brought back the nightmare.

"You're not like him at all. I've never, ever thought that. You've never made me do anything I didn't want to. You'd take 'no' for an answer. Please don't think that," he begged again.

"Shush, it's all right," David whispered, hugging Rob to him, feeling him tremble. "Shush."

Eventually Rob looked up. "I do like it when you touch me. I don't think of anything else, I know I don't. I know you were hurt when I said I just felt safe when we made love but to me that's important. I don't know what I'd do without you. I'm sorry I don't love you. I'm sorry I'm underage." His eyes filled with tears.

"Oh, Rob, it doesn't matter. Don't worry about it."

"Make love to me."

They made love awkwardly as if their bodies were unfamiliar

to each another, stopping at inconvenient moments for Rob to blow his nose.

Afterwards, David kissed him tenderly. "Remember I'm here when you need me." He stared into the darkness, hoping there wouldn't come a time when Rob no longer needed him.

Rob lay awake, too. Why couldn't he love David? David deserved it. It wasn't as if Rob loved anyone else. He didn't think he loved anyone, really, least of all himself. All he was doing was burdening David with all of his hang ups. Oh, God, not again!

He buried his face in the pillow. Then he felt David's arms around him, turning him towards him.

What was the matter with him? Why couldn't he stop crying?

TWENTY FIVE

"Is Rob awake?"

"I don't know. I didn't look in on him."

Mrs Greenaway busied herself pouring out another cup of tea, which she handed to David. "I wasn't sure ..." She hesitated. "It wasn't meant as a criticism – separate rooms, I mean. We didn't quite know what to do, things being the way they are."

"That's all right."

She was reassured by his composure. The evening before, it had been her husband, and not David, who had been nervous of their meeting. David, after all the traumas of the preceding weeks, considered visiting Rob's parents the least of his worries. "Rob's told us not to mention to anyone that you're living together. I wish he'd thought beforehand instead of worrying about it afterwards. Still, he can be a bit impulsive at times. I expect you've noticed."

David smiled.

"I'm glad he brought you to see us. Has he met your parents?"

"No. In fact, they don't know that we're living together, although they may have guessed by now. I want to tell them face to face."

"Is it going to cause problems?"

"It shouldn't. They've had a long time to get used to the idea that I won't be getting married."

"I can't say we were surprised when Rob told us that he'd moved back. When he came home last year, he was very cagey about what he said but whenever he mentioned you, it was always to say something nice. You'd obviously made a good impression

230

on him. I'm afraid we jumped to the wrong conclusion – we thought you'd already been living together. Rob was really indignant – almost angry, in fact – when he realised what we'd been thinking. He said you were just friends." She sighed. "I don't know why he felt he had to run away like that. We understood once he told us."

For a moment, David thought that they knew the real reason, but Mrs Greenaway's next words dispelled that idea.

"After all, it's not such an awful thing. If people are happier with friends who are the same sex, then I don't see what harm it does. We were upset that it took him over a year before he felt he could confide in us. He really didn't have to run off like that. He was doing well at school, too. It's a pity he missed his exams. That's why we thought he'd left – pressure on him to do well. He can always take evening classes. That's if he wants to," she added hastily. "It's not the end of the world."

"I know he regrets leaving school so soon," David said. "He's afraid he's left things too late. I'm trying to persuade him that there's plenty of time. He could even go back to college full-time." David would support him if Rob would let him, would put up with being banished from the lounge while Rob wrote essays or did revision. But at the moment Rob's mind was on other things.

"We'd help, if it's a question of money. We've got a bit saved." She offered David more tea, which he accepted. "We're very grateful to you. Rob told us how kind you'd been. You hear some awful stories about what happens to youngsters who've run away from home. What made you offer him somewhere to stay?"

"We'd been talking for a while – we seemed to find it easy to talk to each other. He looked as if he didn't know what to do next. I suppose even then I felt …" he shrugged, searching for the right word "… protective towards him."

"The age gap didn't worry you?"

David hesitated. "No, it didn't. Well, it doesn't now, not the age gap as such. Sometimes I wish Rob was older."

"It's only a few months until he's twenty-one. Looking at you both, it's difficult to believe that there's ten years between you."

"Oh ... it's not that. It's just that I can't help remembering what I was like at twenty. I wouldn't have been interested in settling down."

"And you are now?"

David nodded.

"You've not lived with anyone before?" she asked cautiously.

"No. There's been no one serious until I met Rob."

"Well, you're the only person he's brought home for us to meet. I know you mean a lot to him." She liked David, and realised that her worries about the influence he exerted over her son were completely groundless. If he influenced Rob at all – and she could see that he cared for her son – it was all to the good. Rob needed someone stable like David. Even if Rob did have a wise head on young shoulders, he was still only twenty. "It's a shame neither of you could make our anniversary party. Rob still looks a bit under the weather. He was very quiet last night. You haven't succumbed?"

"No, I feel fine. We were both looking forward to coming. Rob was very disappointed that he didn't feel up to it."

"Not to worry. Having just the two of you here gives us more time to get to know each other." She looked up as footsteps sounded on the stairs. "Well, I'd better get the toast on. Sounds like Rob and his father are up. No peace for the wicked!"

As David glanced towards the doorway, his eye fell on a calendar. On it he could see that Mrs Greenaway had circled a date and scrawled a reminder to herself to put flowers on her father's grave. It was the anniversary of the death of Rob's grandfather.

David committed the date to memory.

TWENTY SIX

On Sunday, David asked Rob if he was going swimming with Sally. They'd gone the previous week and, if it didn't actually cheer him up, at least it had kept him occupied.

"She can't make it today."

"So you're not going?"

"I don't think I'll bother. It's not much fun by yourself," he added dispiritedly, making it sound as if it wasn't much fun anyway.

"I'll come with you."

Rob looked up. "You don't like swimming."

"I could do with some exercise." He thought activity would take Rob's mind off things for a while and help him relax.

They went.

At first, David found it easy to keep up with Rob; if anything, he was faster; but after six lengths, when he was beginning to think longingly about heated showers and hot coffee, he realised that Rob had only just warmed up. "D'you do this much swimming when you come with Sally?" he asked, holding onto the rail at the deep end and wondering why he felt more tired than he did after a game of squash.

"Sometimes. Sometimes we just muck about, but it's a bit busy for that today." A couple of lanes had been roped off, and David and Rob had been following the more serious swimmers as they went up one lane and down the other.

"Remind me to get revenge by playing you at squash one day."

"D'you want to get out, then?" Rob said.

"Aren't you cold?"

"It's not too bad if you keep moving." They parted, allowing a man wearing goggles to swim up to the end, turn, and kick off. "D'you mind if I stay in a bit longer?"

"No. I've got a book with me."

They smiled at each other, as it was a standing joke that David never went anywhere without a book, and for a moment Rob's face lost its look of defeat.

"I'll see you in the coffee shop," Rob suggested.

"OK. Don't drown."

Rob watched him swim to the steps, climb out, and then walk to the changing rooms. An intelligent, considerate, nice-looking young man with an uncomplicated outlook on life. Until he'd met Rob, who'd heaped trouble after trouble onto him. If only there was a way to undo the things that had happened; to unsay what had been said; to love someone simply because they deserved to be loved.

He hadn't accomplished much by telling David. He felt far worse than he had when he was twelve; worse than when he'd run away from home. All he'd achieved was to upset David, and, now that he couldn't seem to pull himself together, David was worrying about that too, although he was trying to hide it from Rob. Rob wished he'd said nothing: after all, it had all happened a long time ago.

Oh, why did David have to be so bloody nice? he thought, pushing himself off from the side.

Why did he have to fall in love with me?

David glanced up from his book. From where he sat, he could see the pool. He watched Rob as he ploughed up and down, apparently oblivious to the shouts and laughter of the others in the water. He seemed to be swimming as if he had his own private battle to fight or as if it would purge his soul.

"Hi."

David looked up. "Good swim?"

"Mmm."

"I'll get you a coffee." David came back with two cups and put one in front of Rob.

"I still owe you one," Rob said, thinking of the first time they'd met on Waterloo Station. "Oh hell." He found he was crying.

"Close your eyes, breathe deeply, and concentrate on what I say," David ordered gently. He then proceeded, much to Rob's amazement, to give him a mental arithmetic test that grew progressively harder.

After a few minutes, Rob opened his eyes and breathed a sigh of relief. "It's OK. I'm all right now."

"People will just think the chlorine's made your eyes a bit watery. Come on, drink your coffee. I'm not buying you another just because you let that one get cold."

"What was the answer? To the problem?"

"I've no idea."

And, although Rob could have read more into his words, he took them at face value and smiled.

TWENTY SEVEN

David glanced up from his book to find Rob still staring into space. He put down the book and went over to Rob's chair. "Come on, love, what's the matter?" he asked, putting his arm round Rob.

"Don't!"

"Of course not." David hastily withdrew his arm and returned to the sofa.

"I'm sorry," Rob said, moving to sit next to David. "It wasn't what you think. It's just ..." He sighed, wondering how to explain it. "It's just ... when I feel upset and you touch me, all I want is for you to make love to me and then I think I'm just using you."

David touched Rob's face with his hand. "Don't you think I like making love to you?" he asked, smiling gently.

Rob smiled too. "Oh, I know you do, but ... it's not fair on you."

"I don't mind what your reasons are. If you find it therapeutic or if it just takes your mind off things for a while, that's OK."

"But it's so unfair. You never ask for anything. You don't even ask me to love you." His eyes were bright with unshed tears.

"I can't force you to love me," David said. He glanced down for a moment, then looked up. "When you left, I thought I'd give anything to have you back. And then you came back, and I can hold you and I can love you. That's more than I ever expected. I'm just happy you're here. And I'm glad I'm here to help if that's what you want."

Rob swallowed. David's acceptance of the situation always threw him a little, his calmness made him think that things might not be as bad as he imagined. "It is. Even if I don't seem very grateful at times." He paused, then added, "I wish I loved you. I don't know ... Perhaps this is love. Perhaps this is how everyone feels, I just thought it would be more. Perhaps it's me, perhaps this is all I'll ever feel." He blinked. "All I know is I seem to want to hurt you sometimes. It's like I want you not to love me, but I don't know why I do it because it makes me frightened you will stop loving me."

David put his arms round Rob, and drew him close. "It's all right," he whispered. "I won't stop loving you."

Rob drew away. "I'm sorry. I should be over all this. I mean it's a long time since it all happened. It should be getting better."

"But it's not?"

Rob shook his head. "Everything's a mess. I feel like I'm falling apart. I don't know what I'd do if you weren't here. I can't understand it – things were better before I told you. I thought I could cope with it. That's why I came back – I thought I was coping with it. I didn't mean to land you with all this."

"It'll be all right now you've told someone. You'll be able to come to terms with it and consign it to the past where it belongs."

"It shouldn't have been you I told, though. I should have told someone that's not involved. It hurts you just as much as it does me."

"But I can help now I know. I can avoid saying or doing something that might hurt you. It explains a lot of things. Besides, I wouldn't have wanted you to keep it from me. Am I helping at all?" he asked carefully.

Rob nodded. His eyes clouded. "I wish I loved you." he said again.

"Oh Rob, it doesn't matter." Oddly enough, it really didn't seem important now. The fact that Rob wasn't in love with him no longer had the power to hurt as it had before. "It upsets me more to see you worrying about it."

"I can't help it."

"I can't help being in love with you either. I never meant it to be a burden. Just think of it as me being here as long as you need me. Anyway, I know you care. You wouldn't be putting yourself through all this if you didn't. You wouldn't make love the way you do if you didn't care at all."

"When we have sex ..." he didn't usually put it in those terms, but he wanted to be precise although he knew what they did wasn't just about sex "... I'm trying to make up for everything else. Is that love?"

"It'll do," David said encouragingly. Trying to make each other happy. It sounded like a good basis.

"You know when I came back? It was funny. You thought I'd be annoyed because you'd got drunk and because you were nervous about sex. I found it reassuring. It even made me smile." A few short months, and now everything seemed so complicated.

After a while, David said: "I've been thinking about what you said the other night. About the odds. I understand what you mean. And I've been wondering if I've been fair to you. I've only made love to you once that way, and I made it plain I didn't want you to make love to me like that. But I meant it when I said I was willing to try."

"No!" Rob protested vehemently to David's surprise. "You know I said that when we were in bed it never reminded me of what happened? Well, it did. Just the once. That time when I asked you if we could try it. You'd just made love to me and I was about to reciprocate when it hit me: I was behaving just like my uncle. I couldn't believe it. I was horrified that I could think of doing such a thing when I knew you didn't really want to. They say that's what happens: what someone did to you, you go on to do to someone else."

"I never thought of it like that."

"I know you didn't really. But I knew you didn't want to and

I'd been prepared to ignore your feelings."

"Well, you didn't and anyway it can't be that bad otherwise no one would do it," David said.

An early night might help; David felt as if he hadn't slept properly for weeks; but when he came back from the bathroom, he found Rob standing in front of the mirror, lost in thought.

David undressed.

After a while, Rob said, as if he were speaking to himself: "D'you think it's my face? Do you think there's something in my face or the way I look at people that made my uncle act the way he did? What did you think when you first saw me?"

David crossed to the other side of the bed, rested his hands on Rob's bare shoulders, and looked into the mirror, too.

"You want to know what I thought?" He smiled. "I thought you looked nice, and I wondered what you were like. And then when you smiled I thought you were beautiful."

Rob's eyes watched his. "You've never said that before."

"I suppose I thought you knew." From Rob's reaction, he guessed he'd been right. "And then I thought you might find it trivial and worry that that was the only reason I wanted you. Over the years, we all change."

"You mean you'll still love me when I'm old and grey?"

"I hope so." He watched Rob's reflection: a stillness that seemed fixed, then the muscles of his face began to go into spasm. He turned round and buried his head against David's shoulder. "I'm sorry!"

"Come on," David whispered. "You haven't done anything you need to apologise for."

"You don't deserve all this."

"You didn't deserve what happened to you."

"I'm a mess. A complete mess."

"No, you're not. Things'll get better." He held Rob tightly, and soon realised that Rob was becoming sexually aroused.

"Sorry," Rob sniffed. "You said you wanted an early night." He turned away from David, and picked up his pyjama jacket from the bed.

David stopped him. "It's all right. They say we can make do with less sleep than we think."

He still felt an overwhelming sense of joy when Rob touched him. There was still that immediate reaction to his caresses. And to be able to hold Rob and kiss him and then to move his hands down Rob's back until he was pushing Rob's body into his own.

This time Rob hesitated and looked uncertainly at David. "Would you mind making love to me?"

TWENTY EIGHT

"Can I have a look at your book?" Rob asked diffidently. He held out David's copy of Sexual Abuse: Case Histories.

"Yes, of course you can."

Rob got to his feet. "I'll read it upstairs."

David watched him go with a sinking heart; it wasn't pleasant reading, but it might help nevertheless. He'd felt compelled to read the concise, sad stories of childhoods which had been turned into years of fear. Some of the children had grown into compassionate adults determined never to let what had happened ruin their lives and determined to ensure that their own children would never know what it was to hear a voice whispered in their ear at night and to feel a stealthy hand removing the pathetically insubstantial barrier of night-dress or pyjamas.

All the case histories were summarised at their start by a few sentences whose very brevity and objectiveness made David grow cold. But he read the ones about relatives and family 'friends' who had repaid the trust placed in them by abusing the children in their care.

It had become painfully clear to him that Rob's case wasn't unique. Almost all the offenders were men, and, of the victims, a higher percentage than David had realised were boys, some far younger than Rob had been.

Rob, he thought, had coped remarkably well. Several of the children involved had at least considered the idea of suicide; two or three had tried it; one had succeeded. There was a tremendous burden of guilt and shame, and the fear that no one would ever want them even if they remained silent about their ordeal. And most had, at least while the abuse was still going on. (A footnote said that, with the changing climate of opinion, more children were coming forward to report sexual abuse but, taking into account the judiciary's recent handling of such matters, the author thought that this wouldn't last.) One teenager explained how he'd felt when his step-father's abuse, which had started as purely physical, had then become sexual. He said he felt dirty and he hated his step-father for having taking away the innocent sexual pleasures his friends looked forward to.

Suicide hadn't been the only alternative. Some children, as they became older, experimented with drugs or simply became promiscuous. Even the ones who'd had sympathetic parents said they'd usually got into trouble, often by being disruptive at school. One girl, whose next door neighbour had offered her a lift home from school and had then indecently assaulted her and afterwards given her a bag of sweets, stole pounds and pounds of sweets. If she got rid of the sweets, she told her parents who'd been thunderstruck to find that their daughter had been caught shop-lifting, everything would be all right again. Her father went round and hit the neighbour and then they moved away.

Another girl said that her fiancé had broken off their engagement when she had told him. She didn't hold it against him. How could she? It had taken her ten years to learn how to live with it. How could she expect him to be able to do so overnight?

But a lot of people – parents, teachers, husbands, lovers and, in one memorable case, the milkman – had been patient and gentle even though the victims had often become angry with the very person they'd chosen to confide in, as if they hated anyone to see their vulnerability.

And though all the grown-up victims knew the statistics – that often child abusers themselves had been abused as children – most felt that they could cope. Of course, they'd been the ones to receive help. One or two were worried that their own experiences had made them wary of showing affection to their children, uncertain about the demarcation line between parental cuddling and sexual touching.

When Rob hadn't come down after an hour, David went upstairs. He opened the bedroom door and put his head round cautiously, thinking Rob might not want to be disturbed. "Hi," he said as Rob looked round. "Can I come in?"

"Yes." Rob, who'd been lying, his hands behind his head, sat up as David came over to the bed and sat down.

"OK?"

"Mmm."

David looked at him anxiously. There were no signs of tears; in fact, Rob looked, if anything, more relaxed.

"It's funny how you think you're the only one things like this happen to," Rob remarked. He clasped his hands around his knees. "Have you read them all?"

"Most of them."

"They make me feel I'm quite lucky in a way. Did you read the last one? About Mary?"

David had.

"I mean, how could her father just throw her out of the house like that? She was only thirteen. It's unbelievable!"

Mary, or whatever her real name was, had been ten when her father first started to abuse her, and eleven when they had full sexual intercourse. At thirteen, she found she was pregnant. Her father, on hearing this, called her a slut and told her to get out. He, of course, had been the only person she'd slept with.

She'd had an abortion. She'd had no one to help her.

When she was twenty-six, and had been married for five years, she panicked because she still wasn't pregnant. Afraid that the

243

abortion, years earlier, was stopping her from conceiving, she told her husband about it. He, thinking that she and some lad from school had just gone a bit too far, told her not to worry.

She kept worrying. Eventually she told him that it wasn't some schoolboy who'd got her pregnant. She told him who it was.

They stopped making love, and slowly they grew apart. In the end, he suggested that it might be better if he moved out. She could keep the house, he'd stay with his parents for a while until he could find somewhere else. She agreed that it made sense. She could understand him not wanting her. They were still young, after all.

Before the divorce was final, he'd come back to collect some of his things. He'd found somewhere to stay. He gave her the address – things were still very civilised between them. Then he left.

An hour later, as she was pulling the curtains in the bedroom before going to bed, she noticed his car still outside. She thought it must have broken down, so she went downstairs and out to see if he wanted to phone a garage.

In the car, she found her big, strong bear of a husband crying his eyes out. She got him into the house, with a cup of tea in his hands, and finally he talked. He didn't want a divorce, he just wanted them to be together again. They didn't have to have children, he knew it would just remind her ...

It was a complete revelation to Mary. They'd misunderstood each other completely. She'd thought he didn't want to sleep with her, that he couldn't cope with the knowledge of what had happened. He'd thought she didn't really like sex – how could she? – and that getting pregnant would bring everything back to her.

They talked and drank tea until five o'clock in the morning, by which time they'd decided to call off the divorce.

They had three children eventually. The first two were boys, the third, a girl.

I was afraid of having a daughter, Mary wrote. I thought I'd be reminded of myself. I thought I'd end up watching my husband in case ... well. I thought I wouldn't love her.

But it's all right. She's nine, now, and the apple of her father's eye. It's a joy to see them together. And I do love her.

"At least," Rob continued, "I didn't have to worry about getting pregnant. And it wasn't as if it was incest" – could it be incest between men? he wondered – "or even a blood relative. I never got AIDS. It hadn't happened in my own home. Sometimes ..." He paused. "Sometimes I wish it wasn't such an awful crime then maybe it wouldn't seem so awful to be the victim of it. Like when having an illegitimate child stopped being so terrible, actually being illegitimate lost its stigma. Not that there's any excuse for any of this." He stared at the book he'd been reading.

They sat quietly for a while, then Rob said: "It's not as bad as you might think. I mean now, that is," he added. "I don't think of it every moment of every day, for instance. I don't hate everyone I meet, although I'm not as trusting as I used to be." He studied his feet. "I think," he went on slowly, "it's been bad just lately because I told you and I didn't know how you were going to take it. I didn't know how to handle having told you."

"I still want you," David said softly.

"I know." Rob smiled. "It's just asking an awful lot of you. I didn't mean to make you cry."

"It's OK."

"I hated my uncle at first. I think I just despise him now. I blamed my parents for not protecting me, not noticing what had happened. And I feel ashamed and guilty. But mostly I'm angry at my own naïvety and stupidity. You know ..." He paused for a moment. "You know ... I used to talk to myself when I went to bed. I used to tell myself that it hadn't hurt physically and I wasn't going to let it hurt mentally. That it wasn't important. That one day things would be all right."

David waited for him to continue.

"It did help. Saying it to myself. I could almost believe it had happened to someone else. When you think about it, the amount of time … you know … was negligible. I didn't see why it should spoil everything. There've been times when it's been bad again. Just lately, of course, and when I ran away from home. I'm neurotic about photos and I'm not the most confident of people. Sometimes if someone does something nice, it upsets me. That's why I burst into tears when you brought me a magazine when I had the flu. And I suppose inside there's still a bit of me that's frozen. But it's not too bad." He swallowed. "I still don't know if it was luck or judgement which made me speak to you in the first place."

David smiled. "Why me, anyway? There must have been countless people passing through the station."

"I was hungry. You had a sandwich you didn't want. That was the main reason. I'd noticed you looking at me, too. Maybe I thought I stood a better chance of getting a cup of coffee out of someone that fancied me. But it wasn't just that. You looked … dependable." He stared at the door. "When I came here, once I'd got used to you, it was nice. I felt comfortable being with you. I felt safe."

"You put the key back," David reminded him. "Just when I really wanted you, you put temptation in my path by putting the key to your room back in the kitchen drawer. You couldn't have timed it better if you'd tried. I'm just glad I never …" He left the sentence uncompleted.

"But you didn't. And even if you had, it would have been something innocent. Like trying to hold my hand. I wouldn't have screamed the place down over that."

"I always wanted to touch your face," David admitted. "I try so hard to understand you and yet you still know me better than I do you."

"And I try so hard to love you and you still love me more than ..." He broke off.

"It's OK," David whispered. "If I want to love you, it's up to me."

"Liar!"

"I know. But at least it made you smile." After a while, he added: "Love's not all candlelit dinners for two," realising as he said it that they'd never had a candlelit dinner at all, even on that first, disastrous night after Rob had come back. "It's just as much doing the washing-up together. Having an argument as you go round the supermarket. Cooking meals for someone even though you hate cooking."

"And eating them even though they taste awful."

"It's not so bad," David said, unconsciously echoing Rob's earlier words. They both wondered if he just meant Rob's disasters in the kitchen.

TWENTY NINE

It was on a Thursday when the strain of the past few weeks caught up with David. That morning, he'd found himself doubting what he told Rob whenever he sought reassurance: that it would be all right. It was becoming hard to believe that things would ever get back to normal. He tried reminding himself that it had worked out for Mary and her husband. But they had started with an advantage he didn't possess: both partners had loved each other. If only he could be sure that, at the end of the day, Rob would still be with him.

At four o'clock, one of his colleagues had come into the office carrying an end-of-month return due that day which he'd asked her to prepare.

He glanced at it, then looked more closely. It was hopelessly wrong, he could see that even without checking it properly. It was meant to be on Linda's desk by five o'clock. There was no way it could be corrected in one hour.

He lost his temper.

In the pub, Graham looked thoughtfully at David. "You all right?" He'd been an embarrassed witness to David's unusual loss of control, and wondered what had really caused it.

"Yes. Linda didn't hit the roof, thank God." David drained the rest of his half-pint. It was all he dared have as he'd got the car with him.

"I didn't mean that."

"I know."

"It's just that you've seemed a bit ... withdrawn the last couple of weeks."

"I didn't realise it was that obvious. I've just got something on my mind," he said.

"Anything I can do?" Graham asked sympathetically.

David shook his head. "No, but thanks. I expect it'll sort itself out one way or another."

Graham saw that the subject was closed. "D'you want another?" he said, indicating David's empty glass.

"Not for me, thanks."

"How about coming back to our place for a meal? We haven't seen much of you lately. I'm sure Jill wouldn't mind. We could go out for a curry." Even if David wouldn't tell them what the matter was, maybe an evening out would cheer him up.

David was tempted. Out of sight, out of mind, he thought, and instantly regretted it. None of this was Rob's fault. If anyone needed taking out of himself, it was Rob. He wouldn't have objected to David going out, but it wasn't fair to leave him when he was still so depressed.

He sighed. "Thanks, but I've got to get back. Some other time, I promise."

"You're late," Rob said, and David was glad he'd resisted the impulse to take Graham up on his offer.

"I went for a drink with Graham," he replied, staring, bemused, at the group on Top of the Pops. "Oh, I've got to go in early tomorrow."

"Problems?"

"Something that should have been done today and wasn't. It's not really that important."

David was quiet throughout supper, and afterwards sat lost in thought. "Shall we go out tomorrow?" he asked suddenly. Perhaps Graham was right. "For a meal? Nothing special – just a pizza or something? We haven't been out for a while."

Rob thought he sounded dispirited. "OK. Sure you won't be too tired?"

"We don't have to eat late – we could get to the restaurant for seven o'clock."

"How about that Italian place near where I work? I could go there in my lunch-hour and book for the evening," Rob suggested.

David nodded absently.

THIRTY

David shut the bathroom door behind him. It hadn't been such a bad day after all. They'd sorted the report out quite quickly, and Linda accepted the delay with equanimity. The evening had gone unexpectedly well, too, both of them relaxing in the cheerful atmosphere of an unpretentious trattoria run by friendly, exuberant Italians who delighted in re-filling their glasses to the point where David was beginning to wonder if he would still be sober enough by the end of the meal to drive home.

Rob had drunk about the same quantity, which, as he rarely drank wine, had made him more talkative than usual and left him with a tendency to laugh at the slightest thing. Even if technically sober, David wouldn't have let him take the wheel. Rob had joked that if neither of them was fit to drive, they could always sleep it off in the shop, he'd got the keys.

The evening was exceptionally mild, and after they'd got home they sat in the garden which seemed even more peaceful than usual after the good-natured noise of the trattoria. Eventually, however, it grew chilly, and they were forced inside. Rob yawned. They went upstairs.

Taking his tie off, as he went into the bedroom, David asked, "What's that?" The question was rhetorical: it was a medium-sized Paddington Bear propped up against the headboard on his side of the bed.

"It's for you. I thought you were a bit fed-up yesterday, so I bought it to cheer you up. I suppose I only noticed because I've been feeling a bit better this week."

"Idiot!" David said affectionately, putting his arms round Rob. "No one's bought me a teddy bear in years. I don't have to take him to bed with me, do I?"

" 'Fraid so," Rob replied. "I was lucky to get it home – Sally spotted it and wanted it herself. Then she kept asking who it was for. I bought it at that shop next door to the restaurant. Do you like it?"

"Course I do. Thanks."

"I've never really bought you anything before. Just a couple of birthday presents, nothing unexpected. Yesterday, you just seemed really down in the dumps. I thought it was because of me. Was it?"

"Partly, I suppose. I had a lousy day at work. I managed to reduce one of the girls to tears."

"You did?" He hadn't realised things had been that bad.

"In front of Graham, to make matters worse. I didn't feel very proud of myself."

"Have you managed to sort it out?" The thought that all this was really his fault made him anxious.

"Yes. Apologies all round. And we put the report together first thing this morning."

"So you were drowning your sorrows last night?"

"Sort of. Anyway, what was that you were saying? Are you really feeling better?" He looked closely at Rob, hoping that the worn-out, lost look he'd had for the past few weeks had really gone.

"I think so. Better than I was. It doesn't seem to be the end of the world any longer."

"I'm glad. I've been worried."

"I know. Look, I think I was a bit unfair. I know I asked you not to tell anyone else, but I wouldn't mind if you wanted to speak to the Samaritans or someone like that. I mean, I've told you and it's not fair if there's no one you can talk to."

David smiled. "It's OK. I can cope."

"I was always worried that people would find it ... well ... me, I suppose, disgusting."

"No. It just hurts when I think about what happened."

"Can't you forget about it? Not entirely, just most of the time?" He finished undressing.

"Is that what you want me to do?"

"I think so. I get the impression you're treating me as if I'll break." Not surprisingly, he thought, since he'd told David it felt like he had.

"Sorry."

"It is getting better. I feel a lot closer to you now. At first I regretted telling you, but now I'm glad I did." He kissed David.

"I love you," David whispered, feeling a surge of desire.

"We're being watched," Rob said mischievously.

David put Paddington in a drawer. "Is that better?"

"That's the last time I buy you anything!"

"Come here and say that."

"That doesn't sound very threatening coming from someone who's only wearing a pair of socks. Still, I suppose the hard-on looks as if you mean business!"

"Talking dirty again?" David said, advancing towards Rob.

"It's nothing to what you said when you shut your finger in the door last week." Rob stood, his face flushed, waiting for David to reach him.

Then they were kissing again and he felt David's hand move down his body. "Oh God!" he whispered.

THIRTY ONE

Three weeks before Rob's twenty-first birthday, they went up to visit his parents.

David had driven during the first part of the journey, and then Rob had taken over. He joked, as they were standing outside his parents' house waiting for them to answer the doorbell, that David didn't have much faith in his driving – he'd not dozed off once.

Mrs Greenaway opened the door and they went in.

David immediately became aware that Rob had gone very still and, even before they were introduced, David knew who Mr and Mrs Greenaway's other guests for the weekend were.

"Excuse me!" Rob said, and bolted upstairs.

"A touch of car-sickness," David explained to Rob's aunt, who was looking worriedly up the stairs after Rob.

"He did look a bit green about the gills," her husband agreed.

The others turned to go into the sitting-room.

"Pleased to meet you," said Rob's uncle, extending his hand.

David looked through him, as if he hadn't heard, and Rob's uncle eventually let his arm fall to his side.

The man was ordinary, that was what struck David first. Thinning hair, thickening waist, average height. Dressed in dark trousers, white shirt and navy pullover. He wouldn't stand out in a crowd. You wouldn't look at him twice nor would you think anything of passing the time of day with him. You might even discover you both liked gardening.

The eyes. David looked at his eyes. A pale, watery blue, a little guarded – or was he simply seeing what he expected to see? Eyes that didn't seem to smile when his mouth did. Eyes that stared at the floor as if he was concentrating on catching any movement from upstairs. Eyes that didn't seem afraid.

David grew angry. To have done what he'd done, and not to show remorse or fear ...

Rob had been gone for ten minutes. "I think I'll just go and make sure Rob's all right," he said, and left the room.

Leaning against the window in his room, Rob said, "I can't stay here. Not with him." His mother had mentioned that it would be a full house, his uncle and aunt having turned up unexpectedly and been invited to stay. "Can we go home?" he asked tiredly. The thought of driving all that way back just after they'd got there was off-putting, but it seemed preferable to remaining in the same house as his uncle.

"You shouldn't have to leave," David said angrily. They'd missed Rob's parents' silver wedding, and now it looked as if the run-up to Rob's twenty-first was in jeopardy. Rob's parents had planned to give him his presents this weekend. "You've more right to be here than your uncle. He should be the one to go." He sat down on the edge of the bed.

Rob slumped down beside him. "I didn't want this to happen. I hoped you'd never meet him."

"He's your uncle. We'd have been bound to meet sometime. Weddings, funerals ..." He shrugged. In a way, Rob was right: David hadn't been prepared. But would he ever have been? "I think he ought to leave. Do you want me to talk to him?"

"No!" Rob said quickly. "I don't want you involved in any of this."

"I am involved, Rob."

"I didn't mean ... Oh, what a mess!" Just when he thought he was beginning to cope again, this happens. "No horns."

David looked at him, puzzled.

"No horns. No cloven hoof. No way to guard against the devil incarnate."

"It'd be easier if there were," David agreed, recognising Rob's need to be reassured that David's belief in what Rob had told him hadn't wavered. They sat for a while in silence, then David said: "Look, let me speak to him. I'll just say that you'd prefer him to leave. In his position, I don't suppose he'll argue."

Rob considered. It was tempting. Just to leave everything to David. He was never lost for words, unlike Rob. He wouldn't end up shouting or crying hysterically. His stomach didn't churn at the sight of his uncle.

No, it was too easy. And it wouldn't be fair on David. God knows what his uncle might say to him, he could be very manipulative. The memory of David, sitting in the kitchen the night Rob had told him everything, was still fresh in his mind. He knew that for David it had been the worst moment of his life.

It wasn't David's war: it was his.

"No, I'll tell him. After all, it's time I said something. I should have spoken up a long time ago."

"I'll come with you."

"I'd prefer to see him on my own. You can make sure we're not disturbed. And I'll need you to pick up the pieces later." He smiled, not sure if he was joking or not.

"You don't have to do this. We'll go home if you want. I could pretend to phone the office, and then say that something urgent's cropped up and they want me to go in tomorrow. We could go back tonight." He looked at Rob's pale, drawn face and wished there was something he could do to help.

"No, I'll be all right. I haven't got much to say, really." He stared at the floor, thinking, then he looked up. "If I get my uncle to go into the garden, can you make sure no one else comes out?"

"I'll try," David promised.

Rob buried his face against David's shoulder.

"It'll be over soon," David reassured him. "He might already know something's up," he added.

Rob looked up at him. "What makes you say that?"

"I've been giving him some pretty filthy looks. I felt like hitting him only I couldn't bring myself to touch him. I refused to shake hands with him." He squeezed Rob's shoulder. "It'll be OK."

Rob stared at him, wishing he shared his confidence. "Promise you won't make a scene or let anything slip? I don't want my parents to find out."

"No, of course not. By the way, I told everyone you were suffering from car-sickness. I think they accepted it. You looked off-colour when you rushed upstairs. Your aunt seems nice."

"Mmm, she is." He drew in a deep breath and got to his feet. "Better get it over with."

The opportunity Rob had been waiting for – and dreading – presented itself when his mother and aunt took themselves into the kitchen to finish preparing supper.

While David turned to Mr Greenaway and asked him about his local first division football club, Rob suggested to his uncle that they have a look at the garden. For a second, Rob thought he would refuse, but obviously he was conscious of appearances.

Outside, they were both silent for a while, and Rob felt as if the initiative was slipping away from him and that time was running out, but then his uncle made a passing reference to David and this was enough for Rob. Suddenly he felt strong. How dare his uncle mention David! David had been a stranger who, with no ulterior motive, had been kind to Rob; while his uncle, who could have been expected to take care of him, had done exactly the reverse. What he had done all those years ago was inexcusable. Rob told him so. He also told him that David knew. Suddenly, his uncle seemed to age, diminish, both in stature and power. He'd lost his hold over Rob, the invisible bonds linking them had been broken. Rob was free.

David never knew exactly what Rob had said. When he came back into the house, leaving his uncle still in the garden, David had asked quietly, "OK?" and Rob had merely nodded. And then he'd smiled, almost like the Rob David remembered.

He hadn't needed to exercise his self-control at supper as Rob's uncle didn't join them; he had said he wasn't feeling well, and had gone upstairs to lie down. He suggested to his wife that they should leave when she'd eaten.

"He suffers from high blood pressure," she said. "Usually he's good at remembering his pills, but he forgot to pack enough, so we'd better go back tonight. I'll only worry if we stay."

When they'd left, Rob's mother apologised. "They turned up out of the blue."

"No harm done, Mum."

"A pity about your uncle not feeling so well. He certainly looked very pale. Didn't you think so, dear?" she asked her husband.

"Overdid things on holiday, I expect." They'd stopped by on their way back from Wales. "So how's work, David?"

"Fine, thanks."

"I suppose you put him up to it," John Greenaway said to his son. "Getting him to ask about football. He couldn't seem to concentrate on it. When I told him about the great side they had a few years ago, I might as well have been trying to sell him double glazing."

"Dad, after ten minutes of listening to you saying how football's not what it used to be anyone's eyes would glaze over!"

"Well, you've never been interested, that's for certain."

"I used to come to matches with you," Rob remonstrated.

"When you were eight years old!"

It sounded like an argument they'd had many times before. David caught Mrs Greenaway's eye and smiled.

Towards ten o'clock, Rob left the room. Five minutes later, he reappeared carrying some albums. "Photographs," he said, handing the albums to David. He added quietly. "I thought I might as well get it all over with tonight."

"Is he still camera-shy?" Mr Greenaway asked David.

David nodded.

"It's funny," Rob's mother said, "he was all right until he was thirteen or so, then he hated having his photograph taken. We stopped in the end, he looked so uncomfortable. It's a shame. I wish we had a few more photos of him. "

David turned the pages. Baby pictures. Then he smiled, recognising Rob in the little boy with his first bicycle. Posed photos taken at primary school. Family outings ... a shy, sensitive face, a little serious despite a happy smile. As he turned to the next page, he was aware that Rob had tensed. Amongst the other photos was one of Rob and his uncle, the latter's arm round his nephew's shoulder. Rob was about thirteen when it was taken.

"Everyone says I take after Mum."

"You show him that photo of your Mum and me at Blackpool," Mr Greenaway said. "Course, that was a good few years ago, before you were born. You can see the likeness."

David looked interestedly at the photo of Rob's parents, taken when they were younger than David was at present. Rob had the same colouring as his mother and the same build.

"If you look at my mother, it'll give you an idea of what I'll be like in twenty years' time!" Rob joked.

Both David and Mr Greenaway glanced swiftly at Rob, each wondering whether Rob realised that his remark could be taken to imply some sort of permanency in the relationship.

"Well," his father said, "you could do worse."

After they had said goodnight to Rob's parents and had gone upstairs, Rob asked, "Will you sleep in my room tonight? We've got an airbed or a mattress you could sleep on. Mum and Dad won't mind."

"OK." He didn't think he'd have wanted to sleep alone, either, after such an evening.

Rob got the mattress and some sheets and an old duvet, and put them on the floor next to his bed. Belatedly he offered to sleep on the floor himself.

"No. You have the bed. I won't have any trouble getting to sleep tonight." David had suddenly realised how tired he felt. "Are you OK?" he asked quietly.

"Mmm. You?"

David nodded.

As they undressed, Rob said, "I expect my parents'll think we're mad – you sleeping in here on the floor when there's a perfectly good double bed next door. I just didn't want to sleep in there tonight."

As they lay in the darkness, he continued. "You know, I feel free. A sense of release. Like it's all over at last."

"All the ghosts have been laid?"

"I hope so. I hope it's not just a temporary euphoria. I told him I'd told you, by the way. I think that frightened him."

"He deserves to be frightened."

"I'm glad we didn't just go straight home. I'm glad I spoke to him. I can put it all in the past where it belongs." He looked up at the ceiling. "I used to dream about this. Someone being here, someone who knew and didn't mind. About it being over." He leant over the side of the bed. "What did you used to dream about?"

David smiled. "I used to dream that you'd come to my room," he said softly. "I'd throw back the covers, you'd get into bed, and I'd hold you." His imagination had always ended there, certain that it would never happen anyway. His voice became tight. "I missed you so much when you left."

"I'm sorry." His hand found David's. "Is something wrong?" he asked, aware of David's change of mood. Tonight he felt as if all his senses were heightened.

"No, I'm just tired. Goodnight."

" 'Night."

They both lay awake, Rob feeling warm and relaxed, enjoying the sensation that it finally seemed to be over.

It took David longer, despite his tiredness, to fall asleep. He wondered if Rob still needed him.

On the way back, Rob drove. They'd agreed to stop halfway so that David could take over, but as David was still fast asleep Rob drove straight on.

Eventually David stirred and looked out of the window, trying to orientate himself. "You should have woken me," he said, realising they'd gone past the service station.

"I'm fine," Rob said.

"Let's stop at the next place."

"OK. I could do with a coffee." A blue motorway sign indicated three miles to the next services, and, when they got there, Rob turned off, found a parking space and switched off the ignition. They went inside.

"What is it?" Rob asked, as he put his cup on the table and sat down.

"Oh, I was just remembering that day out at the coast. It was over two years ago now, but I still remember what you ate in the café we stopped at on the way home." David stirred his coffee. His face looked pale and pinched.

"Are you all right?"

"Me? Yes. Why?"

"You just look a bit ..." Rob shrugged. "Under the weather."

"Perhaps a little tired," David admitted. His nap didn't appear to have refreshed him. He felt as if he could sleep for a week. "Nothing to worry about. Put it down to the lighting they've got in here." Everyone looked haggard under the pitiless strip lighting. He smiled, but the smile didn't reach his eyes and he didn't argue when Rob volunteered to drive the rest of the way.

"Are you sure you're OK?" Rob asked again when they were home.

"I just feel a little out of sorts. Perhaps it was the shock of meeting your uncle. Perhaps it's a delayed reaction to everything. Now you've come to terms with it, maybe something in me has decided I don't need to be able to cope." He swallowed. "I don't know." He stared bleakly at the floor.

Rob sat in silence, not knowing what to say. He got the feeling that David wanted to ask him something but didn't know how.

David looked up. "I am glad, too, you know."

Rob had never seen David like this. Depressed. It worried him. "I'll lock up," he said at last.

Watching David undress, Rob became aroused. He hoped David wouldn't notice, but when they kissed each other goodnight he saw David's eyes register the touch of Rob's erect penis against his body and felt David's hand go automatically down towards it.

"It'll keep," he whispered, knowing David wasn't really in the mood. "What's wrong?"

"Nothing."

"No lies. Remember?"

David remembered. "I love you," he said, his voice strangely sad.

"So tell me what's wrong."

There was silence while David tried to think what to say. "When you told me ... I was pleased you trusted me enough to tell me. Grateful for the chance to be able to help. Glad that you needed me." He looked away for a moment. "I just don't feel needed any longer."

"I still need you," Rob said quietly. Somehow he had to make David believe him. "It really hurt when we were arguing. I hated it when you thought I'd lied to you because I didn't care. Then everything seemed to be disintegrating and it just went on and on and I was afraid you'd lose patience. But you were always there." To listen, to encourage. A warm, familiar body which could make him forget. "Just because I can cope on my own doesn't mean that I want to be on my own."

"I remember thinking that maybe you'd want to put all this behind you. Start again. I was afraid you'd see me as being part of it."

"You did all that and you thought you'd lose me?"

David shrugged. "Sometimes I wondered."

Rob was appalled at having failed to realise how fragile David thought their relationship was. Had he really been so wrapped up in himself? Looking at David now, Rob realised he looked tired. Older.

He touched David's face. "I want to be here. I want to be with you. I want to prove that I don't just take, that I can give, too. Only, just give me a little time."

"But you still don't love me." David hated himself for having said it. Why now of all times should he want to bring this up? After all, he didn't want lies and he knew well enough why Rob found the words impossible to say.

"I want to." In the heat of passion. Or the gentleness afterwards. Now, when he wanted to cheer David up. But he couldn't. Something always held him back. A brutal kind of honesty? An inability to love? An understanding that what David felt for him was something far in excess of what he felt for David?

Rob wished he knew what else to say. But he didn't, so he just held David tight and hoped that this black mood would pass.

THIRTY TWO

"Here," the doctor said, tearing off a prescription for antibiotics for David's swollen throat and handing it to him. "You look a bit run down too. Have you been overdoing things lately?"

"Not really. Things have been a bit difficult, though."

"Well, that's probably it. These things tend to strike when we're at our lowest ebb. Especially when people allow themselves to relax. It's not the thought of work that causes my surgery to burst at the seams each Monday, it's the result of the 'thank goodness it's Friday' syndrome. And I don't just mean hangovers. Some of it's caused by damn stupid sporting injuries that could have been avoided in the first place. Here," he handed over another prescription, "just a tonic. Take a few days off work. I could give you a certificate, but I think you can certify yourself for a week. Your throat should feel better soon, but don't rush things."

David took the prescription and got to his feet.

The doctor looked up to find David still lingering. "Is there something else?" His pen was already poised ready to update David's notes.

"Could I ask you something?" He thought as he was here, he might as well make the most of the opportunity.

"Yes, of course." The doctor gestured towards the chair and David sat down again.

"Off the record?"

David nodded.

"Of course," Dr Parry concluded, holding the pen between his hands, "it's one of the most publicised ways of spreading AIDS. Even if a condom is used, that only makes things safer. It doesn't entirely rule out the threat. Is that what you're really worried about?"

"No. No, it's not."

The older man looked at him thoughtfully. Many people who visited the Health Centre ostensibly for one reason were in actual fact seeking to have their minds set at ease on a completely different matter. "Statistically, most people need have no cause for concern. Even homosexuals." Dr Parry leaned back in his chair and looked shrewdly at the young man before him. "It is a homosexual relationship we're talking about?"

David nodded.

"Of course, the risks should always be minimised." He stared expectantly at David. "Do you mind telling me what precautions you take?"

David explained that his sexual experiences could be written on the back of a postage stamp.

"And your partner's?"

David paused. "He's had an AIDS test," he said eventually, afraid it made Rob sound promiscuous. "As you were saying, it's better to be safe than sorry." He thought he sounded pompous, preaching to someone who'd heard this all before.

Dr Parry nodded. "Yes. You'd have to be pretty unlucky to have caught AIDS under those circumstances." He sighed. "I'm sorry. That was a crass remark. Please forgive me. If you are at all worried, I can arrange for a test." He looked at him.

David shook his head. The doctor remembered David's original question. He toyed pensively with his pen, his eyes on the desk. "When someone asks a question like that," he began slowly, "about sex, about whether any damage can be done by certain practices, what I usually find is that one partner wants to persuade the other to do something they're not sure about."

He glanced up at David, who remained silent. "It's a difficult thing. I could reassure someone that there's nothing medically against doing something, but if that person held an aversion to doing that particular thing, then nothing I say would convince him. It's not something that's completely logical. And if you persuade that person, against their judgement, to do something they're not altogether happy about, then you've lost something. Trust. Respect. On the other hand," he grinned unexpectedly, "I can tell people what to do until I'm blue in the face and they don't take a blind bit of notice. Ask anyone if they think cigarettes do them any harm and they'll say yes. Ask them why they still smoke and they'll not only tell you it's one of their only pleasures, but think you're mad for even asking." He looked at David, inviting his confidence.

"It's not that, either. Not exactly." He returned Dr Parry's smile, not wanting him to feel rebuffed. "I'm the one who's reluctant," he added after a while, although he realised that Dr Parry had gathered that already. "Rob says he doesn't mind about it."

"But you think he does?"

"No."

It was a bit like drawing teeth, Dr Parry mused. Still, he sensed that David would eventually get round to telling him what it was that was bothering him. His next patient, with an appointment in ten minutes' time, hadn't arrived yet.

"It's just ..." David stopped. He never felt on safe ground when talking about sex. Jeremy was right: he was too puritanical for his own good. "It's not been easy for him, the last few years. I just want to make things as good as they can be."

"You feel you're denying him something? Something he'd enjoy?"

David nodded, glad he'd made himself understood.

The doctor looked at him, considering what to say. It was a pity people got love and sex confused. It was a pity that sometimes they were out of step with each other. "I think," he said eventually, "that you should go home and tell your partner what you've just told me. But there's something you've got to bear in mind."

David looked questioningly at him.

"Just remember that he has as much right to want to please you as you have to want to please him." He broke into a smile, then stood up, signalling the end of the consultation. "I don't think you've any reason to worry. I think you've let things get a bit out of proportion. You can blame your sore throat for that."

David smiled. "Thanks. Thanks for listening."

"No trouble. Look, if you want some literature on the subject, I'm sure I could find you something. We seem to have leaflets on everything under the sun nowadays. There might be a helpline, too, if you want to talk to somebody. But I don't think you need bother. I'm sure if you just talk to your partner you'll find you're worrying about nothing. Am I his doctor, too?"

"I don't think he's got one down here. He hasn't needed one."

"Well, tell him I'm happy to oblige. I never mind taking on a few more healthy people. Makes a change from all the unhealthy ones I get in here. Well, see you again in," – he consulted his notes as to the last time David had been in his surgery – "six years."

They talked when Rob got home. Dr Parry had been right: Rob said it didn't worry him, but if it made David feel better he'd promise to tell him if he changed his mind. At least David sounded more like his old self, thought Rob. As if he could read his mind, David said: "Sorry about last night. It all got a bit serious. I said some things I didn't mean to say."

"It's all right. I'm glad you told me how you felt. You made me take stock. I know I've been hell to live with the last couple of months and you put up with it and never complained." He grinned. "So I reckon it's time I stopped being so selfish and I'll start by making supper."

"And I thought you were supposed to be nice to people who're not well!" David said with a mock sigh.

Strangely enough, it was not even six days, let alone six years, when David bumped, quite literally, into Dr Parry again.

"Sorry!" they both exclaimed automatically, each pulling back the supermarket trolley he was pushing.

"God!"

"Not quite, although a few of my eminent colleagues do tend to act as if they had been deified," the doctor remarked.

"Sorry. Hello."

"Hello. How are you?"

"Fine, thanks," David said, his attention distracted as a boy of about eight sidled through the gap between his trolley and the frozen food display cabinet.

"I think he's one of mine. I've got four," the doctor said apologetically as if he should have known better.

"I can't find the sugar," Rob said, returning to find David in conversation with someone he took to be just another shopper.

"I know where it is," piped up the boy.

"Show the gentleman, then, Joshua," his father instructed, and Rob, a little surprised, followed Joshua back down the aisle.

"You look better," the doctor agreed quietly.

"I feel much better. We had a talk. You were right."

"Good. Ah, you found it!" the doctor said as the others returned, Joshua proudly bearing a bag of sugar which he put in David's trolley. "Where's your mother?"

"Marmalades and jams."

"Where's that?"

"Over there," the boy replied, pointing.

"I don't know why we don't give him the money and let him

do all the shopping. Yes, I do. We'd end up with nothing but fish fingers and ice cream. Oh, well, back to the fray. Goodbye."

"Bye," David said. "The doctor I saw last week," he explained in answer to Rob's unspoken question.

"Looks quite human," Rob said cheerfully.

THIRTY THREE

They drove to Malvern on the Friday, arriving there at lunchtime.

The hotel was small, the receptionist friendly, and the room comfortable. They spent the afternoon looking round the town. They found a park with a willow tree overhanging a lake, and Rob insisted David stand on the little bridge and then he took a photo which caught the reflections in the water as well as the reality. They decided from the brochures they saw in the Tourist Information Office where to go the following day; and then, as the weather was fine, they drove to a nearby village and visited some gardens that were open to the public.

The next day was spent walking the hills. The early morning autumnal chill was soon dispelled by the bright sunshine, and there was no mist or cloud to obscure the view. In places, the grass had been worn away by the feet of the million visitors a year, attracted to the steep bare hills of ancient granite with their views eastwards to the Cotswolds and westwards to the Wye Valley and the Welsh Mountains. No wonder Sir Edward Elgar had been inspired by the Malvern Hills.

The people they met out walking – most of whom, like themselves, had the appearance of casual rather than seasoned walkers – greeted them with cheerful comments on the weather or the scenery.

David had always found that exercise relaxed him, and he was pleased to see that the strain of the last few months had disappeared from Rob's face.

For lunch, they found a café, still open despite the fact that the tourist season was now virtually over, and sat outside drinking tea. Rob, who said he was ravenous, ate a sandwich and two slices of carrot cake. "Must be all this fresh air."

It was nearly five o'clock when they returned to the car, both of them in a pleasant state of tiredness. In the town, they passed the ivy-covered Abbey Hotel, where a pond surrounded by bright yellow flowers was set a few yards in front of the wide steps leading up to the main entrance.

Back in their room, they pushed the twin beds together and then collapsed in mock exhaustion.

"Do you want your present now?" David asked.

"Is this what it is?" Rob said, his eyes mischievous, looking at David's hand on his thigh.

"This is just to whet your appetite."

"I thought you were afraid of me ruining my appetite," Rob reminded him. Then he swallowed as David's hand moved a few inches more. "I'd better have a bath first. I'm hot and sweaty." He tried to get up, but David stopped him.

"Don't. I like the way you smell."

Rob looked at him through narrowed eyes. "Well, I suppose you meant it as a compliment," he said with resignation.

David remembered his promise to tell Rob about the incident with the shirt, when he'd taken it from the laundry basket and held it close to his face.

Rob asked if he still indulged in such practices.

"Not when I've got the real thing," David answered, pinioning Rob's arms and then grinning at Rob's efforts to dislodge him.

"So that's why you play so much squash, is it? You're turned on by sweat."

"Squash doesn't have quite the same effect on me."

"And what effect is that?"

David placed Rob's hand on his groin.

"And I thought you'd go off me once it was legal!" Rob

remarked contentedly.

They made love, then they both slept.

It was seven o'clock when they woke.

"Have I got time for a bath? What time's dinner?" Rob asked, scrambling off of the bed.

"I think it finishes at nine." He watched Rob's naked figure disappear into the bathroom. "Can I scrub your back?" he called after him.

"We'll never get down to supper if you do."

"Can I watch then?"

"Voyeur," Rob muttered and slammed the door. David heard the sound of water filling the bath and grinned.

When Rob had finished, David had a quick shower while Rob put on trousers and a clean shirt. "D'you feel any different?" Rob called from the bedroom. "Now I'm twenty-one?" He repeated the question when David came out of the bathroom, not having heard Rob the first time.

"I suppose I'm relieved that everything's legal now. And talking about being twenty-one ..." He picked up a small parcel. "Happy birthday."

"Thanks," Rob said, taking the present a little awkwardly.

It had taken David several hours before he had found something suitable. He'd wanted something Rob would like and something that would show he cared, but most things he saw seemed too impersonal and too ordinary. He'd wanted something different, but not too expensive as that would embarrass Rob. He'd tried explaining to a few shop assistants, but they would ask who the present was for and had to be diverted.

He was reluctantly coming to the conclusion that it would have to be a watch and was staring into a jeweller's window when he saw it. At first he thought it was a paperweight, then he realised it was the wrong shape. He bought it.

As Rob, now sitting on the edge of the bed, unwrapped the parcel, David watched his face intently.

For a minute, Rob just stared at the heavy piece of glass with the figure of a small bird engraved at its centre. Then he raised his eyes. "It's beautiful. Thanks." His lack of words reassured David.

"No one's ever give me anything like this before," he added quietly after a while. Till then, he'd only had things like books or records or money.

He put the glass object carefully on the bedside table, where it was illuminated by the small table lamp.

He stood up and kissed David.

"Come on, we'll be late," David advised, his voice unusually gruff, and they went out of the room, locking the door behind them.

Throughout the meal, they were both relaxed and talkative. David knew he was looking at Rob through lover's eyes, but didn't care if anyone noticed. "Happy?" he asked impetuously.

Rob, surprised by the question and his own response, nodded.

When they had finished eating and were drinking a second cup of coffee, and, by unashamedly flirting with the waitress, he'd cajoled her into fetching some more mints, Rob said: "Thanks, David. For everything." His eyes stayed fixed on the tablecloth for a couple of moments, then he looked up into David's face.

"My motives are purely selfish," David said.

Rob smiled. He wouldn't argue, although he disagreed.

Upstairs, they half-watched a terrible film on the television.

"Is that John Wayne?" Rob asked.

"No, it's not John Wayne. You always ask me that. He's not in every Western, you know."

They tried to follow the plot for a while.

"Next year," Rob asked, "could we go abroad?"

It was the first time he'd spoken of the future.

"If you like. Where d'you want to go?"

"I remember you saying you liked Austria. We could go there. Or Majorca. Sally says it's nice. If you drive up into the hills you can get away from the crowds." He caught sight of David's expression. "What is it?"

David grinned. "I always thought you were keen on Sally. And don't think I didn't notice you flirting with the waitress!" It wasn't altogether Rob's fault. David had noticed before that girls found him appealing. That was one of the nice things about Rob: he seemed genuinely unaware of the effect he had on people.

"I do like Sally. She asked me, oh, a long time ago and in a roundabout way, if I was gay, but I pretended not to understand."

"When did you realise you were?"

Rob thought. "I'd wondered, ever since I was twelve." David knew the significance of twelve. "I thought it might be just a phase. That's why I went out with a few girls from school but I was never really interested. I liked going out with Sally, though. There was no pressure on me to get involved." He drew the tip of his finger across David's face. "I used to wish you'd find someone, though. I didn't really want you to love me. It was too soon for me. But it was nice that you did. I always felt safe with you. I hope I meet your parents soon. What d'you think they'll think of me?"

"Dad'll ask you your prospects, and Mum'll ask you if you can cook," David joked.

"I hope they'll give me time to pack, then, before they throw me out."

"They'll like you," David said reassuringly. "Even though they might think I'm cradle-snatching."

Rob looked at him, concerned. "You mind, don't you? About the difference in our ages? I thought it was just because I was underage, but it's not, is it?"

"Not so much the difference. It's just that you're so young."

"How old would you like me to be?" Rob asked solemnly, and

David had an irresistible urge to smile. How could he wish away Rob's youth, his enthusiasm?

"Twenty-one," he replied.

"Well, I can manage that. For a year, at any rate." Rob frowned, still serious. "Why d'you want me to be older?"

"I suppose I remember what I was like when I was twenty-one. Not ready to settle down. Not sure of what I wanted."

"Different people want different things," Rob said. "I can't imagine anyone my age wanting to hang around till I'd sorted myself out. They wouldn't have understood, coped with it, been patient with me. I can't imagine sleeping with anyone else, let alone telling them." He grinned. "Anyway, I'm just after your money. I thought you knew that."

They hugged each other.

"We've missed the end of the film, you realise," David said.

"Damn. I was watching that!"

The following day was wet and grey.

David let the curtain drop. "Looks like walking's out. We'll have a look round Ledbury, shall we?"

Rob mumbled something and turned over. Mornings weren't his favourite time of day, at least not until he'd had time to wake up.

David went into the bathroom, had a shave and then soaked for half an hour in a warm bath. His muscles ached a little from all yesterday's walking. So much for squash keeping you fit, he thought, and then remembered he hadn't been playing so much just lately. Graham and Jill had been doing some decorating, so Graham had been happy to forgo the squash, while David had had other things on his mind. He decided he'd make an effort to play more. Thirty-one, he thought lazily, he'd be getting middle-aged spread next. He smiled to himself. Perhaps Rob could do more of the cooking. He was getting better at it. As long as the instructions were on the packet.

He submerged himself.

When he came out of the bathroom, he was still smiling at the thought of Rob's cooking. At least here he got a decent meal.

Rob had woken up, and was watching David. He suggested that David was perhaps still a little tired and might like to come back to bed. Perhaps Rob could remove the towel David had wrapped around his waist, it was a bit damp, after all. David agreed that it did sound like a good idea if he was tired. He added that it sounded an even better one if he wasn't. Rob said he hoped David wasn't. Perhaps they should find out? David said that sounded reasonable.

Immediately David had climaxed, Rob got out of bed. "Don't go away!" he ordered. David wondered what he was up to. He'd been grinning like a Cheshire cat for the last ten minutes, although he'd obviously been trying not to show it. David heard the sound of the shower.

"Breakfast in bed?" he asked, as Rob returned, carrying a small jar of clear honey.

Rob just looked at him, the corners of his mouth twitching.

Suddenly David realised. He gave Rob an old-fashioned look.

"What d'you want me to do?" he asked warily.

"Well," Rob said, holding out the jar, which David stared at in a mixture of disbelief and horrified fascination. "First I thought you could rub it in. And then I thought you could lick it off."

"Off what?" David said, still hoping for a reprieve. He waited in vain. "Oh." He took the pot of honey and looked at it dubiously. Then he took a deep breath and gave Rob the sort of look which the latter interpreted correctly as 'the things I do for you.'

Rob gasped. The honey was cold. Still, he had left it outside all night on the window ledge. What else could you expect?

"Warm it." When David looked totally baffled by the pronoun, Rob hissed: "The honey!"

After which, things didn't go quite as Rob had planned. He got a fit of the giggles and, rather like the story of King Midas, everything they touched ended up covered in honey.

"You're not taking this seriously!" David accused, abandoning his efforts as Rob clutched his aching ribs.

"I'm sorry." As a sensual highpoint in his life, it was a complete disaster; but he hadn't laughed so much in ages. David was grinning too. Mostly, Rob suspected, at his discomfiture.

"Perhaps it wasn't one of my better ideas," Rob admitted.

"I don't think I've ever been as sticky as this. You could have told me what you had in mind and I'd have had a bath afterwards," David complained, trying to unglue his fingers. "I hope you haven't got any more fantasies you want to try out." There was an ominous silence.

"Well, not right at this moment." Rob admitted. "But it might be nice to make love somewhere out in the country. Then I visualise ants crawling around, and being tickled by blades of grass and suffering from hay fever, not to mention having to deal with irate farmers and inquisitive dogs."

"If we did try to make love in the open, just promise one thing."

"What's that?"

"That you'll leave the honey at home. Otherwise your vision of being outnumbered by ants might just come true."

They adjourned to the bathroom. Which was more successful than the honey had been.

Over breakfast, David asked what Rob had been reading lately. Personally he thought he'd never be able to read Winnie the Pooh again and keep a straight face.

Rob ignored him.

At the end of the meal, their waitress from the previous

278

evening came over to their table. She enquired pleasantly if they'd enjoyed their breakfast.

They assured her they had.

Addressing Rob, she asked: "Do you want another one of those little pots of honey to take away, sir?"

David looked steadfastly at the tablecloth.

"Not today, thanks," Rob said, and smiled as if butter wouldn't melt in his mouth. Or honey, come to that.

"You had the nerve to ask her for the honey!" David exclaimed, on leaving the restaurant.

"I thought they might want to re-use the pot."

David looked at him with a jaundiced eye. "I was surprised you didn't return the one in our room."

"I'm saving that as a memento," Rob replied.

Despite the weather, they enjoyed their sight-seeing. Ledbury was a historic market town with narrow streets full of low, black timbered buildings some of whose top halves overhung the pavement. The wide High Street housed the black and white Elizabethan coaching inn, The Feathers Hotel, and nearby stood the Market House on its massive oak posts.

It was six o'clock when they returned to the hotel.

The meal was just as good as the previous evening's. After they'd finished their main course, their waitress disappeared suddenly, looking rather furtive, and then re-appeared carrying a small iced cake with three candles which she placed on the table in front of Rob.

"Did you do this?" he asked David, who shook his head, wishing as he caught sight of Rob's expression, that he had suggested it. "How did you know?" Rob asked the girl, who was smiling conspiratorially.

"Well," she began slowly, obviously wishing to prolong the

suspense, "my sister was doing your room and she noticed the birthday card so she mentioned it to our cook, who's also her fiancé, and he thought we couldn't let a twenty-first go by without doing something. After all, you're only twenty-one once." Her eyes were dancing. "Sorry about the candles – we didn't have enough." She gave Rob an impish grin. "You'd better blow them out before people think there's been a power cut." Then she headed back towards the kitchen.

Rob ran his right forefinger around the top of his glass. "Our first candlelight supper," he said as if to himself.

"I think she likes you!"

Rob hadn't been listening. "You know, this is the best twenty-first I've ever had," he said.

THIRTY FOUR

Then two things happened in a short space of time: the first was Sally's party; and the second David's absence from home.

Rob went by himself to the party and found that he didn't enjoy it as much as he'd thought he would. Oh, the party was fine and he knew David hadn't objected to his going, but he kept wishing he'd asked Sally if he could have brought David along. After all, she'd half-guessed, and they were both over twenty-one now so there was no reason for caution. And he'd wanted David to meet the people he worked with.

The second, David's absence, was caused by his firm sending him on a course for a week. Rob had joked, the Sunday before, that it'd be nice to have the house to himself. Maybe he'd ask Sally round. But he missed David, and when Friday came he was aware that he was looking forward to seeing him again.

Both events gave Rob food for thought.

"When your parents come back, what shall we do?" he asked one Sunday morning as they were lazily reading the papers over breakfast.

"What would you like to do?" David asked carefully, not wanting to suggest something Rob would reject.

"Buy a house or a flat somewhere?" Although they pretended to each other that Rob was always broke, he scrupulously paid David back on every occasion. This time though, he thought, he really couldn't afford even half a house.

"All right." David deliberately kept his voice neutral.

"Some of the estate agents are open on Sundays. Shall we see what they've got today?"

"Anyone would think you couldn't stand it here."

"I love you." The words floated in the air like bubbles.

Caught by surprise, David could only say: "Well, who else would eat what you cook?" He held up the burnt piece of toast he was in the middle of eating.

"You don't have to eat it."

"And I thought the way to a man's heart was through his stomach. Hell!" David stared at Rob and shook his head as if he doubted his hearing. It had taken such a long time.

"You deserve a medal."

"What for?"

"Patience. I think it started that weekend when we went away together. I suddenly realised I'd hate it if you looked at anyone else the way you were looking at me."

"So that's your new excuse for burning the toast, is it? You're lovesick?"

"Make it yourself next time," Rob retorted, getting up and taking the breakfast dishes over to the sink.

David suddenly felt extraordinarily happy.

"It's not really fair on you," Rob began as they sorted through estate agents' leaflets in order to get an idea of what they could afford.

"What isn't?"

"A joint mortgage. I'll be paying less than you, but I'll be entitled to half the house. At least I think I will be."

"Well, I earn more than you and I've got more money saved, so it's logical for me to put in more."

"But it's not really fair," Rob said, unconvinced.

"No, but is it fair that you're younger and haven't been working for as long? Look at it this way: when I've retired, you can keep me in the style to which I'm accustomed!"

When Rob still looked dubious, he added: "Do you really want us each to contribute the same amount of money?"

Rob looked at the price of the house shown on one of the local estate agents' sheets and shook his head. "At these prices, we'd be lucky to be able to afford a garden shed, let alone a house. And building societies can ask awkward questions, can't they, especially when two men buy a house together. They're bound to ask whether we've had an AIDS test. Either I'll have to lie, which I don't want to do, or I tell them the truth and they might ask when I had the test done and they'd find out I was underage and think it was you. I know I'm being stupid, I know that the building society won't be interested, but I just don't want it in black and white. Maybe in a few years it won't worry me, but just now it does."

David thought for a while. "What if you had another test done? Then no one would be interested in the earlier one, and there'd be no need to lie about having had a test."

"If they saw I'd had a test, they're bound to ask you to have one done, too."

"I don't mind."

"But what happens every time you want a new insurance policy?"

"So what do you think we ought to do?" David found himself asking.

"Have the house in your name."

"OK." He didn't mind whose name was on the deeds. "That might mean the mortgage has to be in my sole name." They wouldn't be able to borrow so much if only David's salary was taken into account.

"Back to the garden shed?"

"Back to the garden shed," David agreed. "Rob?"

"You want me to sell my record collection!"

"It won't come to that."

"We could sell yours. What with the age of it, there's bound to be a few collectors' items there."

"I'll bear it in mind. No," he said, sounding more serious, "aren't you worried if the house is in my name? If things didn't work out?" He must remember to make a will when they bought the house, he thought. And to allow Rob to use his credit card. And to tell his parents.

Rob looked at him in astonishment. "I trust you enough to tell you something I've never told anyone else, and you're worried that I might not trust you with my money? Idiot!" he said fondly.

THIRTY FIVE

"I don't suppose you have ..." David named a record that had recently been advertised on television.

"We sold out yesterday. People are buying them for Christmas."

"Already?" David was surprised.

"Yes. We've got some more on order, though. I could put one aside for you when they come in," the girl offered.

"No, I'll take this instead," he said, handing her a tape. "If I don't post this on Monday, it'll be too late. It's a birthday present." He was usually more organised than this, but their search for a suitable house had driven his aunt's birthday clean out of his head.

"Don't I know you?" There was something familiar about him, yet she couldn't place him.

David smiled. "We've spoken on the phone. David Rees."

"Oh, of course. You're Rob's friend." She looked at him with renewed interest. "You should have got him to buy it for you," she said, indicating the cassette. "Staff discount," she added conspiratorially.

"I'll remember next time," he agreed, lowering his voice to match hers. "I blame my aunt – having a birthday only weeks before Christmas."

She grinned. He was quite nice, she thought, remembering how pleasant he'd always been when she'd phoned Rob and David had answered the phone. More mature than the sort of person she usually went out with, but, if anything, that was a point in his favour. She'd have to ask Rob more about him.

"Is Rob here?"

"No, he's just gone out to fetch some milk. We drew lots."

"And he lost?"

"No, he won! Did you want to see him?"

"I just wanted to tell him that I can give him a lift home tonight."

"I'll tell him."

"Thanks."

"Bye." Very nice, she thought. She'd have something to say to Rob, keeping her in the dark like that.

When the shop was a little quieter, Sally went up to Rob. "Before I forget, David says he can give you lift home tonight."

"Oh, thanks. When did he phone?"

"When you went out to get the milk. Actually, he came in. He's nice, isn't he?" She frowned at him as he started to laugh.

"Yes, he's very nice," he agreed.

"What's so funny?" she demanded.

"Nothing. Honestly!" He continued to smile infuriatingly at her.

"Come on, what is it?"

"Well, I like him." He'd been going to tell her anyway. "But then I suppose I'm prejudiced. We live together."

Sally's mouth dropped open, but it was nearly an hour before the shop was quiet again and she could speak to Rob, by which time she was nearly dying of curiosity. "Well?" she asked, knowing Rob had been avoiding her on purpose in order to prolong her agony.

"Well what?" he asked innocently.

"You know very well what! You drop a bombshell like that and then leave me to stew for an hour wondering what you meant. Did you mean what I think you meant?"

"And what did you think I meant?" he teased.

"Rob Greenaway, stop being so exasperating or I'll hit you over the head with this stapler!"

"Then you'd never know what I meant," he said reasonably.

Sally made a strangled sound and looked as if her patience had finally snapped.

Rob capitulated. "Yes, I did mean what you thought I meant."

"But I thought he was your landlord?"

"I suppose he is. Although the house belongs to his parents, but they're in America."

"Why didn't you tell me? We've known each other for more than three years now."

"You are the first person I've told," he reassured her. "Apart from my parents, that is."

"Oh." She was slightly mollified by this. "I did wonder ... So any designs I may have with regard to Mr Rees are doomed to come to naught?"

"Have you been reading Mills & Boon again? Anyway, I thought you were interested in me."

"Huh! I gave up on you a long time ago. What about his parents?"

"We haven't told them yet. They're coming home soon and yours truly's going to come as quite a surprise."

"You mean they don't know David's ..."

"Gay? Oh, they know that. It's just me they don't know about."

"So you're house-hunting?"

"We started a couple of weeks ago."

"That's another thing you didn't quite get round to telling me," she said in an aggrieved tone. Her curiosity took over. "So, tell me everything. What's he like, what does he do, how did you meet, how old is he?"

"Which?"

"All of them! And then maybe I'll forgive you for keeping all this a secret."

Rob laughed. "All right. I'll tell you all about it on Monday. When we go to lunch."

"What about the others? Are they supposed to know?"

Judging from the smirks on the faces of his colleagues, that was shutting the stable door after the horse had bolted. Sally had a very clear, carrying voice whose pitch increased in direct proportion to her excitement. "I don't mind. As long as you understand two things." He raised his voice and waited for the others to stop pretending not to be eavesdropping. Andy and Steve both looked round. "First, that anything you've got to say you say to my face and not behind my back." Too late, as Andy turned a guffaw into a cough, Rob realised the unfortunate aptness of his last phrase. "And second, that it's just between ourselves. Not for public consumption. I don't want to get beaten up on the way home."

"That seems fair enough." Andy grinned. "I may not share your personal tastes, but I defend every masochist's right to choose when and where he's beaten up. Don't worry, Sally, if he's broken your heart. You've still got me."

Sally looked at him. "That was what I was afraid of," she said witheringly.

THIRTY SIX

"So the house is still standing?" his father asked as they headed away from Heathrow in David's car.

"Mostly. Had to get it decorated after the Acid House party, of course."

"The what, David?" said his mother from the back seat, not having caught what he'd said.

It was good to see them after so long.

After ten minutes, however, Mrs Rees decided to sort out one thing that had been bothering her and her husband. "And Rob? Is he well, too?"

"Yes, he's fine," David said, turning left.

Encouraged by his reply, she said: "Will he be at the house?"

"He's at work at the moment, but he'll be back this evening."

"What does he do?"

He told her the name of the shop. "They sell records."

"Oh, I know where you mean," his mother said. The shop in the High Street. So he still worked there.

Once they got home, David went to make them some tea, while his parents wandered in and out of the downstairs rooms and looked at the garden, reassuring themselves that things were as they remembered.

They weren't, quite. Although everywhere was clean and relatively tidy, they noticed evidence of Rob's presence – a few tapes scattered around and copies of a magazine devoted to pop music which presumably didn't belong to David, and a pair of slippers half-hidden by the sofa.

When David brought the tea in, his parents noticed that he looked just a bit awkward. They spoke quickly to hide any embarrassment.

"Why does tea never taste the same abroad?" asked Philip Rees.

"Must be the water," his son replied. He remembered saying the same to Rob once.

"Are you going to tell us about Rob?" his father asked.

"I expect you've guessed, haven't you?"

"We wondered," his father admitted, thinking how much happier David seemed.

"I wanted to tell you face to face," David said. "I know I told you he wasn't homosexual – I didn't think he was – but luckily I made a mistake." He was watching his parents' faces for their reaction.

"Well, it's about time," said his father. "I thought we'd never get you off our hands!"

"Philip!" his wife scolded. "We were going to tell him how pleased we were. I mean ..." She looked a little taken aback at what she'd just said. "Oh, you know what we mean," she said to her son. "We are pleased for you. For you both."

"Thanks." He knew they were sincere. "There are a couple of things I ought to mention," he went on. Actually, it had been Rob who'd made David promise to tell his parents. "First, that we've been sharing the spare room. I could move back to my room if you'd prefer." He looked up at his father, who shrugged and shook his head.

"No. Stay where you are." He smiled at his son.

"Second," David said, unconscious of having taken a deep breath, "Rob's only twenty-one." He saw no reason to tell them, as Rob had wanted, that David had been unaware of his true age when they first slept together.

"Oh!" his mother exclaimed, partly at how young Rob was, but mostly that David had done something illegal. Her stomach lurched as she thought of what the consequences might have been.

"Well," her husband said philosophically, "you're both over twenty-one now so you shouldn't have anything to worry about. What's he like?" David had been very reticent the last time they'd been home, and had obviously not wanted to answer any questions.

David shrugged. He didn't know how to start. "He's nice," he eventually said, his powers of description deserting him. "You'll meet him tonight."

Upstairs in their own room, having decided that they could do with a few hours' sleep, his parents looked anxiously at each other.

"Ten years' difference in their ages and he works in a record shop," Barbara Rees said, voicing their concern. "I know it sounds awful, but that doesn't sound like the sort of person I'd have expected David to want to settle down with."

"No," her husband agreed thoughtfully. "But we haven't met him yet, and you know how stubborn David can be once his mind's made up."

Mrs Rees nodded ruefully. Her husband was just the same, although he appeared not to realise it. "He's just so young."

"Well, David doesn't seem to mind. He certainly looks a lot happier than when we went away."

"I know ..." She sighed.

"But?"

"I just wonder if he's too young. I'm afraid he'll tire of David. You remember how upset David was when he left. Just imagine how much worse it would be if he did it again."

"Let's see what he's like first," Philip Rees said.

It was nearly four o'clock when they awoke.

David heard them and put the kettle on.

"I know I sprang it on you as a *fait accompli*," he said when they were all sitting down. "Rob and me living here together. We've put our names on a couple of estate agents' mailing lists so you should have the house to yourselves in a few months' time."

"You needn't rush to find somewhere. We don't mind you both staying here," his mother said.

"It'll give us a chance to get to know him," his father added.

"What time will he be back?" his mother asked anxiously.

David looked at his watch. "I'll pick him up from work about half five so we should be back by ten to six."

Just as he was getting up to go and collect Rob, his father asked off-handedly whether Rob was like Jeremy at all. He knew that had been at the back of his wife's mind.

David looked at him, surprised. "No. No, he's not."

Barbara Rees breathed a sigh of relief when David had gone. Not that she really had anything against Jeremy. And she was determined to welcome whoever it was that David was bringing home to meet them. She had faith in David's judgement. They both had.

"Christ, Sal," Rob whispered between customers, "they're not going to be overjoyed to come back and find me there."

"Stop worrying," she said for the umpteenth time that day. "What does David say?"

"Oh, he says it'll be all right," he said dismissively.

"Well, there you are, then."

"I know, but ... well, it's not exactly going to be easy for them."

"Doesn't sound like it's a barrel of laughs for you, either. He's met your parents, hasn't he?"

"I know, but it's not as if they had to put up with both of us living under the same roof. Their roof!"

"I expect they're just as nervous about meeting you."

"They couldn't be."

They looked at each other and burst out laughing.

"Sorry." He knew he'd been moaning all day.

"Forget it. Look, if the worst comes to the worst, you can always come and stay at our house. At least Dad won't have to worry about you creeping into my room when he's asleep!"

"Probably won't even let me in the house now," he said glumly.

Sally gave up.

"Come to take misery-guts home?" was Sally's cheerful greeting to David.

"What?" David, puzzled, glanced at Rob to find him glaring at Sally.

"Nothing. No flight delays?" Rob asked hopefully.

"No, the plane was early if anything."

"What did they say when you told them?"

"Dad said it was about time."

"And your mother?"

"She said they were both pleased."

"I expect they're both a bit jet-lagged after the journey."

"They've had a few hours' sleep. When I came out, they were unpacking."

"Oh." So they were up.

"Are you ready to go?"

Rob looked around but today was one of those rare Saturdays when all the customers had left before the shop was due to shut. "I suppose so."

"Good luck," Sally called on her way out.

"I want to get drunk," Rob said.

"Only an idiot takes Dutch courage."

Their eyes met briefly.

The journey home seemed to take even less time than usual. The traffic lights turned green at their approach, no one wanted to use the pedestrian crossings and traffic was light. All too soon, so it seemed to Rob, they were home.

Before they went in, David gave Rob's hand a brief squeeze. "It'll be all right," he said reassuringly.

"Rob, my mother and father," David said rather formally. "Mum, Dad, this is Rob."

Philip Rees saw a pleasant young man who looked as if he wished he was anywhere but there.

Barbara Rees saw a young man who had deeply hurt her son.

"I'm very pleased to meet you," David's father said, extending his hand.

"I've been looking forward to meeting you, too," Rob replied, shaking hands. "Well, until today," he admitted in a burst of nervous honesty, "when I decided that being shot by a firing-squad was preferable." And he smiled, and the smile lit up his face.

Philip Rees looked at David, whose face bore the same expression it had when he'd learnt to ride his first bicycle: happiness and pride. It was clear to him that David was in love. He hoped Barbara had noticed too.

"Hello, Rob," his wife said. She smiled, determined to make an effort for David's sake.

"Hello, Mrs Rees."

"I haven't had a chance until now to thank you properly for the plant you sent the Christmas before last."

Barbara Rees sighed as she got into bed.

"A nice lad," her husband said.

"Mmm," she agreed, wondering if he had heard the doubt in her voice. It would take more than a poinsettia to win her over.

THIRTY SEVEN

"Hello," Rob said as Mrs Rees came into the kitchen. "I've nearly finished." He picked up a second slice of toast and began eating it.

Momentarily taken aback at finding Rob there – she'd forgotten that it was his day off – she recovered herself and told him not to hurry.

Both were aware of this awkwardness between them.

David hadn't noticed his mother's reserve. But when Rob had asked him if his mother had got on well with his other friends and then remarked that perhaps it would be easier for her when they'd moved out, he'd grown concerned and asked his mother whether there'd been an argument.

She'd said no, they hadn't had an argument. "But you do like him?" he persisted, and she'd said yes. She wondered if that was the whole truth. Mrs Rees knew she still hadn't forgiven Rob for making David so unhappy. It was stupid, she realised that, as David obviously had forgiven him.

She had to make an effort to overcome her prejudice before the awkwardness degenerated into friction and alienated her son.

"I'm sorry if I haven't made you feel welcome," she said as she sat down.

More than a little disconcerted at this unwonted frankness, Rob said without thinking: "Well, that's understandable. I know I should have told David how old I was and given him the chance to choose rather than put him in a difficult situation." He looked up. "You didn't know," he stated flatly. "I thought David ..." He broke off, realising why David had said nothing about him being underage.

In an effort to redeem the situation, he added, "It was just that when we met I was only seventeen and I thought he'd tell me to go back to my parents'. I kept meaning to tell him, but I just didn't get round to it."

"I didn't know."

Well, that hadn't helped, he thought, wishing he hadn't jumped to conclusions. "So what was it?" He might as well get it over with.

Rather reluctantly, Barbara Rees said, "I don't want to see him get hurt."

"Neither do I," Rob said, looking levelly at her.

"I didn't mean that you would hurt him intentionally."

"I can't pretend things have been easy," Rob said slowly, "but we've managed to sort them out now. One of the reasons I left was that I didn't want to let things happen out of apathy."

"Then why ..." She broke off, afraid of sounding as if she was interfering.

"Why what?"

She wished she'd held her tongue. "It's just that David's father said that the house and mortgage are going to be in David's name and not in joint names. I didn't understand why. You're twenty-one now, so that can't be the reason. Are you afraid of committing yourself? I can understand it's a big step to take."

"It's not that," Rob said at last. "It's partly because David's putting in a lot more money than me. And then we thought we might have problems getting a joint mortgage. Not all building societies would consider us a good risk." He felt his face becoming flushed. "By the way, we're not – a bad credit risk, that is. I should have said something earlier, I suppose, what with all the reports in the papers about AIDS. David didn't want me to say anything, but I thought you might be worried."

Barbara Rees said nothing for a while. She suddenly felt

ashamed of herself. She'd misjudged him. She really ought to have known better. After all, David had always been blessed with common sense and wasn't likely to have taken up with someone as fickle and irresponsible as she'd imagined Rob to be. Even Jeremy, with his apparently feckless and self-centred nature, had stood by David when it counted.

Impulsively she said: "Look, I was thinking of going into Reading later. I want to look round the shops to see what's available. As we're not moving, I'd like to redecorate now we're home for good. You must still have some things to get for the new house – why don't you come too?"

He bought a Paddington Bear book for David.

Mrs Rees noticed he'd bought something and asked what it was.

Sheepishly, Rob showed her.

"Is that for one of Jeremy's nieces?"

"No, I've never met Jeremy. David phones him from time to time."

"I somehow thought you knew him." In fact, she'd assumed that Jeremy had introduced David to Rob.

"Actually, the book's for David." He shrugged, a little embarrassed. "We'd been going through a rough patch a few months ago and I got him a Paddington Bear to say thanks for putting up with me. You may have seen it – it's on the chest of drawers in our room." He remembered David's parents were careful to respect their privacy. "Well, it's in our room. It started from that – I suppose I've bought him a couple of these now. As a sort of joke." He wondered if she thought he was mad.

She didn't. She thought he was very young and cared a lot for David and she thanked God that she'd realised it before it was too late.

"I thought it was Winnie The Pooh that was a private joke."

For a second, Rob paused, startled, remembering Malvern and the hotel and wondering how on earth she knew.

"He gave you a jar of honey, didn't he?"

Rob relaxed as he realised that she was simply referring to the old-fashioned pottery jar with the word 'HUNNY' hand-painted on it that David had given him for Christmas; if he'd hoped to embarrass Rob, he'd been disappointed.

"With David's father, it was Turkish Delight. He used to bring me some each time he visited. I hated it, but I didn't like to mention it. I used to give it to Poppy, our dog." She smiled. "Eventually I told him, but by then it was too late: we were in love and the dog was hooked on the stuff!"

THIRTY EIGHT

"You'll have to buy a new suit."

Rob looked up. He hadn't realised he was invited.

Nick, David's cousin, and his fiancée were getting married in a few weeks' time, and David and his mother and father had been discussing the wedding.

"Still, you've plenty of time. It's not as if you've anything else to do," joked Philip Rees.

Apart from move house.

Rob smiled. He liked David's father, partly because he felt that Mr Rees liked him. And sometimes he reminded him of David. As for Mrs Rees, well, there had been a definite thaw in her attitude, although it crossed Rob's mind from time to time that that was just when you should tread most carefully.

Now, three weeks later and having just moved, they were getting changed. David had offered to drive, but his father had said he'd pick them up.

"It suits you. The suit." As David said it, he realised how stupid it sounded. He stared at the young man before him and thought how much Rob had been through since he'd turned up on his parents' doorstep nearly three and a half years earlier. They both had.

"Nervous?" he asked Rob, who smiled and sat down on the edge of the bed to lace up his shoes. It was the first time they'd gone anywhere as a couple, apart from visits to each other's parents'. "I expect the groom is," he added before Rob could say anything.

At least that was one thing they were spared, he thought, smiling to himself as he heard the sound of his parents' car. Wedding nerves. The real thing.

Rob was grateful when they arrived at David's uncle and aunt's for the weekend to find that Nick and his best man had already left for the church and that everyone else seemed busy; thus he was spared too many introductions all at once. After saying they were pleased to meet him they ignored him, much to Rob's relief.

The following day, Nick and his new wife came round – they weren't leaving on their honeymoon until the next day.

As they finished their coffee, Nick said casually: "Well, I suppose it's time to open all those presents." He and Alison got up, collected some from the pile in one corner, and put them on the table. They seemed reluctant to begin opening them.

It was Rob who realised first. He caught sight of one of the labels, and glanced round the table, puzzled. Then David recognised the wrapping paper his mother had used to wrap the things she'd bought for his cousin but not the shape of the presents. He, too, looked at the nearest label.

"Did you know about this?" Rob asked suspiciously.

"I hadn't the faintest idea. No wonder Dad was so keen to drive. It would have been difficult trying to smuggle all this into our car. Here …" he handed one of the gift-wrapped shapes to Rob. "You open this one." He picked up another for himself, and began to undo the wrapping.

As they progressed, they realised they were accumulating a set of china. Rob's parents had evidently been in on the conspiracy, as there was a present from them, too.

"So whose idea was this then?" David glanced round the table.

"Well," Nick began, "I was talking to your mother last week and she said it was quite hectic what with Alison and me getting married and you two buying a house, and it struck me that you weren't getting any presents at all. So I asked your mother if she thought it would be a good idea for us to buy you something too."

"I didn't know you were getting all this, but I remember being pumped for information." David stared at the culprit, his mother, who'd asked him which pattern he'd liked. He'd thought she'd been thinking of replacing her own plates. "Three weeks ago," he added meaningfully.

"And I thought it was all my own idea!" Nick said.

"You can change it," Barbara Rees said quickly, indicating the crockery, which they were still unwrapping. "If you want a different design."

They both assured her it was fine.

If he'd glanced up, David might have noticed his mother and his lover smile tentatively at each other.

The ice had definitely thawed.

THIRTY NINE

He bumped into Jeremy quite unexpectedly.

He and Rob had gone shopping and had then split up, Rob to look for a birthday present for his father and David to look round a couple of bookshops.

It was as he was coming out of the second one that he almost collided with Jeremy, who was on his own too.

" 'Hello' is sufficient," Jeremy said, grinning. "You don't need to knock me over to attract my attention."

A few passers-by gave them curious looks.

"Long time no see. How are you?"

"I'm fine," David replied. "And you?"

"Fine, thanks. Still reading?"

"I keep trying to give it up. It's no use."

"Try 'Readers Anonymous'. Their literature is brilliant!"

"What are you doing here?"

"Shopping, funnily enough. Man cannot live by bread alone." Jeremy looked in a puzzled manner at the stick of French bread protruding from his carrier bag. "Damn. Looks like he's going to have to if I don't get a move on."

"You entertaining tonight?"

"Mmm," Jeremy said in a thoughtful tone. "How are your parents? Are they still away?"

"They're back now. Both of them are fine. I've moved out, by the way."

"You've bought somewhere?"

"Yes. I've been meaning to let you know, but it's been a bit hectic lately."

"I hope you're having a house-warming party."

"You'll be the first person I invite."

"Have you got time for a coffee?" Jeremy asked, shifting the weight of his shopping from one hand to the other.

"Well, I'm with someone."

"The Invisible Man?" He pricked up his ears at the hint of a juicy bit of gossip. "That reminds me. Someone told me he'd seen you shopping at Sainsbury's one morning. Only you weren't on your own. He complimented you on your taste, incidentally."

"I've always liked Sainsbury's," David said, pretending to misunderstand.

"So who was it?"

David looked sheepish. "Rob."

"Rob? Another one? I'd have changed my name if I'd realised. Shakespeare obviously got it all wrong. A rose by any other name ..."

"No, the same one."

"I don't understand. The last time I saw you, you were bemoaning the fact that he wasn't gay." He smiled sweetly at a couple of youths walking past who had evidently caught his last few words. "I thought you'd decided not to see him again?"

David grinned. "That's a bit difficult. We're living together."

Jeremy's mouth dropped open.

"Look," David said hastily, having glanced at his watch. "Come round for a meal one evening. What are you doing next Saturday?"

"That depends on tonight." He sighed, in a vain attempt to hide his interest. "Oh, all right. You've talked me into it."

David quickly wrote down his new address on a piece of paper and handed it to Jeremy. "I'd better go. Have a nice time tonight. See you Saturday."

"David!"

But David had gone.

Throughout the meal, Jeremy had behaved in a peculiar manner: impeccably. There were no jokes, no double-entendres, no camp voice, only politeness. He was dressed soberly for the occasion and had brought with him as a house-warming present a perfectly respectable picture.

Rob had looked oddly at David, as if he couldn't understand why Jeremy had the reputation he did.

David couldn't work it out. At first he assumed it was the awkwardness of old friends meeting new ones, but Jeremy maintained his stilted manner too long for that.

It was only when Rob had gone out to make the coffee that David found out the reason.

"I didn't want to let you down," Jeremy said, embarrassed. "I know how much he means to you. I can see how much he means to you. I thought I'd better be diplomatic. It's very wearing," he added, sounding more like himself.

"You moron!" David exploded, touched nevertheless. "So that's why you've been sitting there all evening as if you'd been stuffed! Just be yourself for heaven's sake. I've warned Rob what you're like."

"What d'you mean, you've warned him? Bloody cheek. I didn't come here to be insulted. I even put on a suit!"

"I can't believe it! When was the last time you acted so responsibly?"

"When I met Roger's parents. I was on my best behaviour but Ellie couldn't stand it, either. She told me to stop it, I was frightening the children. "

"Well?"

"Very nice. Has he got a brother?"

"No."

305

"Pity. I don't know what he sees in you, though. And what I was trying to ask you the other day was why the hell did you tell me he wasn't gay? You must have known!"

"I had no idea."

"But you lived in the same house! You must have noticed! Didn't you talk to each other?" he asked despairingly.

"He didn't say and I didn't guess." David poured some more wine for himself, and offered the bottle to Jeremy who waved it away impatiently.

"So how did you eventually find out?"

"He came to the house and asked if he could move back in. I said it didn't sound like a very sensible idea. And that was when he told me he was gay."

"Was it a big shock? Losing your virginity, I mean."

"Do you never give up?" David said exasperatedly.

"I concede defeat where you're concerned. Aren't you going to tell me then?"

"And I thought you knew!"

"I didn't mean generally, I meant specifically." His voice became husky as, tongue-in-cheek, he said: "What was it like for you?"

"Mind your own business!"

"Perhaps Rob will tell me."

Rob had just come back from the kitchen.

"No," David said quickly.

"Tell you what?"

"Who carried who over the threshold. But, seriously, let me know if you want to borrow any books. Sex manuals, that sort of thing."

"No, thanks," David said. "We're doing fine without any help."

"Spoilsport!" Jeremy took the cup Rob held out and smiled at him. "Actually I was beginning to think David was a closet heterosexual, the way he repulsed all my advances." He turned back to David. "How are you coping? I mean, young men can be so demanding. Or is it a case of abstinence makes the part grow stronger? So where did you meet?" enquired Jeremy, abruptly changing course.

"Waterloo."

"Very Trevor Howard and Celia Johnson. What happened?"

"We just got talking."

"You picked him up?" Jeremy said incredulously. "You're telling me you picked him up at Waterloo Station? If you think I'll ever let you forget that …"

"No, I didn't think you would," David sighed. "It wasn't quite like that."

"But you've met each other's parents, and all that?"

"Yes. They came home last November, and we moved in here a couple of months ago."

"You mean you were all living at his parents' house? With his parents there?" Jeremy was aghast.

"Yes."

"Bloody hell. So you get on all right with them, do you?" he asked, turning to Rob.

"I don't think I was quite what they expected." He grinned. "His Mum thought I'd be like you."

Jeremy pulled a face. "No wonder they like you. I expect it's the relief. I thought your Dad was beginning to warm to me, though," he said to David. "Well, at least he'd decided to forgive me."

"What for?" Rob asked.

"It was years ago," Jeremy said. "His father found us in a slightly compromising position on the sofa one evening."

"I think Dad would have taken that in his stride. It was when you said we were playing strip poker and asked him if he'd like to join in that he saw red."

"You said that to David's father?" Rob stared in disbelief at

Jeremy.

"I may have done," Jeremy conceded. "I can't quite remember the exact words. But don't worry, all my powers of seduction failed to tempt him. David, that is, not his father. I think it was at school I first realised I was different. You remember how everyone used to say they fancied the blonde one in Abba? I suppose you're too young to remember them?"

"He works in a record shop," David reminded him.

"Oh, yes. Well, every time someone said that, I always used to ask which one? Took me ages before I found out they were talking about the women!"

FORTY

"We've just been to the cinema," Graham began, "and we were going to have something to eat."

"We thought we'd have a meal. We've just been to see the film on at the Odeon," David said at the same time.

All four of them – Graham, Jill, David and Rob – stood on the pavement outside a Chinese restaurant not far from the cinema. It was half past nine on a Friday night and it was drizzling.

"Great minds …" said Jill. "Shall we share a table?"

"You just want to be able to have the set meal for four!" Graham joked. "Hurry up, I'm getting wet."

"Haven't seen you for ages," Jill said to David, as he held open the door for her.

"I haven't played doubles lately," David admitted, aware that Rob was unsure whether David thought honesty or discretion the better policy.

After the introductions, Rob relaxed as he realised first of all that David didn't mind which, and secondly that despite some fairly obvious clues neither Graham nor Jill seemed to notice anything unusual about their friendship. It was nice to meet someone David worked with at last; after all, David knew everyone from the shop.

As they were leaving the restaurant, David invited Graham and Jill back for coffee. It was only when they reached the house that Jill found Rob had been driving although she recognised the car as David's. She thought nothing more of it until they were sitting down.

She sipped her coffee. "It's a nice house," she said, glancing round appreciatively. "How long have you lived here?"

"We bought it in March," David said.

'We' she thought. 'We bought it.' At the restaurant, a feeling of having missed something had been nagging at her. Suddenly things began to fall into place. Fragments of their conversation during the meal from which it was obvious they knew each other's likes and dislikes. The way Rob had called out to ask if he should turn the heating on. David offering the biscuits to Graham and joking that he'd better take one now before Rob demolished the packet. Things insignificant in themselves, but which struck her as curiously domestic.

She looked from David to Rob, and told herself that she was letting her imagination run away with her. And yet Stephanie had once said that David was very pleasant but she thought he was already involved with someone.

"Would you like to have a look round?" David asked.

She saw Rob look quickly at David, but before she had a chance to answer, Graham exclaimed: "Women!" in a long-suffering voice. "You know what we do on Sundays? We go round every show house within a fifty mile radius, never mind if we can afford them. I wouldn't mind, but we're not even thinking of moving. Don't ever get married," he counselled David.

Out of the mouths of babes and sucklings, thought Jill, wondering how on earth her husband could be so oblivious to the situation. She hoped their hosts weren't offended. Rob, she noticed, appeared to be studying the tips of his shoes with extreme concentration, his face otherwise inscrutable. David, however, met her gaze, his eyes amused. She bit her lip, trying not to laugh. "Oh, Graham!" she whispered weakly.

"What is it?" He looked at David for enlightenment, and then turned to his wife, completely baffled as to why she'd started giggling uncontrollably.

He tried to think. Then various memories began to surface. Speaking to Rob on the phone a couple of times. The photos David had brought in of his holiday – Rob had been in some of those. They'd bought this house together. He stared uncomprehendingly at David. He couldn't be ... He'd have known, wouldn't he? But even as he looked disbelievingly at them, he knew from their expressions that he'd stumbled upon the truth. "I'd no idea," he said at last.

"I'd absolutely no idea," he said again. Rob had taken Jill on a tour of the house.

"I'll wear my 'Glad to be gay' badge on Monday, if you like."

"Sorry. I didn't mean to be rude."

"It's all right. I know it comes as a bit of a surprise." What was it Jeremy had said? First they wonder what you do in bed. Then they think you fancy them. Finally they panic in case you've got AIDS. Even the ones who aren't particularly prejudiced.

"I never imagined ... I just thought, when you didn't mention going out with anyone in particular, that there was no one special."

"For a long time, there wasn't," David said. "I've been meaning to tell you ever since we moved in."

"I thought I would have noticed something. Sorry, I'm making it sound as if all homosexuals are limp-wristed, mincing, lisping queens."

"It's not always obvious," David said reassuringly, trying not to laugh. "I didn't realise Rob was gay."

"It's permanent, the house and everything." More a statement than a question.

"We hope so."

"I'm afraid Jill saw Paddington Bear, but I made her promise not to tell Graham it was yours in case it damaged your macho reputation." There was a mischievous look in Rob's eyes.

"You don't think," David said with equanimity, "that meeting you might have dented it just a little?"

So that was it, Graham suddenly thought, remembering David's anger of the previous year. It couldn't be that easy telling your family that you were setting up house with another man. At least now things seemed to have sorted themselves out. Graham could see that David and Rob were remarkably happy together. He was glad for David's sake.

When they'd settled down with another cup of coffee, Graham asked Rob if he played squash.

"No, I've never played. I used to play badminton at school but I wasn't much good at it."

"Jill and I like badminton. We could have a game of mixed doub…" He stopped abruptly and went bright red.

Jill was caught between horror and hysteria.

"I've never heard it called that before," Rob said, managing to keep a straight face only by not looking at David.

Graham swallowed. "Look, I meant … I mean, I didn't mean …" he gabbled. "It's just that when we've played badminton before we've always played mixed doubles. You remember," he appealed to David, "with Stephanie."

"You'll have to come round for a meal one evening. Stephanie, too." David looked at Jill who had the grace to blush.

Rob, who'd heard all about Jill's match-making attempts, smiled at her. "Never mind," he said. "I'm afraid David always was a lost cause."

The next time David and Graham played squash led to the first – and last, as far as David was aware – embarrassment between them.

They had had a long, tiring game, both were hot and had come off court thinking longingly of a warm, relaxing shower.

Neither had banked on the awkwardness of being the only people in the changing room, each wondering who was going to undress first.

David decided that the only way was to be blunt. "Look, if I ever get an erection when I'm in the shower, it's nothing personal. It's just Nature's way of embarrassing the hell out of both of us."

For a moment, Graham looked shocked and David wondered if he'd gone too far. Then he saw him grin in relief. "I suppose I did wonder ..."

"I got plenty of practice at school on how not to react. It doesn't usually bother me."

"So you didn't have to keep taking cold showers?"

David laughed. "No, it was never that bad. Well, maybe when I met Rob ..." he admitted.

"Good thing he's not here, then."

"Mmm," David said off-handedly. Then he added what he considered a response worthy of Jeremy. "It'd be a lot harder then."

FORTY ONE

On the whole, Rob mused as he planted crocus bulbs in their small front garden, it had been a good year. Odd how he gained the same satisfaction that his uncle must from working in the garden. You didn't expect to have anything in common with someone you'd spent half your life trying to block out or expunge from conscious and unconscious thought. And yet now the thought of his uncle and the events of that night didn't trouble him. It was as if everything had happened to another person, not to the person he now was. It no longer hurt. His anger towards himself and his guilt and shame had burnt themselves out or been quenched by love. Speaking to his uncle had helped greatly in this process: by finally rejecting any blame for what he, a child, had been unable to foresee or to prevent; and by informing his uncle that his actions were no longer a secret shared only by the two of them, he had managed to put the past behind him. His uncle had become diminished in his eyes, no longer a power to be afraid of, the danger of discovery no longer any threat to Rob.

His relationship with David had matured, become more balanced. It was as if a good, rather than a vicious, circle was in operation. As his own insecurities dissolved, he found, to his profound and delighted surprise, that he had fallen in love with David. Something he'd thought impossible had become ridiculously easy.

They were happy.

They'd seen Jeremy a couple of times, but apart from that they'd been rather self-absorbed ever since moving out of David's parents' house. On Sundays they'd go out – walks, a visit to a steam exhibition, a day in Oxford as Rob had never been there before, Kew Gardens, tea shops in picturesque but traffic-congested Surrey villages, a boat trip on the Thames, going to watch a game of American football with Sally.

"D'you think," David said, nuzzling Rob's neck on Christmas Eve, "that your parents would be shocked if they came in and found us making love on the sofa?"

Rob considered the question. "I think they'd be a bit put out if we didn't offer them some tea after they'd driven all that way."

"I've no objection to stopping to make them a cup."

"It can't be the brandy talking." David had found a bottle and said he'd better make sure it was all right before they poured it over the Christmas pudding the following day. "That always makes you fall asleep."

"Am I forever to be reminded of the first night you spent in my bed?"

"Probably. I'm shattered – some of us had to work today."

"What if I put a tea towel round my head?"

"Last time I ever tell you any of my fantasies."

"I love you."

"I love you, too." Rob yawned.

"Would some black coffee help?"

"It might."

While David was in the kitchen, the doorbell rang. Rob's parents, laden with presents and luggage, said they would just put everything upstairs and then they'd say hello properly. The traffic had been chaotic. Were David's parents here? Oh, of course, they were coming tomorrow, weren't they?

They'd come down after a few minutes. Rob, who'd been asleep, thought it was David returning with the coffee.

Still with his eyes shut, he was musing about cranberry sauce. It wasn't as sticky as honey and he was very partial to it. Maybe David wouldn't mind if they ...

"How much cranberry sauce did we buy?" he asked, then, surprised to hear someone else come in, he opened his eyes. "Oh. Hello, Mum. Dad. I didn't realise you were here. Thanks." He took the cup of coffee David held out, avoiding David's eyes in case he started laughing. "I must have dozed off."

It was nearly an hour later when they eventually got to bed.

"Why did you want to know?" David asked, picking up on Rob's earlier remark.

Rob explained. "You know what I really want?"

"I'll go down and get the cranberry sauce." David threw back the covers as if he was about to get out of bed.

"David Andrew Rees, stop making me laugh when I'm trying to be serious!"

"Well, Robert James Greenaway, what do you want?"

"I'd like next year to be as good as this year's been."

"I'd like that, too." After a few minutes, David said, "Shall I turn the light off?" but he got no reply. Rob had fallen asleep.

David smiled to himself and carefully moved his arm so that Rob was no longer lying on it. He switched off the light.

In the darkness, his eyes open, he lay thinking.

All he ever wanted.

THE END

Also Available from BeWrite Books

Crime
Sweet Molly Maguire – Terry Houston

The surreal world of a mean city newspaper swallowed the very toughest or spat them out. This circus of hopeless drunks and heartless back-stabbers was no place for Sweet Molly Maguire. She died, raped and pregnant, and didn't merit a single line of print. But for one reporter, her death wasn't the end of just another story. It was the opening sentence in a search for something rare in the news room ... the bitter truth.

Paperback   ISBN 1-904224-05-9
          $13.50 US/ £9.80 UK/ $21.24 Canada/ €15.55 Europe
Ebook   ISBN 1-904224-01-6
          $6.55 US/ £4.80 UK/ $10.40 Canada/ €7.65 Europe
CD – Rom   ISBN 1-904224-06-7
          $10.25 US/ £7.50 UK/ $16.25 Canada/ €11.90 Europe

Horror   .
Chill – Terri Pine, Peter Lee, Andrew Müller

Dim the lights. Tug up the quilt so that only your eyes are visible. Now, slip into the dark, dark night of this world's greatest masters of macabre. Try not to sleep. Watch for moving shadows. And – whatever happens – *don't* get out of bed ... you may catch your very death ...

Paperback   ISBN 1-904224-08-3
          $13.50 US/ £9.80 UK/ $21.24 Canada/ €15.55 Europe
Ebook   ISBN 1-904224-03-2
          $6.55 US/ £4.80 UK/ $10.40 Canada/ €7.65 Europe
CD – Rom   ISBN 1-904224-11-3
          $10.25 US/ £7.50 UK/ $16.25 Canada/ €11.90 Europe

Crime
Marks – Sam Smith

George Hawkins is a small town detective – low on ambition, lower on glamour. The most exciting part of life is making midnight chalk marks on tyres and roads ... when the marks still match up the following morning, he has proof that someone's been playing away from home. But George's humdrum life is turned upside down within a single day when he witnesses a hit-and-run, his house is burgled, and his girlfriend disappears, leaving him prime suspect.

Paperback   ISBN 1-904224-09-1
          $13.50 US/ £9.80 UK/ $21.24 Canada/ €15.55 Europe
Ebook   ISBN 1-904224-02-4
          $6.55 US/ £4.80 UK/ $10.40 Canada/ €7.65 Europe
CD – Rom   ISBN 1-904224-17-2
          $10.25 US/ £7.50 UK/ $16.25 Canada/ €11.90 Europe

Autobiography
The Golden Locket – A Post-Edwardian Childhood – Dorothy Kathleen Kirby

It may not have mattered to Dorothy Kathleen Kirby that she didn't live to see the book she had written. She had *lived* the memories between its covers. In nine decades that saw the Flanders trenches and the terror attack on Manhattan, Dorothy focused on the simple detail of everyday life, and discovered a wonderful world. Page by delightful page, you cannot help but be struck by the truth that counting blessings one by one can produce a mighty sum.

Paperback   ISBN 1-904224-07-5
          $13.50 US/ £9.80 UK/ $21.24 Canada/ €15.55 Europe
Ebook   ISBN 1-904224-00-8
          $6.55 US/ £4.80 UK/ $10.40 Canada/ €7.65 Europe
CD – Rom   ISBN 1-904224-10-5
          $10.25 US/ £7.50 UK/ $16.25 Canada/ €11.90 Europe

Crime
The Knotted Cord – Alistair Kinnon

The body of a naked young boy hanging in a dusty barn stirs sickening feelings of déjà vu in the detective. As he untangles each knot in the tangled cord of his investigation, he uncovers a murderous thread ... and police prejudices which may have allowed previous killings to happen ... not to mention his own guilt! **Alistair Kinnon** has written much more than a tense, psychological crime novel -- his twisting plot takes the reader into the murky world of child sex-for-sale ... the parent's darkest nightmare and the child's greatest threat.

Paperback   ISBN 1-904224-12-1
             $13.50 US/ £9.80 UK/ $21.24 Canada/ €15.55 Europe
Ebook   ISBN 1-904224-04-1
             $6.55 US/ £4.80 UK/ $10.40 Canada/ €7.65 Europe
CD – Rom   ISBN 1-904224-13-X
             $10.25 US/ £7.50 UK/ $16.25 Canada/ €11.90 Europe

Fantasy Humour
Zolin – A Rockin' Good Wizard – Barry Ireland

Worlds go along happily side-by-side in their own dimensiverses ... until they accidentally bump into each other. Then a wild Glasgow rock band, randy witches, dragons for hire and kings and queens end up rocking where they should have been rolling. And bewildered apprentice wizard, Zolin, is piggy in the middle. **Barry Ireland's** book is to Fantasy what The Hitchhiker's Guide to the Galaxy was to Sci Fi. An adult fairy tale!

Paperback   ISBN 1-904224-19-9
             $13.50 US/ £9.80 UK/ $21.24 Canada/ €15.55 Europe
Ebook   ISBN 1-904224-18-0
             $6.55 US/ £4.80 UK/ $10.40 Canada/ €7.65 Europe
CD – Rom   ISBN 1-904224-20-2
             $10.25 US/ £7.50 UK/ $16.25 Canada/ €11.90 Europe

Romance
A Different Kind of Love – Jay Mandal

More than any other collection, this thought-provoking work will introduce the heterosexual reader to the meaning of *true* gay love, and will afford the gay reader a sigh of relief that – at last – a popular, respected and serious author has cast aside threadbare issues of hatred, brutality, perversion, prejudice and misunderstanding to get to the very heart of the matter ... the honest to goodness love between human beings who ask little more of life than that.

Paperback   ISBN 1-904224-40-7
        $13.50 US/ £9.80 UK/ $21.24 Canada/ €15.55 Europe
Ebook   ISBN 1-904224-39-9
        $6.55 US/ £4.80 UK/ $10.40 Canada/ €7.65 Europe
CD – Rom   ISBN 1-904224-41-5
        $10.25 US/ £7.50 UK/ $16.25 Canada/ €11.90 Europe

General
Odie Dodie – The Life and Crimes of a Travelin' Preacher Man – Lad Moore

Lad Moore builds a collection of tales of stark reality, hanging on the wobbly hook of a phony, money grubbing, licentious gospel-peddler, Odie Dodie and his unholy glory bus.
    Never since Steinbeck and Hemingway has an author written so tightly, entertainingly and honestly about what matters most ... The simple truth!

Paperback   ISBN 1-904224-08-3
        $13.50 US/ £9.80 UK/ $21.24 Canada/ €15.55 Europe
Ebook   ISBN 1-904224-03-2
        $6.55 US/ £4.80 UK/ $10.40 Canada/ €7.65 Europe
CD – Rom   ISBN 1-904224-11-3
        $10.25 US/ £7.50 UK/ $16.25 Canada/ €11.90 Europe

Thriller
Blood Money – Azam Gill

A starkly realistic novel of love and hate in the murky world of international terrorism, mercenary soldiering, dirty banking and underground government agencies. Gill, with the skill of a master story teller and the authority of an actual former insider, writes a gritty story of star-crossed love against a scenario strikingly close to that which may have led up to the attack on the Twin Towers ... and a war far from over.

Paperback   ISBN 1-904224-91-1
              $13.50 US/ £9.80 UK/ $21.24 Canada/ €15.55 Europe
Ebook   ISBN 1-904224-90-3
              $6.55 US/ £4.80 UK/ $10.40 Canada/ €7.65 Europe
CD – Rom   ISBN 1-904224-92-X
              $10.25 US/ £7.50 UK/ $16.25 Canada/ €11.90 Europe

Crime
Porlock Counterpoint – Sam Smith

Sam Smith goes one step beyond the psychological crime novel when he places cynical cops to, like the reader, observe the counterpoint between two levels of criminal. The middle-aged, middle-class couple smuggling hard drugs for their avaricious dreams and the desperate young couple who 'borrow' their car simply to get to hospital in time for the birth of their baby. The quartet may never meet ... but their lives, worlds apart in terms of social rank and the definition of 'crime', collide with shattering results.

Paperback   ISBN 1-904224-15-6
              $13.50 US/ £9.80 UK/ $21.24 Canada/ €15.55 Europe
Ebook   ISBN 1-904224-14-8
              $6.55 US/ £4.80 UK/ $10.40 Canada/ €7.65 Europe
CD – Rom   ISBN 1-904224-16-4
              $10.25 US/ £7.50 UK/ $16.25 Canada/ €11.90 Europe

Short Stories
The Miller Moth – Mike Broemmel
The miller moth flutters through Mike Broemmel's pages like a phantom - sometimes benevolent, sometimes threatening. A shade of human life itself. Characters you'll meet are ordinary people in ordinary situations - made extraordinary with the touch of a modern Steinbeck. You will recognize yourself, family and neighbours in this collection of deceptively simple stories crafted with the intricacy, delicacy and humanity of a master wordsmith.

Paperback   ISBN 1-904224-15-6
          $13.50 US/ £9.80 UK/ $21.24 Canada/ €15.55 Europe
Ebook   ISBN 1-904224-14-8
          $6.55 US/ £4.80 UK/ $10.40 Canada/ €7.65 Europe
CD – Rom   ISBN 1-904224-16-4
          $10.25 US/ £7.50 UK/ $16.25 Canada/ €11.90 Europe

N.B The price for paperback and CD-Rom excludes postage and packaging.
Prices correct at time of press.

All the above titles are available from

www.bewrite.net

Printed in the United Kingdom
by Lightning Source UK Ltd.
101078UKS00001B/7